The Path
to Piney
Meadows

Gail Sattler

Abingdon fiction™
a novel approach to faith

Other Books by Gail Sattler

The Narrow Path

The Path to Piney Meadows

Copyright © 2013 by Gail Sattler

ISBN-13: 978-1-4267-3355-0

Published by Abingdon Press, P.O. Box 801, Nashville, TN 37202

www.abingdonpress.com

Library of Congress Cataloging-in-Publication Data

Sattler,Gail.
The Path to piney meadows / Gail Sattler.
    pages cm.—(The Path to Piney Meadows)
ISBN 978-1-4267-3355-0 (binding: paper, pbk. / trade: alk. paper)
I. Title.
PR9199.4.S3575P38 2013
813'.6—dc23

2013007209

Scripture quotations from the Authorized (King James) Version.
Rights in the Authorized Version in the United Kingdom are vested
in the Crown. Reproduced by permission of the Crown's patentee,
Cambridge University Press.

Printed in the United States of America

1 2 3 4 5 6 7 8 9 10 / 18 17 16 15 14 13

Dedicated to Martha Thiessen—
Thank you for all the great translations,
and thank you especially for not laughing at my
horrible accent.

Honorable mention to Shelley Bates,
writing as Adina Senfit,
for all the Chickin Pickins,
and for letting me know why chickens don't snore.

Blessed is the man that endureth temptation:
for when he is tried, he shall receive the crown of life,
which the Lord hath promised to them that love him.

—James 1:12

1

Chad Jones stared into the bottom of his empty mug.

Since noon, peals of drunken laughter had echoed down from the office Christmas party of the business on the floor above him.

Chad sat alone, on Christmas Eve, working. Without coffee. But he could smell the dregs from what was left in the bottom of the near-empty pot. Everyone else had gone home.

Chad glanced around his private office, not much bigger than a closet. He had barely enough square footage for his desk and chair, one filing cabinet, and one guest chair. Not that he had many guests. It was embarrassing. The building looked passable from the outside, but there was a reason the rent was cheaper than other buildings in the same area.

Gary, however, had spared no expense in renovating his own office, which was nearly the size of Chad's living room.

Upstairs, someone turned up the volume of "Jingle Bell Rock."

Chad gritted his teeth and tilted his head up. "I hate 'Jingle Bell Rock'!" he called up, even though they couldn't hear him. "Can't you pick something else?"

With every thump of the bass, the tape dispenser on Chad's desk vibrated.

He stared at the pile of paper Gary had plunked on his desk before he'd walked out. Gary had left early to be with his family. Chad didn't have anywhere to go, and Gary knew it, but that wasn't the point.

After all this time, he could finally admit that his boss had no intention of making him a partner. Everything had been a ploy to get more work out of him. The only thing that would shake greedy Gary into really making him partner was if Gary actually had to do all his own work.

Chad peeled off a sticky note and started writing.

I quit!

Chad

He smiled and pressed the paper to the center of his monitor. As he pulled his hand away, the note fell.

Chad's smile also fell.

Mr. Cheapskate couldn't even buy decent quality sticky notes.

Chad sank his teeth into his lower lip, picked up a pushpin, poked it through the note, and aimed it at the monitor.

Testing the screen, Chad poked it with his thumb. His monitor at home was a plasma screen—hard, with a glass front—but this was an LCD and was . . . pliant.

Even though he had no intention of really doing it, he speculated what would happen if he pushed the pin into the soft surface. Would the screen go blank? Would it blow up? Would there be a spark? It gave him a small degree of satisfaction to imagine Gary's expression when he saw a hole in his precious bargain-basement monitor.

Slowly, Chad pressed the pin against it, just enough to make an indentation but not enough to cause actual damage.

Someone turned up the volume on "Jingle Bell Rock." Again.

A sharp bang resounded above him. The rickety overhead light rattled. Keeping his hand pressed against the screen, Chad looked up at the same time as something about the size of a quarter fell down from the ballast and landed on his head.

Chad pushed his chair back and jumped to his feet, swiping the top of his head with both hands until he knocked something off. He stilled and stared down at a huge, dead, dust-covered spider in the center of his desktop. Then he looked at his monitor, his note pinned firmly to the center of the screen.

The area around the pin distorted and a black oozy liquid leaked out.

Now he knew.

He sank back into his chair, flicked the dead spider into the wastebasket, and watched as the yellow note soaked up the black goo.

Either Gary would make him pay for a new monitor, or he'd fire Chad for willful destruction of company property.

Chad sighed.

Gary wouldn't fire him. Chad worked too hard and too long for too little pay and zero appreciation.

As he continued to stare at his note, he crossed his arms over his chest. Nothing was ever going to change if he continued to put up with the way Gary treated him.

Not only had he not taken a vacation in two years, he was stuck working on Christmas Eve when everyone else had gone home. Scrooge had even locked up the coffee supplies.

Chad squeezed his eyes shut. He'd finally had enough.

He turned his head to the door, in the direction of Gary's office, and called out, "Gary, even though you can't hear me, I'm telling you right now, I quit." Out of habit, he reached to turn off the damaged monitor. "Oh, and Merry Christmas," he muttered as he pressed the button.

When he pushed himself away from the desk, as usual the broken wheel of his crappy chair locked.

He squirmed out of the seat, stood, spun around, and gave it a hefty shove.

The chair banged against the wall with enough force that his framed college diploma shook and then hung crooked.

Gently, Chad removed it from the wall. "For all the good all my years of college did," he mumbled as he pulled the tail of his shirt out of his pants and wiped the dust off the top of the frame. Cradling his hard-earned diploma beneath his arm, he picked up the small plaque with his name on it from the desk, retrieved his coffee mug, grabbed his coat off the coat rack, tossed his small cache of personal effects into an empty box, and headed for the door of what had once been his dream job. "Attention everyone," he said to the empty chairs as he walked past them for the last time, "Elvis has left the building." Except Elvis would have had an entourage to carry his stuff to his car.

After setting the box on the passenger seat and starting the engine, Chad got out of the car to unplug the block heater. As he wound the cord, it occurred to him that he didn't know what he was going to do. He had nowhere to go. Everyone he knew was busy getting ready for friends and family on Christmas day. He couldn't intrude. Especially not in his current mood.

Rather than go home to an empty apartment, Chad simply headed north. Maybe if he drove far enough, he would find Santa. Maybe he would even make it as far as the Canadian border, which had to be close to the North Pole.

As he drove through the city, the more decorations he saw, the worse he felt.

When he approached the city limits, rather than turning around and driving past the depressing sights again, he followed the sign pointing to the entrance for Highway 10 North and kept going.

The recent snowfall had left a stark white covering on the fields beside the highway, almost sterile, unlike the brown slush and Minneapolis muck created from the mix of ever-increasing volumes of salt and sand that kept the roads clear, deiced, and safe for thousands of frantic rush-hour drivers every day.

As he drove away from the city, his stress levels melted, without the necessity of industrial-grade salt.

Instead of turning on the radio, since he didn't want to hear Christmas music, Chad simply let the hum of the tires and the monotony of the bumps when he hit the expansion seams on the concrete highway soothe his shattered nerves.

From inside his pocket, his cell phone beeped. "Whoever you are, leave me alone," he grumbled as he reached into his pocket and hit the mute button without checking the call display. He didn't want to explain his actions to anyone, especially when he couldn't explain them to himself.

Because there was no traffic, Chad took the turn to go onto route 371, which turned into route 200.

He passed a sign that read Manhattan Beach, although he wondered what kind of beach would be up here and how big such a place could be, but the only Manhattan he could think of was New York City.

Which was the last thing he wanted. More crowds.

Chad kept driving until the sun had almost set. He flipped on the lights and started to think about turning around to go back and which highway he'd come off when a beep sounded and the gas light came on.

Chad winced. He had no idea how far he could go before he ran out of gas.

He didn't want to take the chance of becoming stranded in the middle of nowhere on a cold winter night, but he had no idea where he was and he couldn't remember the last time he'd passed a gas station. He'd declined the option when the car salesman had asked if he wanted a GPS, and now he was sorry he'd been so cheap.

A sign pointing down a country road directing him to a town called Piney Meadows nearly made him shout for joy. He hadn't heard of the town before, but if Piney Meadows had a sign, it had to have a gas station. He turned onto the dark, narrow road.

Fortunately, he didn't have to go too far before he saw the glow of lights in the distance. Not only did he need gas, he also had to use the facilities.

The main drag was only a few blocks long, but he could see the sign for one gas station.

It was dark.

Chad smacked the steering wheel with his fist. The station was closed. Everything was closed.

He pulled to the side of the road, turned the car off, and reached into his pocket for his cell phone. Despite it being Christmas Eve, he could call his best friend for help. Brad would google the town of Piney Meadows and be here in a few hours with a can of gas. Even though Chad knew he'd never hear the end of it, another blow to his already damaged pride wasn't as bad as freezing to death in the metropolis of Piney Meadows, home of one closed gas station.

Chad flipped open the phone and hit the unlock button, only to see the warning note for a low battery appear for three seconds before the display went blank.

Chad stared at the phone, then looked up at the glow of lights in the distance that had guided him this far.

The building was bigger than a house and smaller than a mall, but whatever it was, if it meant people, it was where he was going.

Instead of using the auto start and hoping that starting the engine manually might save a few drops of gas, Chad turned the key. The engine whined, chugged a few times, then died. He dropped his head to the steering wheel, muttered a phrase he hadn't said for a number of years, and then looked up. Ahead of him at the end of the block, two people walked on the street toward the lit area. Behind him, the headlights of another car appeared in the distance, confirming that something was indeed going on at the source of light.

He got out of the car, hit the button to lock the doors, pulled up his collar as best he could against the biting wind, and walked toward the light, hoping he would make it before his nose turned white with frostbite. Above the building in the distance, beaming with a golden glow, was a cross.

He nearly groaned out loud.

A church.

He didn't know whether to laugh with relief or smack himself for his own sarcastic attitude. This town was so small it didn't have what he really wanted, which was a mall bustling with people before it closed for the holiday. Instead, the hub of activity was a church.

Just like the other buildings he'd passed, it was old and exactly what he imagined a picturesque little country church to be, although it really wasn't so little. It was about the same size as the church his parents had dragged him to every Sunday, when he'd believed in such things. But God obviously had a sense of humor, because the church was the only place open that was warm and sheltered, and he was almost at the point of desperation.

If it were the same here as where he'd grown up, on Christmas Eve there would be free coffee and snacks. And a men's room.

Just the thought of food, even stale cookies and weak coffee, caused his stomach to grumble painfully. He hadn't eaten since breakfast, and he was so hungry he was starting to feel sick. If his queasy stomach wasn't bad enough, his teeth chattered so hard he hoped he wouldn't shake a filling loose. His leather jacket looked good, but it didn't protect him from the wind. Here, in the roaring metropolis—no sarcasm intended, at least not much—of Piney Meadows, he wouldn't have to wait overnight in his car to freeze to death.

He'd never experienced wind like this in his life. In the city, when he ran from his car to the office building, the leather protected him. But here the buildings were too far apart and too small to offer protection. He'd heard the terminology on the radio, that the temperature was minus 5 but felt like minus 20. Now he knew what that felt like—the hard way.

Chad quickened his pace.

2

Chad made his way across the small parking lot and headed for the door, weaving his way through the throngs of people milling about. Strangely, many in the crowd were dressed like characters from a historical novel. Some of the women wore white bonnets.

Often when he'd flown out on business trips he'd seen small groups of women wearing such things. What their names were escaped him, but he knew it had to do with some religion. They weren't nuns. Hutterites or something like that.

Chad sucked in a deep breath, then nearly coughed from the sharpness of the cold. Church was the last place he wanted to be, but the costumes meant this wouldn't be a regular service; instead it would be a holiday pageant. If that were the case, then it wouldn't be so bad, and he could suffer through it. He would sit in the back row until the production ended. Then he would find someone who could siphon some gas out of their car into his, and he would be on his way. It was either that or spend the night in his car until the gas station opened up on Christmas Day and hope he didn't freeze to death.

He forced himself to look relaxed, exhaled a breath in a white puff, and entered the building.

Near the door, a row of wide-brimmed hats hung on pegs.

Just like the crowd outside, even the building looked like something out of a historical novel. Old pinewood planks, worn pews, and lots of old, worn wood everywhere.

Even the people who weren't in the play looked odd.

About half the men wore long, dark gray coats. Some coats were fastened, but those that were open showed plain-colored dark suits beneath. Not a single man wore a tie.

But he wasn't there to check out local fashion blunders.

The moment he came out of the washroom, a man approached him, smiled, and extended his hand.

"Welcome to Piney Meadows Full Gospel Mennonite Church. Our drama is about to start. Let me find you an empty seat. We have a full house, but I am sure we can find a spot for you to sit."

After Chad returned the handshake, he forced himself to smile politely, hoping he looked more sincere than he felt.

The man asked a bunch of people in one of the pews to shuffle and make room to allow Chad to squeeze in.

"Enjoy the performance," the man said, still smiling. "And I hope and pray you have a very merry Christmas."

Chad's head spun. "Yeah," he mumbled. "Merry Christmas."

The play began, allowing Chad some time to let his head clear. As the plot unfolded, he actually began to enjoy the show.

Until the last couple of years, Chad had been to many Christmas performances, but this one was different. Most were expectedly preachy, but not this one. It was almost like two different plays were going on at the same time. For a while, the scene was the predictable storyline surrounding the actual birth of Christ, except that every once in a while the biblical characters were joined by a group of Mennonite people, who shouldn't have been there but somehow fit the progression of the story. At least, he assumed they were Mennonites, because the person who greeted him said this was a Mennonite church. About halfway through the drama, the two groups started talking, interacting in the strangest presentation of the Christmas story he'd ever seen.

He liked it. Not only was it unique, the music was energizing to his weary soul.

It almost made him want to go to church again.

Almost.

By the time it ended, Chad's throat tightened and he felt oddly moved, even though he knew the Christmas story inside out from seeing it almost annually. As the actors shuffled to the front and began to form a line, applause erupted throughout the audience, so he openly joined in.

Center front onstage, the woman who played Mary, a woman with the voice of an angel, held hands with the woman who played an angel character, along with the bearded man who played Joseph. When the whole cast had lined up, they all joined hands and bowed awkwardly. The audience stood and the applause increased to a roar.

These people were good.

As soon as the applause died down, most of the cast fled the stage like a flock of lemmings, leaving only Mary and a few other key characters, who started to unplug microphones and wind cords.

Being at the back, Chad arrived at the refreshment table first. He grabbed a cookie and ignored the coffee, then looked around the room for the least populated spot, which happened to be near the musicians' area. Only one person remained—a guy about his age who had been playing the piano. He looked like an honest fellow, and Chad needed a huge favor.

"I really enjoyed your play," Chad mumbled around a mouthful of cookie.

"I am glad you enjoyed it, it was our pleasure." The man paused in piling up his music and sighed. "This was our final performance." He straightened and turned to Chad with a somewhat sad smile. "Are you from a nearby town? We have clear highways tonight, so you will have a pleasant drive home."

Chad stopped chewing and looked at the man. He had the same accent as the older man who had directed him to his seat.

"Funny you should mention that. The gas station down the street is closed. Do you know somewhere else I can buy gas?"

"*Ja*, there is another gas station in the next town, about thirty miles east."

"I can't go thirty miles. My tank is completely empty. My car died on the street down the block."

"Brian will not open the gas station tonight or tomorrow."

In a town this size, Chad found it amusing, but not surprising, that the piano player knew the name of the person who owned the gas station. "Then I'm going to need a favor. I won't be able to get home unless someone can siphon some gas out of their tank into mine. I'll pay a fair price." He jerked his thumb over his shoulder, toward the wooden cross on the wall above the stage. "I'll even make a donation to the church." He swiped his hand down the side of his pants to wipe the crumbs off his fingers and extended his hand. "My name's Chad Jones. I'm from Minneapolis, so I'm going to need a fair amount of gas to get home."

The man's brows knotted, and he returned Chad's handshake. "Ja, you will. My name is Ted Wiebe. You will need more gas than I have in my own car right now, because I must also drive all the way to Minneapolis tonight and then home again. All of the people here from my own congregation have walked. Everyone else is strangers, so I do not know who I can ask such a thing."

Ted's interesting accent almost made Chad smile, except he'd started to feel a welling of panic in his gut. Not only did it look like he wasn't getting home, he didn't think a town this small would have a hotel. As the overnight temperatures continued to drop, he wouldn't be alive if he had to sleep in the car overnight.

Ted glanced at the door, then back to Chad. "You are a long way from Minneapolis to be traveling with an empty gas tank."

"I didn't expect to be so far from home." He shrugged his shoulders. "I kind of quit my job and didn't have anywhere to go, so I just got in my car and kept driving without thinking of where I was going until I got here." Not that he wanted to play the sympathy factor, but after all, this was a church. "So I need to look for a gas station and then I need to look for another job, but that will wait until after Christmas." He gave a lame laugh. "Know anyplace that needs an office manager? I've got references."

Ted stopped moving, and his eyes widened.

"I am looking for a general manager. Do you have business college or experience?"

Chad sighed. "Yeah. Two years of college, three years of management experience."

"Why did you travel so far from Minneapolis? Are you moving out of the cities?"

Chad pictured the quaint little area he'd driven through that was Main Street in this little town. He hadn't really thought about it, but he'd never liked the hustle and bustle of the city or the rat race that his job had become. He'd received an eviction notice anyway, so he needed to find another place to live by the end of December, besides needing to find a new job. And a tank of gas. Maybe he should move to a small town. The rent and the taxes would probably be lower, too. "Yeah. I just might move out of town. Maybe even a place like this. What's this place called? Piney Village?"

"It is called Piney Meadows. If you are interested, I would like to interview you for a job as general manager for our local furniture factory. We handcraft old-style Mennonite furniture and ship it all over North America."

"That's not something I've done before, but it sounds interesting. When's a good time to talk? I assume you don't want to have that kind of conversation here, at the church."

Ted checked his watch. "No, I must talk to someone in a few minutes, and then I must take her to the Minneapolis airport. I will not buy gas on the Lord's birthday, but when I return we can siphon out what I have left in my car and you can be on your way. In the meantime, you are invited to stay at my house."

Chad's chest tightened. He'd expected a member of this quaint church to be nice, but not this accommodating. "Don't worry about rushing back from the airport on my account. I don't have plans for Christmas day, so it doesn't matter what time you return." It would probably be better if he could sleep on Ted's couch until daylight, so he didn't have to drive without sleep on a dark highway he didn't know.

Ted smiled. "I only ask that, while you are at my house, you give me your car keys and your driver's license. I am sure you understand."

Chad grinned back. He could see that this guy was a good manager, thinking ahead.

He reached into his pocket. "I'll do better than that. Here's my keys, and take my whole wallet. You'll also have all my credit cards, bank card, birth certificate, and a couple of hundred bucks in cash."

"*Danke shoen*," Ted said as he accepted Chad's keys and wallet.

As he slipped them into his pocket, the lady who played Mary ran up to them, holding her floppy skirt up awkwardly so she didn't trip, showing bright red tennis shoes on her feet instead of the plain leather sandals that people in Bible days would have worn.

Ted turned to the woman. "Miranda, it is a good thing you are here. I must talk to you, it is very important. But first, I would like to introduce you to Chad Jones. I think you will find that Chad has an interesting story to share."

She turned to Chad and smiled graciously. "Good evening, Chad. I don't mean to be rude, but please excuse me." She handed a red cell phone to Ted. "I don't know who this person is, but someone called for you a few minutes ago. It must be terribly important for them to call on Christmas Eve like this, and I thought I'd give you the phone so you can call them back."

Ted pushed the button to activate the call display. He nodded when the number appeared on the screen. "Excuse me. I must find a quiet place and call him back. This is very important. I will not be long."

As Ted rushed off, Miranda released the voluminous folds of her skirt, straightened it, turned to Chad, and smiled. "I hope you enjoyed our play."

Chad returned her smile, in a much better mood than when he'd first arrived. "Yes. I did. It wasn't at all what I expected to see in a place like this." Thoughts of the productions at the church where he'd grown up flickered through his mind. They hadn't been as good as this one, yet this place was in the middle of nowhere. His own words replayed in his head, causing his smile to drop. He really had worded his thoughts badly—he'd meant it as a compliment, but it hadn't sounded like one. "Please don't take that the wrong way. It was very,

very good, which is why I was so surprised. You have a very talented group of people."

"Yes, we do." Without moving her head, her eyes shifted from side to side. At the same time, Chad struggled to think of something to say and wished Ted would return quickly.

Miranda cleared her throat and looked at him again. "Where are you from? I'm curious to know how you found out about our play."

"It's funny you should ask that. I actually didn't intend to be here. I was driving around and got lost, then I ran out of gas down the block. The gas station was closed, and the church looked like something was going on with all the people and lights, so I walked in and got a very pleasant surprise."

Her smile faltered. "I'm glad you enjoyed it. We—" Her sentence was cut off by Ted's abrupt return.

Chad didn't know why he hadn't noticed it before, but Ted was holding a hat, the same kind of hat that the Mennonite men in the play had been wearing as part of their costumes. In the back of his mind, he wondered if maybe this hat wasn't a costume but really was his own hat, since Ted was a musician, not an actor.

As Miranda looked at Ted, her expression turned sappy. She blinked a few times and turned back to him. "It was nice meeting you, Chad. I'm going to go change and then Ted and I have to leave quickly. I have a plane to catch."

Ted shook his head. "I will be dropping Chad off at my house before we go. He is going to stay for the night."

Before Chad could explain, Miranda grasped Ted's elbow and hauled him off. "Are you crazy? You don't know him or . . ." Her voice became softer the farther away she dragged him.

Chad felt caught between wanting to hear the rest of their conversation and being polite.

Since it looked like the man could one day be his boss, he decided being polite was the better choice.

Out of the corner of his eye, Chad saw Ted grin as he displayed Chad's keys and wallet to his lady friend.

He turned away, but Miranda's cell phone beeped, drawing Chad's attention back to them. With a speed he hadn't seen in a long time, Ted grabbed the phone out of Miranda's hand and held it over his head. Miranda sucked in a deep breath, squatted just a bit, and just as he thought she'd do, jumped like a star basketball player and grasped Ted's wrist.

Chad nearly laughed. From the look on Ted's face, the poor guy hadn't seen it coming. Brittany would have done the same thing if he'd held her cell phone over her head. Except that Brittany wasn't as tall as Miranda, so she never would have gotten it.

Chad's chest constricted.

He didn't want to think of Brittany now. She was gone. The next time he saw her would probably be in court.

Thinking of Brittany and what should have happened versus what actually happened, Chad couldn't take his eyes away from the young couple.

Ted dropped to one knee, pressed his hat to his chest, and looked up at Miranda with an expression so besotted it was obvious what was happening.

The man was proposing. In a church. The crowd had begun to disperse, but plenty of people still lingered.

This time should be the happiest in a man's life, when the woman he loves accepts his proposal. At least, it is supposed to be.

Chad held his breath, waiting, unable to tear his gaze away. However, instead of the expected hug and kiss and declarations of love forever, the two of them were having a conversation.

He'd had many conversations with Brittany, and none of them had turned out the way he wanted. Especially the last one.

He didn't know these people, but he wanted them to be happy. The kind of happy that lasted seventy-five years, give or take.

Just as Chad pictured Miranda leaving Ted hanging, the same way Brittany always left him hanging, Ted jumped up and grabbed Miranda tight, spun her around, and kissed her so intensely it made Chad's heart pound.

These people were in love. The way it should be.

"All right!" Chad called. He clapped a couple of times, then stuck his fingers in his mouth and whistled.

An elderly lady grabbed a teenaged boy by the sleeve, gave Chad a dirty look, then tugged the boy in a straight line away from Ted and Miranda, who were still smooching. "Do not look," she hissed to the boy, and both made a beeline for the door.

The place emptied quickly. Only the middle-aged man who had helped him find a seat, the man who had played the pastor—it was announced he really was the pastor—and a lady who was probably his wife, remained. Strangely, he didn't remember the wife being on stage, but she wore the same kind of costume, including the bonnet, as the women on stage in the non-nativity part of the play.

He turned around to see Ted, now wearing his hat, and Miranda walking toward him.

Ted looked so starry-eyed Chad almost laughed, but really, he felt happy for the guy.

"We are getting married," Ted said, blushing.

"Yeah, I can tell. Congratulations." He shook Ted's hand, really meaning it.

"Come. It is a long drive to the airport. I will take you to my house, and then we must leave."

The drive was only three blocks, so there was no time to start a conversation. Inside Ted's house, the living room contained more boxes than furniture. "My house does not usually look like this. These boxes, they are all Miranda's things. A truck will be by next Wednesday to pick everything up. There was no room for everything where she was staying, so we are doing it this way."

Ted showed him the kitchen, told him to help himself to anything he wanted to eat, and as soon as Ted pulled the key for the house off his key ring, Ted and Miranda were gone.

Compared to his own kitchen, Ted's was quite bare. It didn't even have what Chad considered the basics, including a dishwasher.

Chad's stomach grumbled painfully, reminding him that all he'd eaten was one cookie. It was a good cookie, but it hadn't done much to appease his hunger, so he went straight to the fridge to check it out. The first container he opened contained a casserole, so he spooned a healthy-sized serving onto a plate and put it into a microwave that looked brand-new.

While the casserole heated, he walked into the living room. Since he was going to be here for probably eight hours, he wanted to check out what was on TV.

Except there was no television.

He heard the microwave beep, but instead of returning to the kitchen, he walked down the hall, peeking in each room, looking for the den, where the television would be since it wasn't where he'd expected.

The first bedroom was obviously Ted's. Its furnishings included one double bed and a very solid and old but pristine dresser, with a matching armoire and night table. Plain, light blue curtains matched a fluffy bedspread as well as a small knitted thing under a lamp on the table beside the bed. The room was neat and tidy, and unlike Chad's, the bed was made. But there was no television in here, either.

The next room looked to be a well-lit office with a large desk and computer. But no television.

The third bedroom looked like a den, containing a small couch, an electric piano, a bookshelf piled with music and books, as well as a small desk and a guitar on a stand.

Still no television.

He felt invasive, but he walked down the stairs into the basement, which contained only a workbench, some piles of wood, tools, a plug-in heater that wasn't plugged in, and a set of shelves containing jars of preserves. It was cold and damp, and there was no television here, either.

Chad shivered and crossed his arms over his chest. The first thought that ran through his mind was that maybe he was being set up. He was going to be accused of stealing Ted's television. This didn't make sense, because Ted had the keys to his car, so Chad had no place to hide anything, especially something as large as a television.

He returned to the living room.

All the boxes were neatly stacked in the corner nearest the door. The furniture had been moved slightly to make room for the pile.

Chad took a quick inventory. Couch. Love seat. Recliner. Coffee table. Bookshelf. End tables. Lamp. Fireplace. Christmas tree.

He walked to where the television should have been, according to the layout of the room. There was no stand for a television, no speakers, and no DVD player. There also were no indentations on the carpet to show that anything had ever been there.

There really was no television in Ted's house.

Chad ran his fingers through his hair and studied the bookshelf lined with many great mysteries and thrillers, both new and classic.

He could see what Ted did with his time. Some of the books he'd already read; most he hadn't. Most were by Christian authors, something like his book collection had been, until the last few years.

He picked up a book that looked like a recent purchase. He'd bought the same book but hadn't started it yet. He brought the book to the table and began to eat. He didn't know what kind of casserole it was, but it was delicious. Not only was this Mennonite food good, the book was good, too. Instead of moving to sit on the couch in the living room, he stayed seated at Ted's kitchen table, reading Ted's new book.

He was about halfway through when the phone rang. His gut clenched. The only time anyone ever phoned in the middle of the night was if something bad had happened.

Since it was Christmas Eve, he hated to think that someone Ted knew or loved had died.

Chad picked up the phone. "Ted's house," he mumbled, struggling to remember Ted's last name.

"This is Ted. I am calling from the airport. I only have a minute to use the phone. There is an empty seat on the plane, and I can go to Seattle on standby to be with Miranda's family for Christmas. But you are at my home and I have your keys and your wallet in my pocket. You had said that you did not have plans for Christmas, and I do not like to ask this of you, but you are welcome to stay in Piney Meadows for Christmas. I can courier your keys and wallet back to you the day after Christmas. But if you wish to go home, I will not buy the ticket and I will be back in a few hours."

"Christmas on the coast with the future in-laws. That sounds like fun." Chad glanced around Ted's kitchen. He didn't care if he didn't make it home for Christmas. He'd received an invitation from Todd's parents, which he'd turned down because he didn't want to be a third wheel, or worse, hear the inevitable "I told you so" from Todd. His own parents were in Florida in the land of eternal sunshine, blissfully unaware of what had happened in the last two weeks. Not unusual. These days, they mostly were blissfully unaware of Chad. So instead of spending time with family and friends, feasting on turkey or ham with all the trimmings, he'd planned to barbecue hamburgers for one on his balcony. With the luck he'd been having, it would snow overnight and cover the grill anyway.

The leftovers in Ted's fridge would keep him fed better than anything he could ever cook. Here, he was just as alone, but one day he could look back and consider this an adventure. "You go to Seattle. I don't mind staying here. In fact, I've already dug into your library, and you have lots of good books I haven't read yet. I'm unemployed now, so I don't have to rush to get back to Minneapolis after Christmas. Have fun."

"I will call you when I can so we may talk about the job. I must hurry to move my car and get back so I can get on this plane. Thank you again. Merry Christmas, Chad."

"Merry Christmas, Ted, and again, congratulations."

After he hung up, Chad rested his fists on his hips and looked around the kitchen. When he'd gotten up for work this morning, never in his wildest dreams could he have imagined this.

The fridge certainly held enough food, and there were enough books that he wouldn't be bored. He could also check out Ted's guitar. They had the same taste in books; possibly they had similar tastes in music.

Just as Chad looked down the hall toward the den, the phone rang again.

"Ted's house," he answered, expecting it to be Ted again.

But it wasn't Ted's voice.

"This is Anna, I am Ted's secretary. He has called me to say that you are staying at his house until after Christmas. Rather than eating leftovers from Ted's fridge, I would like to invite you to join my family for Christmas dinner tomorrow. Do not be shy. It will be our pleasure to have you here."

One thing no one had ever called him was shy. Since the Mennonite leftovers were so good, he could only imagine what a Mennonite Christmas dinner fresh out of the oven with all the trimmings would be like.

"That sounds great. It would be an honor to come. Thank you for your hospitality. Just give me directions, and I'll be there. I just need to go find a pen and paper."

Anna giggled. "You do not need a pen and paper. We are next door. Please come at three o'clock. I will see you tomorrow."

3

*A*nna Janzen inhaled deeply to calm her nerves, telling herself to stop her hands from shaking or else she would spill the *oft mooss* before their guest arrived.

Beside her, her mama and Sarah, her *sesta*, worked diligently preparing the Christmas meal, making sure they would have enough food for their unexpected guest, in addition to her papa and David, her *brooda*. As if they wouldn't. Even though everyone knew they would have enough food to feed double her family, her mama still insisted on preparing an extra dish at the last minute.

At the thought of their visitor, Anna didn't know whether to be more nervous or more excited. Ted had told her that this man, Mr. Chad Jones, was from the cities.

Except for Miranda and those Ted invited to Piney Meadows to visit the furniture plant, she'd never actually spoken to anyone from the cities. She'd only been outside Piney Meadows once, when Miranda borrowed Ted's car and they had gone to deliver curtains and jars of fruit to their friend Theresa and her husband, Evan, who had moved to the cities.

That day, upon their arrival, all Theresa and Evan had talked about was the baby that was on the way and nothing about what it was like to move from Piney Meadows and live in the cities.

Even though Sarah and Miranda had become close friends, Miranda had always avoided talking about her life before she'd come here, even with Sarah. The hours Anna had spent in the car with Miranda and Sarah had been no different.

When Ted's clients visited the furniture factory, they only talked about business before she escorted them to their meetings with Ted.

All her life she'd been taught that even though there were some God-fearing people there, mostly the cities were full of sin and wrongdoing. As a child, she had believed this because her parents and pastor and the elders of the church would never preach a mistruth. As an adult, she had learned their words to be true because every time Ted returned from a business trip, he became extremely quiet, retreating into his office with the door closed and saying little for days until he regained his bearings.

Yet many people had left Piney Meadows to live in the cities, and she needed to know why. It couldn't be as bad as her parents told her or no one would leave Piney Meadows. Most of all, Miranda had come from the cities. Even though Miranda never fit in with their community, Miranda was a wonderful woman who loved God. When Ted phoned from the Minneapolis airport, during their short conversation, he told her he'd asked Miranda to marry him—of course, everyone knew he would. When they packed up the stage after the last performance, all had been surprised Ted had not asked for Miranda's hand in marriage. Instead, he proposed after they all had left, making Anna the first to know. She could hardly wait until after Christmas dinner to tell everyone it was now official.

Anna smiled and sighed, recalling Ted's short version of the evening. Perhaps it hadn't been the most romantic proposal, but it was from his heart.

One day, the same would happen to her.

Anna's smiled dropped.

The same would never happen to her here in Piney Meadows. Even though arranged marriages were no longer a strict part of their culture, parents still helped select mates for their children. Her parents had made it very clear they expected her to wed William. While he was a dear friend, she was fond of him only in a brotherly way and could not imagine life wedded to William.

Worse, she couldn't imagine being with William every day as his workmate, then going home with him as his wife.

One day, just like in the books she read, she would have a career and meet a handsome young man, fall in love, and live happily ever after.

This would never happen if she stayed in Piney Meadows.

Her only chance for happiness was to leave and live in the cities. However, the only people she knew who had moved to the cities were Theresa and Evan, but she couldn't even write them a letter to ask about their new lives. Her parents would see the mail before she did and ask what they'd said. She also couldn't ask anyone who would tell her parents about her questions.

But she could ask this man Ted had welcomed into his home. Mr. Chad Jones.

As if her thoughts had summoned him, the doorbell rang, loud and clear, sending her heart racing.

"I will answer the door," she muttered to her mama and Sarah, who both stood beside the stove.

"*Ach*, Sarah and I have everything under control here," her mama muttered while spooning the juice over the turkey. "This is nearly cooked. See to the door, and stay with our guest and make him comfortable."

"Danke shoen, *Mutta*," she replied, then turned to scurry from the kitchen through the living room, past her papa and David, who sat talking on the couch. Since they saw her hurrying to the door, neither got up, silently acknowledging that Mr. Jones was technically her boss's guest and therefore her responsibility.

At the door, Anna paused, straightening her posture and preparing herself the same as she did when she welcomed Ted's visitors to his office at the factory, hoping she could hide her nervousness.

Wrapping her fingers around the doorknob, the thought flashed through her mind that she didn't know anything about her guest other than his name, Chad Jones, and that he'd become stranded after their Christmas performance at church. Being Christmas Eve, the church had been filled with both guests and her people. On the stage, with the spotlights in her eyes, she hadn't been able to see the number of people seated in the sanctuary. She'd heard every seat had been filled, with more people standing at the back, crowded together. After the performers had taken their bows to those in attendance, the house lights had come on. As if being onstage hadn't been bad enough, she'd nearly fainted when she saw the sea of people, most of whom she didn't know, and she knew almost everyone in the town.

Mr. Jones had been one in that sea, and now she was about to meet him.

She didn't know how she could talk to him in private with her papa and brooda in the living room, but the need to ask about living in the cities burned within her.

Although, if she talked about the factory as Ted had asked her to do, her papa and brooda would soon become uninterested. Then she could easily move to a more secluded area of the living room and ask the questions she needed to ask.

Anna pulled the door open, reminding herself to smile.

As the door opened, she gasped, and stared.

Perhaps because Ted had spoken of him in a manner similar to the way he spoke of the visitors to the factory, she'd thought he would be an older gentleman. The opposite of what she'd expected, Mr. Jones appeared to be closer to Ted in age, but even that wasn't so shocking. Before her stood the most handsome man she'd ever seen.

Unlike the dark-haired men in Piney Meadows, Mr. Jones had blond hair and blue eyes, a strong jaw that contrasted with his fair coloring, and a smile that made her nearly forget to breathe. Unlike the men who worked on the farms, he had a thin build and was quite tall. Wearing an expensive-looking waist-length jacket, and without a hat, he was woefully underdressed for December weather.

A gust of cold wind brought her to her senses.

"Come in, Mr. Jones," she muttered, glad to find her voice, as she backed up to allow him entry.

He grinned and shook his head as he stomped the snow off his boots. "Please. I'm not Mr. Jones. Mr. Jones is my father. I'm Chad."

Thoughts of his age caused her to look more closely at his face, drawing her attention to dark circles under his eyes.

Ted had asked her to make sure Chad was comfortable, because Ted hadn't been sure he would be able to get a flight back on standby the day after Christmas, so Mr. Jones—Chad—would be staying in Ted's home for at least another night.

"Ted has asked me to be sure that you have been comfortable in his home. Did you not sleep well?"

Chad smiled, but the smile wasn't as cheerful as his earlier greeting. "I was quite comfortable." He glanced from side to side then looked out the window at the endless drifts of snow. "But I have to admit that I had trouble sleeping. It sure is quiet here in Piney Meadows. I mean, really quiet. Like . . . nothing is out there. And it's really dark, too."

Anna's lips tightened as she tried to understand what he meant. "Of course, it is quiet. It is winter. It is only during planting and harvesting seasons that the machinery will start at dawn." She had no idea what he meant about it being dark. Of course it was dark at night.

One side of his mouth twitched up, and he ran his fingers through his hair. "That's not what I meant. In Minneapolis, I live on a main street. The traffic never stops. There's always something moving. Horns blowing. Sirens. Cars driving by, even in the middle of the night. Planes overhead on their way to and from the airport. There's constant noise, like the hum of the lights and computers." He looked up at the light fixture, which made no noise at all. But she knew what he meant. At the office, the fluorescent lights emitted a constant noise, as did the computers. Both she and Ted found it disturbing, but there was nothing they could do about it.

"There's always something going on," he continued. "Not as much as during the day, but there's always something making noise. Here, there's nothing. Absolutely nothing."

Anna tried to think of the sounds of night. In the summer the crickets chirped most of the night, and the birds began their songs at the break of dawn, but in the winter, he was right—nothing made noise on a winter night.

He again turned his head to look out the window. "It's also really dark. No streetlights. No traffic, nothing. All the lights in all the houses are out, and the houses are really far apart.

There's absolutely nothing moving out there. It's as though the whole town shuts down. Completely."

"Of course, the town is silent. People are sleeping."

He shrugged his shoulders. "Of course. It's just that I'm not used to a total shutdown like this. But it was nice. I think I could like it. It was just a little unnerving because I've never experienced it before. This is like camping, except in a house. And even quieter."

Anna had read books about people in the cities going camping. They would leave their comfortable homes and beds and deliberately sleep in tents, on the ground, then cook their food outside over an open fire instead of in a well-stocked kitchen. She couldn't imagine something so ridiculous.

He patted the pocket of his jeans. "Before Ted left I got my spare charger for my phone out of my car. Otherwise, it would have been dangerous."

A chill ran through her. "You had to phone someone in the middle of the night? Were you ill?" She didn't want to think that a man his age needed to be near a phone in case of a medical emergency.

He grinned. "No, I was fine. I used it for light."

"Light?"

His grin widened and he reached into his pocket. Her breath caught. Chad Jones was truly handsome. He flipped his cell phone open and held it up. It glowed with a dull light, just like Miranda's had.

"It's not much, but in the utter blackness, it sheds a lot of light. Just like at a concert."

"Concert?"

"You know, when everyone holds up their phones and then sways to the music."

"I do not know about that."

He shrugged his shoulders and returned his phone to his pocket. "It's not a flashlight, but it worked." He bent to remove his boots and then set them on the mat beside the door. "I want to thank you for inviting me for Christmas dinner at the last minute. Is there anything I can do to help?"

"*Nein.* There is not. My mama and sesta are in the kitchen, and they have told me to stay here with you to visit."

She led him into the living room. Immediately the men in her family stood. "Chad Jones, this is my papa, Peter, and my brooda, David." The men shook hands to greet each other, then her papa and brooda sat. But Chad did not sit. Instead, he turned and looked at the entrance to the kitchen, toward the echoes of pots and spoons. "My mama and sesta are in the kitchen."

She hadn't meant it as an invitation, but as soon as the words were out of her mouth, Chad turned and started walking toward the kitchen.

Anna stared, unable to believe he was going into the kitchen. He was halfway there before she could get her feet to move. She dashed after him, skidding to a halt at his side as he stopped in the doorway.

Both her mama and Sarah froze at the sight of a man in their kitchen—a man they didn't know.

Anna cleared her throat. "Mutta, Sarah, this is Chad Jones, our guest. Chad, this is my mama, Susan, and my sesta, Sarah."

Chad smiled brightly. "Ladies," he said with a slight nod, "I'm pleased to meet you." He looked toward the open oven door with the turkey sticking out on the rack, ready for her mama to baste it. "That looks heavy. Would you like me to take it out of the oven for you?"

"Ach, nein," her mama said, shaking her head. "You are our guest. Please go sit down. We will call everyone when supper is ready."

"Are you sure? I don't mind. I always lifted the turkey in and out of the oven for my mother. I know how heavy they can be, and that's the biggest turkey I've ever seen."

Her mama stepped back, probably out of shock, but Chad seemed to take it as an answer. He stepped forward, slipped her mama's oven mitts onto his hands, and proceeded to pull the heavy turkey out of the oven, resting it on the stovetop and then closing the oven door.

He wiped the steam from his forehead with his sleeve. "Wow. Now I know for sure that's the biggest turkey I've ever seen. How many other people are coming?"

Her mama's eyebrows knotted. "No one else is coming. Please, go be comfortable in the living room. We will call you when everything is ready."

"Sure. Just let me know when you want that turkey back in the oven," he said, as if he didn't understand what her mama had clearly said. She would not call him back into her kitchen. She would only call him to the table, when everything was ready to eat.

Anna glanced toward her mama for instruction, and the sweep of her mama's hand in the air told her to stay with their guest in the living room, with the men, perhaps to keep him out of the kitchen.

Anna had never *not* helped in the kitchen for Christmas dinner. It would be strange, but she would follow her mama's wishes.

She directed Chad back into the living room, and this time he sat on the couch with her papa and David.

Pape smiled brightly. "I welcome you to Piney Meadows. Anna has told me that you came to see our church's Christmas presentation and have become stranded."

Chad smiled back. "Not directly. I actually got lost and this is where I found myself. I must say it was a pleasant surprise. You have a very talented group here."

Pape's smile dropped. "Then God has a reason you are here. Do you know yet what it is?"

Chad's eyes widened. "I . . . uh . . ."

Pape only nodded. "For all things, God has a purpose. If you have only just arrived in our community, let us tell you something of it."

Anna sat and listened while Pape told Chad a short version of the history of their town, the crops the farms grew, and a little about the furniture factory, which she suspected Chad already knew—after all, he was technically Ted's guest.

She tried not to show that she was practically squirming in her seat. While she naturally wanted to be polite to their guest, she also wanted to ask him many questions about living and working in the cities, which she couldn't do in front of her family.

She'd never seen her papa talk so much, yet, despite some repetition, Chad graciously listened, smiling and nodding at all the appropriate moments. She thought he listened even more closely when her papa spoke of the furniture factory. He then asked questions about it, and what it was like to work there.

Which meant this was her opportunity to get Chad alone.

She gently rested her fingers on her papa's forearm. "Pape, I can tell our guest many things about the furniture factory."

Pape's face froze, and his smile faded. "Yes. Anna has been working for Ted for a few years, but she does not work in the factory with the rest of the ladies. Anna does not sew; she works with Ted and William and uses the computer."

Anna's insides quivered as her father continued to explain the history of the factory without her help. Many people in their community were pleased with the way Ted had expanded the furniture factory. When it started, only Ted's *onkel,* Bart, and a few of his friends were building furniture, and Ted's *Taunte* Odelle sewed all the cushions. After a few years of selling the furniture at all the nearby county fairs, Bart started getting orders from furniture stores in the cities, so the business grew. Then when Ted came back from college and took over the management from his onkel, the business expanded even more, so that now dozens of people worked at the factory instead of having to move away because there weren't enough jobs on the farms.

Now, not only men but many women also worked at the factory. Of course, Anna was the only woman who did not sew, but she enjoyed working in the office and being Ted's secretary.

That she worked at the factory displeased her papa, even though he allowed it. He was even less pleased that she had chosen to work in the office, instead of doing typical women's work. But Ted knew her well—they'd nearly grown up together, living next door to each other since they were *fonn kgleen aun,* babies from young on. He knew she liked working with the numbers better than sewing, so he took her out of the sewing pool and asked if she would be his secretary.

He had been very brave to ask her father's permission to give her the job. Her papa had not been pleased, but because it was Ted, he allowed her to work in the office. Out of gratitude, she always did her very best for Ted.

Now, she wanted more than to marry and work at the furniture factory until she had babies. While many of the people of Piney Meadows left to go to college, less than half returned to work and live there. Most of the people who went to college didn't come back, and she needed to know why—and if she could do the same.

Finally, her papa seemed to be finished talking.

She turned to Chad. "I can tell you all about the furniture factory now."

He smiled. "Thank you. I'd like that."

She stood. "I know Pape does not need to hear this. He hears much of what happens every day. Let us go sit across the room where we will not disturb them."

Chad stood as well. "Uh . . . sure . . ."

They hadn't taken more than three steps when her mama and Sarah began to carry bowls to the table. "Anna," her mama called out. "Come help, and we will eat sooner, before everything becomes cold."

Anna knew that would never happen.

Chad turned. "You mean your mother lifted that huge turkey herself? She didn't call me or your father to help lift it."

"Do not worry. Please sit with Pape and David, and we will call when it is time to eat."

Anna tried not to let her disappointment show to Chad or to her family. She hadn't had an opportunity to talk to Chad about the cities, and now she didn't know when she would. It was probably a sin to pray that Ted would be unable to get a flight back tomorrow, but she knew she would anyway. If that happened, tomorrow, instead of going to work, she could walk with Ted's guest to give him a tour of Piney Meadows, and then she could ask him all the questions she wanted to ask without anyone listening.

A sense of peace filled her, making her wonder if God was telling her that He had heard her prayer.

4

Chad stood, staring at the refrigerator with his hand pressed over his stomach. Instead of opening it, he continued to stare at the closed door.

During the first night in Ted's home, the complete silence had unnerved him. But last night, he'd slept longer and deeper than he'd ever slept in his whole life. It made him think that if Ted couldn't get a flight back for a few more days, he'd get so used to the soundlessness that when he got back home the noises that used to lull him to sleep would jolt him like a clanging gong all night long. He'd never experienced such peaceful silence in his life. He could get used to the nighttime void that was Piney Meadows. Without the stresses of the job eating at him like they usually did, even in his dreams, and without having to block out the clatter of the night, he felt like a bear waking after a winter-long hibernation.

Except unlike a bear, he wasn't the least bit hungry, despite knowing the volume of delicious leftovers waiting for him when he finally opened the refrigerator door. He'd eaten so much for Christmas dinner he technically shouldn't need to eat again until sometime next week.

Piney Meadows was unlike any place he'd ever been. Outside, it was almost as quiet as it had been all night. Since today was a normal working day and he didn't have a job to go to, today was his chance to find out if Piney Meadows was as peaceful during the daytime as it had been at night. He suspected not just Christmas Eve and Christmas Day quieted the people of Piney Meadows; it looked like the whole town shut down every day once the sun set, and it didn't appear too active in the daytime, either.

His mind jumped over all the possibilities for his future. If he really did move forward with the job Ted had spoken of, he'd never again need to force himself to sleep through the never-ending white noise of the city. If he didn't get the job here, of course he would go back to Minneapolis. Besides looking for another job, he needed to find another place to live, since he'd received an eviction notice.

His heart sank at the thought of the kinds of places that might be available to him. He doubted any decent place would let him sign a lease given his current economic status. The possibility existed that he could put the few pieces of furniture he had in storage, and he'd find himself sleeping on a friend's couch until he found a job and could sign another lease and buy more furniture.

When he found another job, he was also going to have to pay money to find Brittany, and the sooner the better.

With an unsure future in front of him, he started mentally kicking himself for being so impulsive as to quit, but as the saying went, hindsight is twenty-twenty. Being here in Piney Meadows without the means to get home slammed a number of doors shut. By now, Gary had not only seen the damaged monitor and that Chad's personal effects had been cleaned out, he would also have seen the note, which hadn't been the most respectful or professional way to terminate his employment.

Even if he went back to Gary begging on his hands and knees, Gary wouldn't take him back—everyone in the office would have seen the statement he'd made when he left. Gary's pride would never allow him to hire Chad back.

So for now, Chad would make the best of this time off. Even though Ted had promised to return the day after Christmas—which was today—Chad doubted that Ted would be able to book a flight. He also had doubts Ted could get a seat on standby.

Still, no matter how long it took Ted to come back, Chad wouldn't starve. Susan had given him enough leftovers to last a week, even though he'd told her he expected to be leaving within a day. Now he hoped he wouldn't be. He could take the enforced time here to think and plan.

Chad let his mind wander to summarize the previous day. Anna was a sweet woman, and her family, except for her father, were just as sweet and pleasant as she was. Her father seemed to have strong opinions on what was right and wrong, but still, Chad could tell Peter was a good man—just a little regimented.

Their home was even simpler than Ted's, which he found surprising, because Ted lived alone. In addition, their house was smaller, yet five people lived in one small three-bedroom bungalow.

The first thing Chad had noticed when he entered their living room was that, just like Ted, they didn't have a television.

Then, when he'd gone into the kitchen to meet his hostess, he'd tried not to let his mouth drop open when he saw Susan and Sarah both wearing the same kind of bonnets that the ladies on stage had worn during the play, as well as the same ugly dresses. Anna had also worn the same kind of dress, but it seemed to fit a little better.

Now that he thought about it, at the church, many of the ladies in the audience were wearing the same type of outfit, including the bonnets. During the play, he'd thought it might have been some kind of dress-up event, but apparently, it was the ladies' normal mode of dress.

He'd read of such communities in the newspaper but never paid much attention. Now he wished he had.

He now had to think most of the people he'd seen on Christmas Eve who were residents lived a similar lifestyle—simple, old fashioned, and deeply set in the ways of their faith. And they all went to bed early.

While he waited for Ted to phone, Chad decided to turn on Ted's computer and google this place to see what kind of future he might have if he stayed.

The computer wasn't new but it was certainly good enough for what he needed. He turned it on, waited for the operating system to boot up, then clicked the browser.

Instead of one of the search engine sites for the home page, a note came up that he wasn't hooked up to the Internet.

Chad's mouth tightened into a frown. He didn't want to do anything to upset Ted's system, and he hoped all he had to do was reboot the modem. Except he couldn't find it.

He got down on his hands and knees and crawled under the desk, just in case the modem was on top of the tower . . . but it wasn't.

Chad ran his fingers through his hair. He'd looked in every room in Ted's house to discover that Ted didn't have a television. But Ted had a computer, and while he'd been talking to Anna, she'd mentioned Ted connecting to his office from his home, so Chad knew his computer was online.

He sprawled all the way under the desk, and using his cell phone for light, looked at the back of the computer and wiggled all the connections.

Oddly, he didn't see a black cable to connect to the modem. He did find a telephone line coming from the back, which was odd because Ted didn't have this room set up as an office, so he doubted Ted had a fax line for his computer. Just in case, he traced the phone wire to a jack in the wall, telling him that Ted had an ISDL hookup, which didn't make sense, because there still should have been a modem.

Then, sitting on the floor, he stared at the monitor.

In the corner was an icon that said "Internet."

He reached forward for the mouse and clicked it.

A dial tone sounded, followed by the beeps of numeric dialing. A hiss sounded, then an electronic screech, two digital bong-like tones, ending with a long electronic hiss.

All Chad could do was stare. He'd heard these sounds while watching a documentary on the Internet. This was . . . a dial-up connection. He'd heard of it but never experienced it. A documentary had said that about five percent of the population still used dial-up.

As quickly as he could, Chad pushed himself up to his knees and worked the mouse to close the connection. He didn't know enough about dial-up to know if Ted might be paying for long distance charges for his Internet connection.

Chad shook his head.

No television, no cable modem or wireless . . . Yesterday—Christmas Day—Anna, her mother, and her sister had worn little white bonnets and old-world dresses that looked like something out of the 1800s—just like what the women in the play had worn on stage, only this was real life.

And yesterday he couldn't help noticing the disparity of the division of responsibility—it was like watching old reruns of *Leave It to Beaver*, only worse.

Yet, the ladies didn't seem unhappy. It seemed . . . normal.

What kind of place was this?

He tried to get a mental picture of the town but couldn't. During the journey from the church to Ted's house it had been dark, and he'd been in the back seat of Ted's car, not able to see much. In the daylight he'd only experienced what he could see as he walked from Ted's house to Susan and Peter's house next door.

Just as he pushed himself to his feet so he could look out the window, the phone rang.

"Ted's house," he answered.

"This is Ted. How are you, Chad? I hope you had a merry Christmas."

"I did." Although, maybe that was because it had been so different from anything he'd ever experienced. It felt like home, even though the home and family weren't his. "I hope you did, too."

"I did. But I am calling to say that I could not get a flight, and that everything is full yet for a few more days. Are you still interested in applying for the position as general manager at the furniture factory? If you are, everyone is back to work today, and my Onkel Bart would like to interview you, since I cannot."

Chad gulped and stiffened, even though he was alone. Maybe more alone than he'd ever been in his life.

The old saying made up of half truth and half sarcasm flashed through his mind—*this is the first day of the rest of your life.*

This was it—that proverbial first day.

He could thank Ted for his kind offer, go home, and beg Gary for his job back, and maybe if he ate enough crow, it would happen. He could get his professional life back on track, but was that what he wanted? The reason he was stranded here in Nowheresville, USA, was because he'd been driven past his level of tolerance. He couldn't go back to that.

A shiver ran up his spine recalling Peter's words—even though Chad was only here because he had run out of gas, Peter believed the real reason was because God had a reason. Chad couldn't imagine God getting involved in his life now. God hadn't done anything in his life for years, and if God really cared, he wouldn't be in his current situation, either professionally or personally.

Peter was obviously mistaken. But the fact did remain—the need for a change burned in Chad's gut. But when he'd walked out on his job, he hadn't seen the change being this big.

If he actually got the job here in Piney Meadows, he couldn't project how his life would change, only that the change would be big. He'd only been outside the city limits of Minneapolis once, when a friend had taken him fishing. The first thing he'd done when he got back to the city was to head straight for Starbucks.

Chad doubted Piney Meadows had a Starbucks.

Piney Meadows only had one gas station. And it was closed by 5:00 p.m. on Christmas Eve.

Piney Meadows. Where there was no television, limited Internet, and definitely no Walmart.

He didn't think he'd have to go very far and he'd find . . . cows.

He'd wanted a change in his life, and he couldn't see anything being more of a change than this.

Chad cleared his throat. "Yes. I'd love to set up a meeting with your uncle."

This was it. The first day had begun.

5

$\mathcal{A}$nna typed the figures into the spreadsheet, thankful this portion of her job didn't require too much thought. Anger still bit at her that her father had sent her to work instead of allowing her to take a day off to escort Ted's guest around Piney Meadows. Ted not only would have allowed it, he would have encouraged it.

Thinking of Ted, her fingers stalled over the keyboard. When Ted told her that he and Miranda were to be married, it came as no surprise. Now, back at work, the reality of everything fitting together in life suddenly hit home. Ted and Miranda could not be married if she were to live at her home in Seattle and Ted were to live in his home in Piney Meadows. One of them would be moving.

Most of their people in Piney Meadows truly liked Miranda, despite her different ways. But there was no doubt she did not fit into their community, despite how hard she tried—and she had tried. Ted often traveled to the cities, and everyone knew how much he disliked going. Anna especially knew, as she was the one who saw how he withdrew upon his return.

It didn't happen every time he left Piney Meadows. Some of their customers were fellow believers, and when Ted returned from those trips, she could see the strength emanating from him upon his return. The times he withdrew were only when the clients he had visited were not men of their faith, or any faith. Ted never spoke of the places those people had taken him as a visitor to their cities. He'd only told her that talk of such places was inappropriate and he was happy to be home.

Being with Miranda, her family, and her church would be different. There, Ted would be with members of their extended church family and the family and friends of his future wife. Nothing there would be inappropriate or uncomfortable for him. The opposite—there would be more people his age; and even more, Ted was quite different from the other men in Piney Meadows. Here, the only people she knew well who had gone to college besides Ted were William and Brian, who had gone to trade school. A few others had gone to college and returned, like their teachers, doctor, dentist, and other professionals, but she couldn't ask them what she needed to know. The fact was that few of their people who were born and raised here obtained a higher education.

Ted had been one of those few. Even as a boy, Ted had been different from the other boys his age. When the other boys, including her brother, went fishing or played ball, Ted preferred quiet activities, and he'd always loved to read. It had been no surprise to Anna when Ted went to business college instead of learning a trade or working on one of the farms.

Now, as a young man, Ted's management skills had brought prosperity to Piney Meadows because of the way he ran the furniture factory.

Anna stared at the closed door to Ted's office—where instead of Ted, Bart worked at Ted's desk, doing Ted's work.

She knew what was going to happen. Ted would be leaving Piney Meadows.

As his friend, she was happy for him. He would be with people with similar interests—professional people like him—and he would be happy there, involved in a large church and surrounded by fellow believers. But that also meant that once he and Miranda married, he would be leaving Piney Meadows and the furniture factory.

And that meant once again Bart would be in charge—running the plant, making all the decisions, and doing the marketing. Bart had started the business and made it successful as a small enterprise, but the business had reached a plateau. The best business decision Bart had ever made was to send Ted off to college and hand over the reins when Ted graduated. If Bart once again ran the factory, she could see it slipping back to what it once was, without the strong leadership Ted provided.

Anna's stomach made a flip. She didn't know when Ted would be back or how long he would stay. All she knew was that he would certainly be coming soon, because even with Bart running the factory, Ted would never abandon his guest. Such rudeness was not Ted's way.

Thinking of Ted's guest, her mind wandered back to the previous day, to the time spent with Chad Jones.

She'd never met a man like him, although admittedly her experience with men was extremely limited. No man except for her papa and brooda had ever entered her mama's kitchen, and certainly neither had offered to help with the preparation of the Christmas meal.

Both during the meal and afterward, when her mama and sesta had finished cleaning up, Chad had spoken equally to everyone in her family, making sure no one would be left out of any conversation, including herself, regardless of the topic.

He had asked a few questions about Piney Meadows, yet she'd been unable to ask anything important about living in Minneapolis.

The image of Chad seated at their family table appeared in her mind's eye. Not only was Chad charming and sociable, he was also the most handsome man she'd ever met, and working beside Ted, she'd met many more men than any of her friends. Only unlike so many of the men who came to visit Ted, Chad's smile seemed genuine, and when he laughed, she could tell it came from his heart and was not done just to be polite.

As if thinking about him could make him appear, Chad stood in the office doorway, wearing the same leather jacket he had worn yesterday. Looking at him closely, she could see his teeth chattering.

"How did you get here? Ted told me that he has the keys to your car. Did you walk from Ted's house without a good coat?"

He nodded, slapping his upper arms to regain his circulation.

"Why are you here?" As soon as the words escaped, by reflex she wanted to cover her mouth with her hand. While she wanted to know why he had walked all this way without an adequate winter coat or a hat, she hadn't meant to sound so rude.

He smiled, as if he hadn't noticed. "I'm here to see Bart. Ted wanted me to talk to him."

Anna glanced at the office door. "Bart has had the door closed for a long time. I will go tell him you are here. But first, would you mind if I asked you a question?"

He smiled. "Not at all."

She looked first to the right, then the left, just to make sure no one but Chad would hear her words. "What is it like to work and live in the cities? Is it difficult to find a job? Is it difficult to get from place to place? Do you have a good place to live?"

His smile dropped. "That's more than one question, and I have to ask you a question first before I answer. Why are you asking?"

Again, she looked from side to side before answering, then spoke softly. "I am wondering about leaving Piney Meadows and living in the cities, as many of our young people are doing. But my mama and papa will not let me speak of this, so I have questions while I am considering it."

"There isn't a quick answer. I'd need to know what area you're looking at."

"I do not know any areas."

His brows knotted. "What parts of the city have you seen, then?"

"I have never seen any parts. I have only been to Minneapolis once, when we went to visit my friend Theresa and her husband, Evan. I do not know enough of the cities to know what area that was. But Evan was able to find work, so I should also be able to do the same."

Chad stiffened. "Are you saying you want to move to a big city like Minneapolis, and you've only ever been there once?"

Anna nodded. "Ja. Can you not answer my questions?"

At the same moment as Chad's mouth opened, so did Ted's office door, and Bart stepped out.

"Chad, I am glad you have come. I hope you did not wait long. Please come in so we may speak."

Before Anna could ask if his answer would be a yes or a no, Chad stood. "We'll talk later. Excuse me." He turned to join Bart in Ted's office, and closed the door behind him.

Anna stared at the closed door. All she could do was take solace in the fact that her questions had been asked and that Chad had promised to answer. She only had to wait until he came out.

The longer the door remained closed, the more she was tempted to press one ear to the door to listen to the conversation. In order not to feel so frustrated, she busied herself with the filing and other tasks not requiring intense concentration.

She was nearly ready to scream in frustration when the office door opened.

Bart nodded at her. "I am going to give Chad a tour of the plant so he may see the operation. I am expecting some phone calls. Please tell them I will call them back tomorrow."

Before she could ask him who he was expecting to call, the two men left the office and disappeared down the hall toward the plant.

Anna sighed. She could have given Chad a tour of the plant, and in fact, she should have been the one to do it in order to allow Bart to focus his concentration on Ted's job. When Ted was busy or expecting an important call, he often asked her to give a short tour of the plant to his guests. In the cities, women could do such things.

The thought that Ted would be leaving and Bart once again running the plant made her stomach churn. Bart's marketing was quite poor compared to Ted's. In time, they would get fewer orders, and fewer orders meant a downturn in production, causing many of the people there to lose their jobs—one of them probably her. She suspected that Bart was well aware that Ted did a better job than he did, because she'd never seen him as stressed as he'd been today.

Now, more than ever, she needed information about moving to the cities and finding a job.

The longer she waited for Bart and Chad to return, the more anxious she became.

Two minutes before it was time to go home, Bart and Chad returned.

For the first time that day, Bart smiled; Chad did not. Bart stepped closer to Chad, resting one hand on Chad's shoulder. "Anna, this is Chad Jones. He is going to take over for Ted and manage everything. Chad, this is Anna Janzen, your secretary."

⁓⁓

Chad watched as a myriad of emotions playing like a movie in slow motion passed over Anna's face. Disbelief, confusion, shock, then almost as though the words scrolled on her forehead, fear over what she'd told him less than an hour ago. At most businesses, telling the boss you were looking for another job meant instant dismissal, especially in a position where that person knew the company secrets, like an executive secretary would. Of course, finding a job here wasn't as simple as in Minneapolis, where anyone could either check the want ads or take a bundle of resumés and walk from business to business handing them out. Often, depending on the industry, a person could put his or her name out to competitors hoping to get the inside scoop, and it wouldn't be long before a person had a new job offer.

It wasn't like that here. Bart had told him their factory was pretty much the only employer in town. All the other businesses in town were small and family-owned. When anyone needed help, they simply asked a family member or a friend of the family. Of course, this was a family-owned and operated business as well, but it had grown because unlike any of the other businesses here, this one marketed beyond its own small town to the big cities.

Both Bart and Ted had said a lot of good things about Anna. Even if she planned to quit, it would be a long time before that happened. In the meantime, he would make the best of it. He smiled at Anna to reassure her that her job wasn't in

jeopardy because of what he knew. "I look forward to working with you."

That she sagged with relief was unmistakable. Beside him,
Bart turned his head and looked at him, his expression asking
for an answer that Chad didn't want to give.

Chad had experienced tenfold what it felt like to be dis-
satisfied, which was why he'd left his job the way he had.
However, unlike him, Anna wasn't in a position to walk off
the job and jump into another one. He knew nothing of her
skills. But from what Bart had told him, this was her first job,
and she hadn't taken any business courses, because there was
no place here in Piney Meadows to take them. He also knew
she hadn't taken any courses online, because during Christmas
dinner her father made some very disparaging remarks about
computers, so he knew there wasn't one in her house.

From what he'd learned in his meeting with Bart, this business wasn't quite on the ground floor, but it was close. He'd
also learned that they liked it that way.

Bart stepped back. "Just in case you agreed to accept this
position, my wife has made a special supper, and I would like
you to be my guest."

Chad's mouth opened, but he couldn't think of anything to
say. This had definitely been the strangest job interview he'd
ever had. It hadn't taken long to describe his qualifications—
he'd handwritten a resumé while Bart watched him, including
when Chad counted on his fingers the years he'd worked at
previous employers. Bart and Ted had gone off the speaker-
phone for an alleged private conversation. Since they hadn't
asked him to leave the room so they could talk in private, he'd
heard every word Bart said. When they put Ted back on the
speaker for a few more questions, it also hadn't taken long for
Chad to say that he was more than ready to move away from
Minneapolis and settle down in Piney Meadows.

What hadn't been so easy was when, still on the speaker-phone, they'd started questioning him about his belief in God, and his life as a believer.

He hadn't known what to say. While what they'd done was illegal, Chad wasn't ashamed, and wanted to be upfront with them. He agreed with everything they said and he'd been a faithful churchgoer all his life until the last couple of years. Yet Bart and Ted had asked him questions he'd never had to think about and didn't really have answers to.

Still, in all things, he was honest. If they were looking for a super-religious, pious, holy man, it wasn't him. He honestly told them he hadn't been to church for over a year, and at that point he'd felt they were ready to escort him to the door. After a very telling silence, Ted's voice came over the speaker, asking if he prayed every day. Chad had answered honestly. He didn't pray every day, but he did pray most days. He didn't tell them he felt God had stopped listening to him a long time ago. Maybe some foolish part of him hoped God might hear just one small request, even though it never happened.

God hadn't answered a single one of his prayers. He had a demanding and overbearing boss who lied to him, or at least he'd had one until he quit his job on a whim. His fiancée, whom he'd been living with, left him while he was at work and didn't leave a forwarding address. Since the lease was in her name, when she pulled out he got evicted from the apartment, because he could no longer afford it on one salary. His friends were too busy to spend much time with him, especially now that he was single again and all of them were in relationships. Even his parents were too busy to spend much time with him. They'd bought a motor home, signed up for a time-share, and were seldom in town now that they were retired.

The only thing that had gone right for him in the last year was happening right now. These very nice, honest, albeit rather caught-in-a-time-warp-old-fashioned people had offered him a job. All he could do was be honest about everything and promise that he would do his best.

And they gave him the job.

Chad looked at Anna, who was looking up strangely at him. For a moment, his breath caught. The first time he'd seen her had been during the Christmas play. She'd been an angel then, and she certainly looked like an angel now, which he really needed. His nerves were still on edge with this situation, but just looking at her calmed him. Completely unadorned with makeup, she was still pretty. Without a fancy, expensive haircut, her soft brown hair should have been boring, but it wasn't. But what held him were her eyes. Big, beautiful, hazel eyes. Honest eyes, with depth that went all the way to her soul. Eyes that told him that everything would be all right.

He spoke to Bart, while he was looking at Anna. "I would love to be your guest."

Bart spoke behind him. "That is good. Anna, I will call your parents so that you may come and we will talk."

She nodded and didn't speak.

From Anna's reaction, this appeared to be a normal event, so Chad told himself that he didn't have to be nervous, but he still was. He'd never had a job where he was invited into the home of the owner. He couldn't help feeling this interview wasn't over, but at the same time, he felt good. For the first time in a long time, something in his life had gone right.

Since Bart and Ted felt that praying was so important, tonight, maybe, he'd pray that everything would keep going this way.

Bart turned and walked back into Ted's office. "I will get our coats. Let us go. Odelle has been busy cooking all day, and I do not wish to make her unhappy if we make her wait."

6

Chad dabbed at his mouth with the napkin, using it in an attempt to stifle a burp. The only other time he'd eaten so much in one meal had been yesterday, at Susan and Peter's home for Christmas dinner. He'd expected today to eat Bart and Odelle's leftovers, but everything today was fresh-cooked, maybe with a few recycled ingredients, but nothing obvious. Odelle had cooked a meal fit for a special guest, and he didn't know how to feel about that.

He wasn't special. He was just an ordinary guy. But the conversation had made him feel like he was a miracle dropped in on them from God. Everything he'd seen had shown him a solid company base, even if all their systems were a few decades behind the times. But then, that was the backbone of the company—building solid and well-crafted, heritage-type, old-fashioned furniture that looked like it had been built in another century. It wouldn't be hard, after a few software updates, to bump their fiscal operation up to the current decade. It also wouldn't be hard to update their marketing efforts with their current clients. Of course, first he'd have to spend some serious time with Anna, who apparently knew more than the owner about what made this business tick. But it was ticking, and ticking well, just a little slow.

Odelle smiled at him. "I know Susan would have sent much food home with you. But I hope you will at least take home some of my *Schinkje sleesch* to enjoy."

Chad nearly choked on the sip of his coffee. Home. He didn't have a home. Not in Minneapolis, and not here in Piney Meadows, either. For now, he couldn't even sleep in his car if he wanted to, despite the fact that he would probably freeze to death if he tried. Ted still hadn't sent his keys, his drivers' license, or his wallet.

Even if he had the money and his credit cards, Piney Meadows didn't have a hotel or motel. Since the town wasn't a tourist mecca, he also doubted he would find a bed-and-breakfast. Come to think of it, he wondered if a town like this even had an apartment building where he could find a place to rent, which is what he'd assumed he would do.

He forced himself to smile back politely. "I would love to take home some of the . . . uh . . . what you said. It's delicious, and you're making me feel very spoiled. You're a fantastic cook."

Odelle waved one hand in the air and blushed. "Ach. You are being kind. But I do love to cook. It is good to have more people to cook for, since my daughters are married." At the word *married*, Odelle turned to Anna. "I also had planned to invite William today, but he had told me of other plans. He had made promises for tonight."

Interesting. Today at the factory William hadn't been at his desk, he'd been in the factory taking stock of the materials. Chad had met William briefly, but hadn't had a chance to talk to him or be introduced as his new boss. The first person he'd need to talk to in order to become more familiar with the business and their financial status would be the company accountant.

Now, Odelle's words reminded him that in addition to assessing everyone's skills and level of responsibilities, he'd also need to be aware of the relationships between the employees. Nothing had been said during her family's Christmas dinner, but apparently there was more between Anna and William than merely being fellow employees.

Tomorrow, Bart would officially introduce him to all the staff, he'd be given an initiation into each department, and then, when things settled down, he would talk privately with Anna to learn the personal details he needed to know. Here, he wasn't just the new kid on the block; he was an outsider to this lost-in-time community. He would always need to be aware of all the interpersonal relationships so he didn't cross any lines or offend. He'd also have to learn more about this community in order to interact effectively with them.

Since Anna was his new personal assistant, he needed her to advise him.

He turned to Odelle. "Thank you for a wonderful supper. I'm honored that you would prepare such a special meal just for us."

Odelle blushed, turned, and muttered something in German.

Bart stood. "Come. Let us sit in the living room to talk."

Chad also stood, waiting for the ladies to precede them out of the kitchen. They both stood, but instead of leaving the room, they began clearing the table. Chad understood that they would need to pack up the food and get it into the fridge, so he followed Bart to the couch.

Just as had happened with Peter, Bart talked fondly about the town of Piney Meadows. And as during his time at Anna's parents' home, the women not only put the food into the fridge, they also cleaned the kitchen and washed and dried the dishes before joining the men in the living room.

Leave It to Beaver, with bonnets.

He didn't know how he was going to get used to this, but if he was going to live here, he had no choice.

He told himself with each day he'd become a little more accustomed to it. Even more, he was going to need Anna's help to do this. Fortunately, Anna was easy to talk to, and best of all, he had something to offer her in trade for her help.

They continued to chat about nothing in particular, until he saw his hosts starting to show signs of fatigue. It dawned on him that while he had slept the morning away after enjoying a big turkey dinner the day before, they had arisen early and gone to work. Also, since he'd seen how the town shut down not long after nightfall, he suspected that his hosts, unlike himself, were the early-to-bed-early-to-rise type.

Chad stood. "Thank you for a wonderful evening, but I think it's time we called it a night. What time should I be at the factory tomorrow morning?"

Bart stood. "I will be there at six o'clock, but it is fine with me if you start later. How is seven?"

Inwardly, Chad grimaced. He'd started at eight o'clock at his old job in Minneapolis, and there, he didn't have to slog through half a mile of snow in the dark. He'd merely taken the elevator to the underground parking area, where it was sheltered, made a trip to the drive-thru for a fresh cup of coffee, and driven to work on nicely plowed, salted streets. Likewise, at the end of his workday, even though at work he'd had outside parking, he always had both the block heater and the in-car heater plugged in, and he'd always had a comfortable drive home.

Bart, the owner of the company, didn't own a car. They'd walked to Bart's home, and likewise, he would have to walk back to Ted's house. He would also have to walk to work until he got his car keys back. Or, maybe he'd have to walk to work all winter. He'd noticed on the way here that the streets had been hand-shoveled, and he hadn't seen a single car or car tread in the soft snow. He didn't know if Bart chose to walk to work, or if he perhaps didn't own a car.

Anna also stood. "I also thank you for a wonderful meal. I will see you tomorrow at work, Bart. Odelle, I will see you at church on Sunday."

Once outside, Anna pointed to the right. "We are to go in that direction."

"Thanks. I would probably get lost without you, and I sure don't want that to happen tonight." Already, his teeth were chattering.

Anna nodded as she raised her fingers to touch the scarf she'd wrapped over her head and around her neck. "You must feel very cold. Would you like to use my scarf since you do not have a hat?"

He eyed her pink scarf and nodded. Without the scarf, she still had her bonnet protecting her head from the biting cold. In Minneapolis, he wouldn't be caught dead wearing a pink scarf, but here, no one would see him, so he was safe. "That would be great. Thank you."

"Do not let her know I have said this, but my mama asked yesterday why you had no hat, and she is knitting one for you. It should be finished by morning. I can bring it to you before work tomorrow."

He nearly stumbled. "Your mother is knitting me a hat? She doesn't even know me."

Anna smiled. "My mama has a good heart. She has asked me if she can sew you a good winter coat, but I told her you no doubt had a warm coat at home."

"I do," he muttered. But it wasn't anything like the knee-length double-breasted coat that Bart had been wearing. In Minneapolis he had only needed a coat warm enough to protect him from the elements between his car and the office door. He had a feeling he was going to be making a trip to the mall very soon.

If they had a mall in Piney Meadows. Or maybe when he went home to pack up, he'd go shopping on the way back.

He nearly stumbled again. Thinking of clothes, he didn't have anything to wear tomorrow. He'd felt horrible wearing the same thing to Christmas dinner as he'd worn the day before, but he'd had no choice. Before he'd gone to Bart's office, he'd used some of Ted's laundry soap and washed his shirt and personal items in the sink before bed. He'd needed to look fresh for the interview, and now he was glad he had, because he'd been seen by all the employees. However, tomorrow, when introduced as the new general manager, he needed to look professional. On his first day as manager, he should be wearing his suit, which was in his closet in Minneapolis. Instead, he would be wearing the same clothes four days in a row. Even with them freshly washed, it wasn't right. Some things even laundry soap didn't fix.

He couldn't even take the liberty of borrowing or buying something out of Ted's closet. He was about four inches taller than Ted, and Ted had a stockier build. He didn't even have to look to know that nothing would fit.

"Is there a place we can go shopping on the way home?" Even if that meant the chance some of his future staff would see him wearing a pink scarf.

Anna shook her head. "It is after six o'clock."

Chad didn't know why he'd asked. Of course, everything was closed. The winter sun had set.

In his mind's eye, he watched any potential nightlife he'd envisioned going down the proverbial drain. Mentally he shook his head. No, those days were gone. He was done with a party nightlife and lack of focus. It was time to get his life in order, and this new job was the start.

"Is there anything open here after six o'clock any day?" he asked, already knowing the answer but saying the words anyway.

"Nein," she answered with a completely straight face. "Of course not."

One day he'd tell her that in the month before Christmas, most of the big-box stores were open 24–7 in the big cities.

Chad struggled not to quicken his pace, keeping in mind the height difference between them, which caused him to walk faster than Anna did. However, it was obvious from the white puffs of air as they walked that he was breathing much harder than Anna. It hit him that she had to be in much better physical condition, because he was getting out of breath and she wasn't. She walked everywhere, including through the thigh-high snowdrifts, and he drove only on plowed streets. In fact, in addition to a new coat, he needed to buy new boots and a man-colored scarf. His ankle-high boots had become packed with snow and his feet were as numb as his nose.

He walked with Anna to her front door. It shouldn't have shocked him that she simply reached for the doorknob, ready to open it, knowing it was unlocked even though it was dark out.

"Are there any stores within walking distance of Ted's house where I can buy some new clothes? Or make that close to work. I'd like to do some shopping on my lunch break, if you can loan me a little money until I get my wallet back."

He turned his head to see her smile.

He liked her smile. It was honest and sincere, and suddenly, he didn't feel quite so cold anymore.

Even if he did have to walk everywhere, if everyone was as nice as Anna he really would like it here.

"Of course. About ten minutes away, that is where the stores are. You do not need money. Just tell them I sent you and your name. They will sell you what you need and wait for you to get your wallet back." She giggled. "Besides, by tomorrow at lunch time, everyone will know who you are, anyway."

She stopped talking, and he mentally filled in what she hadn't said. Within hours, everyone, not only people who worked at the factory, would know that he was taking over Ted's job, and by the nature of the job, his credit was good.

A scary thought.

Anna opened the door. "Good night, Chad. I will see you tomorrow morning. We can walk to work together, and I will make you some coffee before Bart goes over everything with you."

⟿

Anna sat at her desk, her eyes focused on the door to Ted's office—or rather, Chad's office—and smiled.

She'd never seen a man so happy. Just before the lunch break, the courier service delivered a package containing Chad's wallet and keys. Instead of eating his lunch, Chad had gone shopping, and he had returned wearing a new knee-length coat and new boots, carrying an armful of bags. It did her heart good to see that despite the new store-purchased clothing, he still wore the cap her mama had knitted for him.

Since Bart had gone into the back to check on something, Anna rose from her chair and walked into the office to check on Chad.

A new pair of padded mittens lay in the middle of the desk alongside the hat, and he'd deposited the bags onto the chair.

"You look warm." Except for his red nose and pink cheeks.

He smiled, wider and brighter than he had since she'd met him. Her heart began beating in double time. He truly was a handsome man.

His grin widened even more. "Yeah. This coat is great. The lady in the store helped me pick it. The lining zips out for when it's not so biting cold, and it's also got a wind protector panel in the back. I didn't know they made them like this." He clicked his heels together. "And nice padded boots, too. I feel like a kid at Christmas." As he shrugged out of the coat and draped it on the coatrack, Anna noted he also wore what looked like a new suit, a new shirt, and a tie. "I asked Bart to hold off on the general meeting to introduce me until after lunch." He rubbed his palms together. "That's now. As soon as I fix my hair." Instead of going to the mens' washroom, Chad looked at his reflection in the window and finger-combed his wavy blond hair. "They didn't have my brand of hair gel, or actually, they didn't have any hair gel, so this will have to do." He straightened, wiggled his tie, and turned around. "When Bart comes back, it'll be official."

All Anna could do was stare. With his new clothes, Chad looked even more handsome, and he even seemed taller.

Anna cleared her throat. "Here he comes."

With a quick stride, Bart entered the room, then skidded to a halt and looked up. Beside Chad, Bart looked . . . messy. And definitely harried. Also, just as she'd thought earlier, there did appear to be a bit more of a height difference with Chad's stiff posture. Bart looked up and down at Chad's new clothes, stopping at the tie. "I have called everyone into the lunchroom. Let us go."

As soon as Chad stepped into the lunchroom, all the chatter ceased. "Everyone," Bart called out, "I would like you to meet Chad Jones. Starting today, Chad is taking over for Ted. As you know, Chad is new to Piney Meadows, so please give him a warm welcome."

Odelle stood beside one of the tables taking the plastic wrap off a cake she'd brought, then began to fuss with folding the napkins.

At first only a couple of the men came forward, but when everyone saw how easy Chad was to talk to, more of the men came to shake his hand and greet him. After he'd shaken hands with all the men, Chad walked to the back of the room and introduced himself to the ladies, who were helping Odelle serve the cake.

When Chad had spoken briefly to everyone, Bart took him back to the office, and Anna stayed behind to help the ladies clean up.

Elaine approached her first. "Who is this man? Where did he come from? I have never seen him before." Her voice lowered. "He looks like he is from the cities."

Anna nodded. "Ja. He is."

Martha came to Anna's other side. "How did Ted find this man? I saw Ted speaking to him at church, after our Christmas play. Then he left with Ted and Miranda. I hear he is staying at Ted's house until Ted's return." Her voice lowered. "I have seen his car parked near the church since Christmas Eve. It is very fancy and looks like it goes very fast."

Before Anna could answer, Elaine spoke again. "Sarah told me Ted and Miranda will be married soon. When is Ted coming back?"

Anna cleared her throat. "I do not know the answer to all your questions. Today when Ted phoned for Bart, I spoke to him first for a little while. He is not sure when he is coming back, as he has been hired at a new job in Seattle and he cannot leave his job to come here. He said he must wait until a weekend, when he can get flight times that will be good. But he said that Chad will do well for us. He has phoned Chad's former workplace and told me that they spoke very highly of him."

Ted had told her more than just that. He'd spoken to some of the people Chad supervised before speaking to the owner of the company. All of them spoke very highly of Chad and not at all highly of the president of the company. Then when Ted spoke to the company president, he spoke even worse of Chad than the other people had spoken of *him*. Oddly, he'd told Ted to tell Chad that if Chad came back and begged, he would give him the job back. This told Ted that the decision to hire Chad was the right one, and Chad was hired.

Ted had also reminded Chad's former boss to forward Chad's vacation pay and all money owed promptly or he would take legal action.

Anna couldn't believe Ted would have said such a thing.

She turned to Elaine as she put the last cup into the cupboard. "I must go back to the office now. I do not know what will happen, but surely many things will become different now that we have a new manager."

A new manager from the cities.

7

"*A*nna!" a female voice called out. "You must come quickly. It is Chad!"

Anna fumbled with her coffee cup, then set it down so quickly that coffee splashed out onto the desk. "What is wrong? Where is he?" The last she'd seen him, he'd told her he was going to the kitchen to get himself more coffee. Anna had offered to get his coffee for him, just as she did for Ted, but Chad had told her that he didn't want to interrupt her work and left the room with his empty mug before she could respond.

At the desk next to her, William grunted and kept working. The financial statements Chad had asked William to prepare were unlike anything he'd ever had to do for Ted, and William had complained all morning. "I do not know where he has gone," William muttered and kept punching numbers into his calculator.

Knowing Chad had gone to get his own coffee, she'd had a difficult time returning her concentration to her work, which was an order confirmation she should have sent out yesterday. She now noticed it had been nearly half an hour since Chad had left the room.

He had obviously done more than just pour himself a cup of coffee.

She sprang out of the chair and ran after Martha. Instead of going to the factory, where Anna was sure she was going to find Chad lying half dead on the floor, Martha turned into the kitchen.

Anna skidded to a halt behind her.

Chad stood with his back to them, at the sink, his shirt-sleeves rolled up to his elbows, with his hands immersed in soapy water. Beside him Elaine stood holding a towel, wringing her hands in distress as a man—not just any man, but the new general manager—washed dishes.

He ran a plate under the water and placed it on the rack, beside a couple of other plates and some cups. "There we go. Now it's time to get back to work." He lifted his cup from the stack, poured himself a cup of coffee, and turned toward the door, and toward her.

As his eyes met Anna's, his face tightened and his eyebrows clenched. "Are you looking for me?"

"Is something wrong?" she choked out.

"No. I just realized what time it was and made myself a late lunch. Did you need me for something?"

"I . . ." her voice trailed off as she looked at Elaine, who looked like she was about to cry.

Chad blew across the top of his coffee, grabbed his suit jacket, which he'd slung over the back of one of the chairs, and dangled it over his shoulder by one finger while carrying his coffee mug with his other hand. He began to walk toward the office. "Okay, let's see what you're having trouble with and don't want to tell me about," he said as he walked past her into the hallway and toward the office, probably expecting she would trail behind him.

Instead, Anna looked toward Elaine. Lowering her voice so only Elaine could hear her, now that Chad was almost at the office, she stepped closer to Elaine. "What is wrong? Why was he cleaning? Was the kitchen dirty? Is he displeased?"

Elaine shook her head. "I do not know. I could see nothing wrong. We all cleaned the kitchen yesterday, with Odelle." Elaine wrung her hands again. "*Daut es mie onnbekaunt.* I did not know what to do." She held out the dishtowel with a shaking hand. "He told me to dry the dishes and did not allow me to wash them."

Anna lowered her voice even more. "I will find out what was wrong, and I will let you know so it can be fixed. I must go."

She turned and ran back to the office, where she found Chad seated at her desk, reading the spreadsheet she'd left open.

"I don't see that you've done anything wrong," he muttered as he added a comment to one of her entries. "But I do see that we need to get a better quote on shipping prices to the Eastern states. What were you having trouble with?"

Anna cleared her throat. "It is not me. It is Elaine. Can you tell me why you washed the dishes?"

Chad stopped typing. "Oh. Elaine. Thanks. I couldn't remember her name. I will now. I told her she could dry, I'd wash, and it would be faster."

Anna shook her head. "But she was going to wash your dishes, and you did not allow her."

He stiffened in the chair. "Allow? What are you talking about? I made myself some lunch and washed what I used because the dishwasher was already full and running. The kitchen was so nice and clean, I didn't want to leave a mess in the sink. I wanted to be a good example and show that everyone should clean up the mess they make. The kitchen at my old office was disgusting, and I don't want that to happen here. Everything goes in the dishwasher, or it should be washed right away. Nothing gets left in the sink."

Thinking of the dishwasher, Anna bowed her head and pressed her fingertips to her forehead. "I remember when Ted bought the dishwasher. Everyone was very unhappy. The men were angry because they do not wash dishes at home, they did not want to rinse their dishes and put them in the dishwasher here, but Ted insisted. Then the women were angry because they thought Ted bought the dishwasher because he did not think they did a good enough job cleaning the kitchen. He told me he did it so everyone would spend less time doing dishes and more time building furniture."

"Ted sounds like a smart man."

Anna raised her head. "But it made everyone very unhappy. The men were angry that they were told to wash dishes like the women, and the women were angry because they did not like the way the dishwasher washed the dishes."

"Then the dishes weren't being rinsed before they went into the dishwasher, or they sat for days with gunk caked on." He visibly shuddered. "That can be disgusting. But if the dishwasher is run every day, it's more sanitary than washing by hand."

"Then you are not displeased with Elaine?"

"Of course not. You mean she's worried because I helped wash the dishes?" He sighed. "I knew I would have to learn about your culture here, but I had no idea how much. I have a feeling I'm going to be putting my foot in it often. I'm going to need your help. A lot."

Anna looked down at his feet in his brand-new boots. "Why would you step inside the dishwasher? That would not be sanitary."

He sighed again. "It's an expression. 'Putting your foot in it' means to say something that puts you in an awkward spot. I've said something to Elaine and unintentionally hurt her feelings. How do I make it better?"

Anna turned her head to the door, mentally picturing Elaine back at her job painting the wood. "I will speak with her and tell her this is how it is done in the cities. And you are not unhappy with the kitchen."

"Thank you." Chad checked his watch. "I'm going to be leaving soon. I decided to go back to Minneapolis tonight instead of waiting until Saturday morning. I have a lot to do, and I must get it all done in one weekend, because I won't be back. Anything I don't get out this weekend, the landlord is likely to put out on the street for the vagrants."

"Will you need help?"

William, who had remained silent until now, raised his head. "If you need help, I can go with you. I can help you pack and carry your furniture. What are you going to move?"

Chad's posture sagged. "I really don't have much—I can handle it. I've been in contact with a few of my friends and they're going to help, and I'm going to store my stuff in a corner of one friend's basement until I know what I'm going to do with it. For now, I just need to pack and vacate the premises."

William nodded. "When you will be moving your furniture, there are many of us who can help you. You do not have to do this alone."

Chad gave William the saddest smile Anna had ever seen. "It's okay. I don't really have much stuff. Most of it wasn't mine, and it's already gone. It's mostly just odds and ends left."

Anna blinked and stared at Chad. "Do you not have furniture?"

He stared blankly out the window. "It's a long story." He checked his watch and stood. "I should go now. It's going to be dark soon, and it's a long trip to Minneapolis. I'll see you both bright and early Monday morning."

⁓

Chad stood in the middle of the now-empty space that used to be his living room.

He remembered moving in, and it had been nothing like this. He'd thought when he mixed his things in with Brittany's that it had been the most important day of his life. It was a melding of like minds and lives, almost like getting married. Only they never got married; the engagement went on forever. Apparently, he'd wanted to get married much more than she had. Every time he asked about actually setting a date, she had some supposedly good reason for another delay and he'd had no choice but to go along with it.

In hindsight, he wondered if she'd intended to marry him at all, or if she'd just used him for his half of the rent on a place neither of them could afford separately. Since she obviously valued his money more than she valued him, his gut told him that he'd probably find the expensive engagement ring, on which he'd spent a large chunk of his savings, on sale in a pawn shop somewhere, as well as some of the other expensive gifts he'd given her.

Yet, he really didn't care about any of that, the ring, or the money. Brittany had taken something far more valuable away from him, and even if he had to use up everything he had, he was going to get it back.

He looked at the boxes piled up in the corner, leaned his back against the wall, and sank to the floor, landing with a thud.

He'd thought he'd have more, but Brittany really hadn't left him with a lot. When they first moved in together, Brittany said she liked her colors better than his, so they'd sold almost all of his furniture, one piece at a time, until there was almost nothing left. The few things they'd bought together, each putting in fifty percent of the cost, had disappeared the day she moved out.

He'd gotten home from work expecting to go out for supper to find not only that Brittany was gone but that she'd taken almost everything with her.

The only significant furniture left was his TV, stereo, computer, a desk, one chair, and his barbecue.

It didn't take a lot of work to pack up his computer or his stereo. The television was packed and ready to store at Todd's place, at least for now. When he found out how to get cable hooked up, then he'd be back for his television and a few more bulky items. He'd thought about getting satellite, but at least in the initial stages of trying to fit in with the community, he didn't want to be the only one in town with a television.

He looked at the ratty recliner that had been his father's favorite chair before his parents moved into a smaller place and gave it to him. Brittany hadn't wanted it in the living room, but he'd insisted. Maybe he would take it to Piney Meadows when he found a place of his own to live, but for now, he couldn't take it to Ted's house.

He turned and stared blankly out the window.

For now, all he could take was what fit in his car.

He wondered if his new employer had an employee discount or purchasing plan so he could buy some of the furniture the factory manufactured.

Or, if he wanted to be cold and practical, he didn't know how much furniture Ted would be moving versus selling. It was a long way to ship furniture from Minneapolis to Seattle, and expensive. If Ted's situation was the same as his own had been, Miranda probably already had an apartment full of nice furniture, and Ted would probably be selling at least a portion of the furniture he had to leave behind. If so, Chad hoped he got first dibs.

Chad stared at the one photo of him and Brittany left on the wall. Ted's situation wasn't anything like Chad's.

Ted and Miranda were getting married. No doubt about it.

It was also totally obvious, even though he'd only met them once, that Ted and Miranda were completely in love, and they were perfect for each other.

He couldn't remember the last time Brittany had said she loved him. He now wondered if she'd ever loved him at all.

But it didn't even matter anymore. What did matter was she had something he would always love. And he was going to do everything he could to get it back.

Chad pushed himself up to his feet, walked around the boxes, plucked the photo off the wall, and dropped it into the garbage bag. He didn't even want to salvage the frame.

He'd been packing all weekend. Todd and Matt would arrive in a few minutes to put everything in either Todd's truck or Chad's car. They'd stack what little furniture he had left in the corner of Todd's basement, and then Chad would drive back to Piney Meadows and stay.

For today, he didn't want to call this a bitter end but a new beginning. It wasn't all bad. He could see great possibilities in the business, and he had the experience and education to make it work.

All of the staff were very pleasant and honest people and he liked that, too. Besides Anna, the person he'd be working with the most would be William, the accountant. Even though William wasn't very talkative, he was a pleasant fellow, and he'd found William to have an unexpected sense of humor.

The best part of Piney Meadows, at least so far, was Anna. He was tired of all the petty games and self-seeking and back-stabbing that surrounded him here.

When he looked at Anna, all the truth and honesty in her soul showed through her eyes, making him feel that life could be good. If the rest of the residents of Piney Meadows were half as sweet and pure of heart as Anna, he could be convinced that maybe, just maybe, God hadn't forgotten him and left him in the dirt after all.

Things were good and would continue to be good. By the time Anna decided to leave, he would be settled in and would be fine without her. Yet, already, after only a week, he knew he would miss her, but the difference—now he was wiser. She wasn't his friend or his lover. She was only his administrative assistant, and therefore, when she left, he wouldn't feel like his heart was being ripped out of his chest.

When she left, he would deal with it. Until then, he would take every day as it happened.

8

*A*nna reached for her coffee mug without looking at it, and while skimming an order on the computer, she raised it to her lips. Instead of soothing warmth, her lips met only air.

She lowered the mug and looked up at the clock. Like yesterday, she didn't know where the day had gone, but it was nearly time to go home.

This was now the second week without Ted, and things were going well—so well that Bart had only been in for an hour yesterday and today he hadn't been there at all. Bart's confidence in Chad felt reassuring. William also seemed comfortable with Chad, which said a lot, because William had always been cautious.

The other employees also felt it, because all the work had continued with a minimum of disruption as Chad continued to learn Ted's job.

Tonight, however, she knew they would all be staying late. They needed to complete a quote for a new client, and they needed to prove to each other they could carry on with a minimum of disruption.

Anna picked up her mug and stood. She reached for William's mug, but he covered it with his hand and shook his head.

Anna had learned quickly that her new boss was a heavy coffee drinker, so she turned and stepped into his office, knowing she didn't need to ask if he wanted more coffee—he always did.

Again, Chad was concentrating so much on the computer screen that he didn't appear to notice her enter the room. Not wanting to disturb him, she stepped beside the desk and reached for his mug while he continued typing a long e-mail.

She nearly dropped the mug. This was the first time she'd seen him type long sentences instead of notes or numbers. Ted had complimented her on her typing because even though Ted had gone to college, Anna could type just a little faster than Ted.

She almost expected to feel a wind pushing her out of the office door at the speed of Chad's typing. She didn't know a person could type so fast.

Even though she probably shouldn't have looked at the screen as he typed, she couldn't help watching the words form on his computer monitor. No mistakes and his sentences were complete and coherent thoughts, including correct capitalization and punctuation.

Chad stopped typing in the middle of a sentence and looked up at her as she stood beside him. "Yes? Do you need to ask me something?"

"I came to get your mug so I may bring you more coffee, but I have become distracted watching you type." She wouldn't say it out loud, but her boss appeared to type at least double or triple her speed. Maybe even faster.

He turned his chair so his whole body faced her. "Speaking of that, I've been meaning to ask you, do you have any idea what your typing speed is?"

"I do not know." She'd always felt a good sense of accomplishment because she'd learned to type and use the computer when no one else she knew, except William, could use more than two fingers to type a short message.

"I know you don't have a computer at your parents' house. Would I be correct to assume the only time you type is here, at work?"

She nodded. "Ja. That is correct." She would have liked to type at home, but her father would not allow a computer in the house.

"Please take this only in the right way it's meant, but I've been watching you type, and I'd like to see you improve your speed. Also, if you really want to move to Minneapolis and find a job there, you're going to have to improve your speed significantly. Watching you, I doubt you're typing any faster than twenty words a minute. Even for an entry-level position, you'd be expected to type at least thirty-five words a minute."

Anna tried to imagine calculating how many words she could type in a minute.

Chad swept one hand in the air to encompass his own typing on the computer. "That means without mistakes. No going back and making corrections."

She turned to look at Chad's monitor, which was completely filled with sentences and paragraphs in the e-mail he was typing to a client. "How fast do you type?"

Chad shrugged his shoulders. "Last time I took a test, it was seventy-eight words a minute. I know I'm faster now. It's a skill you've got to have if you work in an office." He reached under his desk and pulled out a small, thin satchel that looked almost like a miniature suitcase. "I'd like you to improve your typing skills, so I'm going to loan you my laptop. Take it home and practice, and I'm sure you'll see an improvement real soon."

"What do I type?"

He looked around the office. "I'm not really sure what I can give you to practice on. Letters probably wouldn't be the best to practice with because they're short and concise. What you need is something with lots of words."

One eye narrowed and his lips tightened. "I know. Take your favorite book, and copy-type the book." He grinned. "Just don't get distracted with the story and lose track of what you're trying to do. Although, if you pick a good book, then it will be an incentive to type faster, so you can read faster and see how the story goes. Do you read a lot? Do you have books at home?"

Anna nodded. "Ja. Many books. I like to read." What she liked to read were romance novels, where the man and woman in the book always fell in love and were either married or engaged by the end of the book. Such a thing would never happen to her in Piney Meadows. But when she moved to the cities, she would be able to join a big church, and if it were God's will, she would meet a good Christian man to fall in love with on her own, a man whom her parents had not previously chosen for her. Of course, she would need her parents' approval for such a relationship, but they couldn't refuse if he were a man of faith.

One day, that would happen.

Chad grinned. "I was going to ask you to pick a book you don't necessarily like, because you'll need both hands to type so you can't be holding a book open. You'll have to rip the binding to lay the pages flat."

"Nein! I cannot destroy a book!"

"I guess you can use an e-book reader, but you won't have as much to type before you turn the page, because they only show one page at a time, not two." He shook his head. "Forget I said that. You don't have a computer, so you wouldn't have an e-reader."

Anna knew she wouldn't feel right about destroying a good book, or any book. Wasting things or destroying something someone else could use was wrong. But she had a goal that could not be reached any other way; therefore it would be a tool, not willful destruction.

Knowing her boss typed faster and better than she did was humiliating. It was her duty to type for him, but his typing was far superior to hers.

"I will do it."

Chad ran his fingers through his hair. "It's been a long time since I learned to type. It's something I've just always done. There might be a better way, but I can't think of anything. It's different typing words as you think than copy-typing something you see, but it gives you volume to blast through, so this will help." He checked his watch. "I need to get this sent in a few minutes if I want to catch him before the close of business today."

Anna picked his cup up from the desk, which was why she'd come into his office. Standing beside him, she looked down into Chad's face, her fingers wrapping around the cup's handle. With Chad occupying this chair, she realized for the first time that this was Chad's office and Chad's desk, not Ted's.

He leaned back in the chair and tilted his head slightly to one side. "Why are you looking at me like that?"

Anna could feel the warmth of a blush on her cheeks. "I was wondering when Ted will be coming back. I know he will be able to show you things that Bart cannot."

"I got an e-mail from him about an hour ago. He says he'll be coming back this weekend. The flight times weren't the best, but he can't wait any longer because he's paying a fortune for parking his car. I know he put it in the long-term parking lot before he left, but that still is going to add up."

Anna nodded. Their people learned to be careful stewards from an early age.

She backed up. "I will go get you more coffee so that you may finish your e-mail."

As she walked to the lunchroom, she felt her heart quicken. Chad taking over Ted's position no longer worried her. Chad appeared to be a good manager, and nothing in the business had suffered. In fact, the opposite had happened. She'd helped Chad put together some new quotes that would probably get them additional customers. All the people who worked at the factory had accepted him.

However, he wasn't having the same success in the community because not many people had met him yet. Last weekend he hadn't been at church; he'd gone back to Minneapolis to move his belongings and say goodbye to his friends. Very similar to Ted, Chad had not been very cheerful for a couple of days after his return, but she didn't know him well enough to ask why.

This weekend he would be able to attend church. Ted and Miranda would be back, which could be both good and bad for Chad. It would be good for him to have Ted help introduce him to everyone, and Ted showing his support and approval of Chad would help others get to know him.

On the other hand, with Ted and Miranda coming, everyone's attention would be on them, especially since their engagement. She worried that with all the excitement, Chad might get lost in the crowd when instead he needed to make a good first impression on so many people.

It also meant that in the evening, when all activities were done, Miranda would go back to Lois and Leonard's home for the night and leave Ted and Chad together at Ted's house without distraction or interruption, allowing them time to talk.

Now that she'd thought about it, this was exactly what Chad needed to fit into their community.

This worked well both ways—Chad was helping her gain some skills for moving to the cities, and Ted would help Chad with his move to Piney Meadows.

Anna smiled. Everything was falling into place.

Chad shook hands with Ted. "Congratulations. I must say this was a surprise."

Not that Ted and Miranda being there at 5:30 a.m. surprised him. The only flight they could get left Seattle late in the evening. Adding the late hour to the flight time, then the time change between Washington and Minnesota, plus the drive from the airport to Piney Meadows, they'd made good time.

The surprise was the matching wedding bands on their fingers. He hadn't heard they'd already had their wedding. Anna hadn't known, either. No one did. In fact, when he'd talked to Ted less than twenty-four hours ago, Ted had told him they hadn't set a date yet, and Miranda wanted to have a spring wedding. It was a long way from spring.

"I didn't know, uh . . . Mennonites eloped." It wasn't as if they'd run away from disapproving parents. They were both adults, and they'd been living in the home of Miranda's father, who was the pastor of a large and established church.

If it wasn't Chad's imagination, Ted blushed. "Miranda's father had made a joke about this trip being like a honeymoon, except we were not yet married. We already had our marriage license, then Miranda made a joke about running away to get married, and our trip here could be our honeymoon. We all got carried away, because before we thought about it very much, we went to the church and were married by Miranda's father. Let me say that it is very easy to get married on short notice when your future father-in-law is a pastor."

Chad grinned. "I guess it was a small wedding."

Ted grinned back, and this time, Miranda broke out into a blush.

"Not as small as anyone would think," Ted said. "Word spreads just as fast in Miranda's church as it does here. Many people were at the church before we were."

Beside Ted, Miranda sighed. They dropped each other's hands, Miranda leaned into Ted's chest, and Ted wrapped one arm around Miranda's shoulders. "It was soooooo romantic," Miranda murmured, then pressed herself more firmly against her new husband. "One of the ladies who rushed to the church brought her wedding veil from when she was married forty years ago. Another lady works at a florist. She brought some flowers for a bouquet. Everyone was taking pictures. My best friend was there, crying her eyes out, and someone even took pictures of us with my cell phone. We showed everyone on the plane."

Ted grinned. "Nein. You are the one who showed everyone on the plane."

Chad stared at the barely married couple. On the outside he grinned, but on the inside his heart sank.

He'd planned to stay at Ted's house while Ted and Miranda were in town, but he wasn't going to sleep in the same house as a newlywed couple. Even though it would be daylight in a few hours, it was still technically their wedding night.

They looked happy but had circles under their eyes. "You both look exhausted. I guess you didn't sleep on the plane."

They turned their heads and grinned at each other like . . . a couple of newlyweds.

"Nein," Ted said, still smiling, his eyes not leaving Miranda's. "We did not."

"Then you haven't slept all night, have you?"

Both shook their heads, without commenting.

Chad forced himself to smile. "How about if I quickly change the sheets and you two have a nap?" He would find something to do outside the house for a few hours, despite the fact that it wasn't dawn yet. At this time of year, the sun wouldn't rise until a little before 8:00 a.m. Piney Meadows didn't have a twenty-four-hour convenience store, but he could go to the office, get some work done, make himself a pot of coffee, and then drink the whole thing himself. His only other choices were to drive around the town until he ran out of gas or walk around until he froze to death.

Compared to that, work wasn't so bad.

"If you're hungry, there's lots of food in the fridge. Anna's mother invited me over for supper yesterday, and she gave me some great leftovers to take home. There's plenty, help yourselves. While you grab a snack, I'll go change the bed."

It didn't take long, and Chad was out of the house and scraping the car windows before Ted and Miranda were out of the kitchen.

He had a lot to think about, mainly where he could stay for the weekend in a town that had no hotel or motel. He wouldn't intrude on a couple of newlyweds, especially since this was going to be a very short honeymoon, with both of them having to go back to their jobs Monday morning.

As he drove toward the factory, Chad's heart quickened.

Inside the building, a light shone. They never left the lights on at night. William counted every penny of the money spent on electricity.

Someone had broken in.

His jaw tightened, and he clenched his teeth. Anna had laughed at him for locking his car, saying there was no crime here. Their people were not like that, and people did not steal from others here.

However, someone would apparently steal from the biggest business in town.

He slowed the car, trying to think of what to do. This town was too small to have a 9-1-1 service, and he didn't have the number for the police station on his cell phone. Even if he did, there wouldn't be anyone there at this hour.

Besides, even if there might be a police officer on duty, he couldn't go back to the house to look up the number. He refused to take the risk of walking in on Ted and Miranda's honeymoon, because he doubted they were sleeping.

Chad wasn't a fighter, but if he found some kind of weapon, he could at least scare off a midnight bandit. Although really, there wasn't anything worth stealing inside a business that made furniture. There was no money, only raw materials inside. No one was going to just walk off with a heavy wooden dresser, which was the bulk of the product line.

However, they did have three computers. They weren't new or high quality, but they were computers, and they had no security cables like many offices back in the city used.

Monday morning, he was going to change that.

Chad pulled his car into the single parking spot beside the building, which was a mystery, because as far as he knew, no one ever brought a car to use the space.

The only thing in his car the least bit intimidating as a weapon was the metal bar from the jack in the trunk, but it was better than his bare hands.

He closed the trunk as quietly as he could and ran to the door.

It opened without a key.

His teeth clenched. The crime rate in Piney Meadows was obviously low and the riffraff inexperienced if a thief would leave the door unlocked while he ransacked the place.

Closing the door with the softest click, he shuffled through the lobby, his heart pounding, and tiptoed toward the office.

He heard a noise.

The boot-up tones of the operating system.

As he suspected, the thief was after the computers. A foolish thief who took the time to make sure they worked before he ran off with them. If he was checking to see if they used a current Windows operating system, he was going to be seriously disappointed.

Chad sucked in a deep breath and stiffened, gathering his strength and courage. He mentally counted to three and jumped into the open doorway. Holding the metal bar at his side, ready to strike, he deepened his voice to sound as intimidating as possible. "Freeze!" he yelled.

9

$\mathcal{A}$ scream split the air.

A female scream.

It came from behind the monitor at Anna's desk . . .

Where, on the floor beside Anna's desk, sat Anna's purse.

"Anna?" He lowered the metal bar and then whipped it behind his back.

In slow motion, Anna, her face as white as the sheets on Ted's bed, rose from behind the computer monitor. "Ch . . . Chad? Wh . . . what are you doing here?"

"Me?" He checked his watch, even though he knew very well what time it was. It was 5:38 a.m., when the rest of the town, except for Ted and Miranda and himself, and apparently Anna, were fast asleep in bed. "Never mind me. What are you doing here? Do you know what time it is? How did you get here?"

Some of the color slowly flowed back to her face, and she blinked. "I got here the same as I do every day. I walked. How did you get here?"

He could only stare at her. Except for one day that he'd slept in, the two of them had walked to work together, so he knew what that walk entailed. Being pitch black outside at this early hour this time of year and wading through snow that was thigh deep where it had drifted, he'd felt it somewhat of an adventure. But that was when the two of them were together. Today she'd made the trip alone. Not only was it midnight black, the temperatures, which were normally coldest just before dawn, had taken a seasonal dip. Even with his new Piney Meadows-style clothing, he still felt chilled to the bone to walk that distance. "I drove this time. What are you doing here at this hour?"

Her cheeks darkened slightly, but her face was still pale. "I came to use the computer, to practice typing."

"But it's twelve below zero." With the wind chill, it would be even colder. Not that it was much warmer at dawn, but it felt colder in the dark. "I gave you my laptop to use at home. Where it's warm."

She paused, as if she was trying to think of what to say. "It is better for me to practice typing here, where I am alone."

Now, as his heart stopped pounding and he was starting to feel normal, he began to relax. "I can't see how typing on a laptop would be disturbing to anyone, even before dark."

She lowered her head, staring at her keyboard as she spoke. "I do not have a desk, I must practice my typing in the kitchen. My papa gets up early, and it is difficult to practice with him watching and listening. Then on the weekend, during the daytime my mama is in the kitchen. She needs the table for cooking. Also, my papa would prefer me to help mama prepare meals, not to sit and type on the computer."

Unfortunately, having been to her home a number of times, he understood what she meant on both counts. The first thing he'd learned about Anna's father was he hated computers. He'd also learned her mother's kitchen was her castle, and a computer was out of place there, too. Not to mention that being in a room with flour floating in the air wasn't the best place for a laptop. "I can see your point."

Anna pushed her keyboard away from the edge of the desk and folded her hands on the desktop. "What are you doing here? Is there something important that we should be doing? You did not call me."

He pulled William's chair out from the empty desk, wheeled it toward Anna, and sank down so he could talk to her at eye level. "Nothing important on a business level, but the reason I'm here is that Ted and Miranda just arrived."

She looked up at the clock on the wall. "Now? I thought they had made a plan to stay in a hotel at the airport tonight. I do not understand why they would drive so far on the dark highway."

He didn't know Ted well, but he did know that by reputation Ted was very careful with money. "I have a feeling when Ted saw the price of parking his car for two weeks at the airport, he didn't want to pay for another day or for a hotel bill. Mostly, though, I think he just wanted to bring Miranda home. They got married last night."

Anna's eyes widened. "Married? But Miranda had sent me an e-mail yesterday to say they were planning to pick a holiday weekend for their wedding, to give those who could go to Seattle an extra day. What has changed their minds?"

Chad shrugged his shoulders. "I have no idea. But from what they said, I think it was an impulse and they went with it. So now they're at Ted's house, and I'm here to give them some privacy."

She looked at him, directly eye to eye. "That was nice of you."

He felt his cheeks heat up, and he knew he was blushing. "Not so much nice as self-preservation. This is technically their wedding night."

Anna blushed as well. "You will need someplace else to stay while they are here. We had planned for Miranda to stay at Leonard and Lois Toews' home. She stayed with them for the year she lived in Piney Meadows. Since they are prepared for a guest, they will probably ask for you to stay with them."

Chad sagged. "That's kind of awkward. I've never met them. How could I stay at their house?" Although, he really didn't have any other options. Besides, he hadn't known Ted. He still didn't really know Ted. Yet, he'd been living in Ted's house for nearly three weeks, and now he had taken over Ted's job, with Ted's blessing.

These people were like no one he'd ever met before in his life.

Anna smiled. "Lois is a wonderful hostess. She had not met Miranda before Miranda stayed in their home, yet they became close. I will call Lois and tell her what has happened." Anna raised one hand to her mouth and began to giggle. "And once I tell Lois that Ted and Miranda are now married, it will not take long, and everyone will know." Her smile dropped, and she lowered her hand. "Since they are married, we must have a wedding celebration, but this does not leave us much time. We must have the dinner tonight, because they will be leaving for Seattle on Sunday."

This time, Anna looked up at the clock. "I must call Lois now. She will be angry with me if I do not. Tonight, we will have a celebration."

Before Chad could remind her that it wasn't yet six in the morning on a Saturday, Anna had already started dialing.

He could tell the woman she'd called was at first confused by the early morning call but recovered quickly as Anna told her what had happened.

Anna reached for her coat the second she hung up from a very short conversation. "We must go. You have brought your car, so it will not take long to get there. Lois was very excited. It is an honor for her to organize this wedding celebration. By the time we arrive at Lois and Leonard's home, they will be ready for us. Lois and I will spread the word, and everyone will bring something."

Chad started to open his mouth to ask why they would cook. On short notice, they could just call a caterer so that everyone could simply be a guest. Then he thought of what he'd learned of this community so far. Very few women had outside jobs, and for those who did, it seemed almost every one of them except Anna worked for their family's business. For the most part, a woman's place was to be a housewife; this was a community of Mrs. Cleavers. Only Mrs. Cleaver didn't cook like these Mennonite women. He'd never experienced such great food in his life. From what he'd heard, all the Mennonite women cooked like this, so even though he'd never heard of having a potluck for a wedding, this would be better than any catered wedding he'd ever been to.

Anna went through the sequence to shut down the computer, pressed the button to turn off the monitor, then turned to him. "This is also very good, because it will give you a chance to talk to Lois, but also at the same time, unfortunate because she will be so busy she will not have time to get to know you better with a wedding dinner to organize. Let us go. We all have much to do. I am sure you will be staying at Lois and Leonard's home tonight."

Chad found it interesting that all the talk had been about Lois and nothing about her husband. Somehow, it made him wonder who really ruled the roost.

There was only one way to find out, and he didn't have any choice.

He stood. "Okay, let's go."

Anna sank into the seat of Chad's car, let her head fall back against the headrest, and closed her eyes, hoping she didn't fall asleep while Chad scraped the windows.

It was done. Her people had put together a grand celebration for Ted and Miranda's marriage in only a few hours. Everything had fallen into place as if it were God's plan and timing all along.

But just to make sure the happy couple didn't ruin their surprise, while Ted and Miranda were sleeping, not long after sunrise Chad had gone back to Ted's house and very quietly sneaked into the basement and shut off the electricity to the bedroom so Ted's alarm clock would not wake them, and then he unplugged the phone. She didn't how Chad had come up with such a good idea, but everyone in the town thought he was quite ingenious. After their long day, long flight, and long drive, Ted and Miranda had slept the whole day away. Chad had left a note on top of Ted's hat to meet him at the church when they woke up. All the church had prayed for good timing as they worked to put all the pieces together for the celebration. When everything was ready, and Chad was starting to call Miranda's cell phone, the two newlyweds arrived at the church door. Then the celebration began.

It had been grand, and they had been surprised. Miranda cried when she saw what everyone had done, but everyone knew they were tears of joy. Everyone except Ted, but he did come to understand after Chad took him aside to talk to him.

Now, it was over. Anna and Chad were returning to Lois's house to clean up the kitchen, while Lois stayed at the church with the rest of the ladies to clean up there.

Anna hoped she would be up to the task. She'd never been so tired in her life.

In all her days, she'd never fallen asleep in church, but she feared she would tomorrow. In fact, she feared she would fall asleep before they arrived at Lois's house. She felt herself starting to doze but couldn't do anything about it.

When the car door opened, a blast of frigid air jolted her awake, at least until Chad closed his door again.

Now sitting behind the steering wheel, Chad turned to her as he fastened his seatbelt. "The car's warm enough to go. Are you sleeping?"

"Nein," she muttered, trying to keep her eyes open.

"If you want, I can take you straight home."

She shook her head. "Nein. I must go clean up. Lois did so much work, she did not have time to clean up the mess before the party." She forced one eye open to watch Chad as he put the car into gear and started to drive. "I do not know why you are doing this, but I am very glad for your help. I am hoping we will be finished by the time Lois returns home. She has worked so hard. It will be good for her heart to come home to a clean kitchen." Lois would not sleep until her kitchen was perfect, even though she had to get up early for the church service Sunday morning.

Chad shrugged his shoulders. "It wouldn't bother me. I'd leave it until the next day. But if it would bother Lois, then I want to help. She really made this all happen without a hitch."

As he drove, once again Anna felt herself starting to doze.

She barely registered the sound of the glove box opening and closing, but then some music started to play. "This will help keep you awake," Chad said as he turned up the volume.

It wasn't loud, and the singer's voice was reasonably pleasant, but the heavy drumbeat and booming bass line prevented her from falling asleep. She opened her eyes and stared at the knobs, trying to decide if she should let the music annoy her to full wakefulness or try to figure out how to turn the volume down.

Beside her, Chad grinned. "Not my favorite band, but it's good driving music, so I thought it would wake you up."

Since it wasn't so loud they couldn't talk, she decided to leave it be. Since its purpose was to keep them both awake, it was certainly doing its job.

She turned to him. "I am very surprised that you helped Lois with her cooking." She was almost more surprised that Lois allowed him to help, but then, they all had so much to do, Lois couldn't turn down anyone's help, even a man's. "All the other men were at the church, moving tables and setting up the banquet room."

Chad shrugged his shoulders. "Yeah, but there were certainly enough of them doing that without me. I wanted to help where it was needed the most. Besides, I like cooking more than I like moving furniture."

Anna frowned. "I have never seen a man cook. I know that Ted made many of his own meals, but I saw what he brought for lunch. He would make sandwiches for lunch, or he would bring leftovers made by someone else. He has never cooked like you. Until he met Miranda, when he returned to us from college many of the mamas invited him for dinner hoping that he would marry their daughters. Then they always gave him food to take home."

Chad's eyes narrowed and his jaw tightened. "I cook my own meals, and I do just fine."

Anna froze at his reaction. While she'd been on the phone organizing all the details, she'd been unable to help Lois. But without asking, Chad had immediately stepped in to work. Instead of waiting for a step-by-step of what to do, he'd required no assistance other than initial instruction on how to prepare things that were unfamiliar to him. He'd chopped, mixed, and even kneaded the dough for the buns. He even knew how to pinch off pieces of dough to shape the buns properly.

Everyone had thought it odd that when Miranda came from the cities she was a terrible cook. Eventually Lois had helped teach her to do fairly well in the kitchen, but this had not been an easy task. Now they had another person from the cities who was exactly the opposite. Chad was an excellent cook—in fact, he was a better cook than Anna.

Which was rather humiliating.

"It is odd for a man to cook like this. I do not understand."

"I've been on my own for a while. It's not a big deal."

She turned to watch him as he concentrated on driving through a drift of snow that had blown across the road. He now wore his new coat, but beneath it he was sharply dressed. Not only were his clothes well-chosen and well-fitted, they had been neatly pressed. Yet no one selected his clothes nor had anyone done his ironing.

After the banquet, many of the single ladies had gathered around him. He'd impressed many people with his smile and fine manners as well as his good looks. All night he'd moved from group to group, talking to many people. Everyone seemed to like him, even elderly Mr. Reinhart. This man from the cities charmed everyone he spoke to.

Even Fidette, Lois's dog, liked him. She'd seen him sneaking Fidette bits of food when Lois wasn't watching.

All feelings of sleepiness fled. "Do you like it here in Piney Meadows?"

His jaw tightened even more. "Yeah. I do. All the people here seem like good folks. I have to admit this is like no place I've ever been. Sometimes I feel like I'm in the *Twilight Zone*, and in a flash I'm going to find myself back in my old office, listening to Gary tell me I've got to work another weekend."

She blinked. "What kind of zone?"

"Never mind. You wouldn't get the reference. My point is, this is so different from what I'm used to, and it makes me certain I've done the right thing. Everyone here seems so honest and . . . nice. What you see is what you get, if that makes any sense."

It did. Her people carried no deceit in their hearts. Hearing him say it, though, told her this was not the way of the people he knew, and it made her heart ache.

It was good he felt he would be content to live in Piney Meadows, but he hadn't been here long. Only today had he met everyone in her church, without spending much time with anyone in particular. Talking at a banquet was not the same as living within a community. The more time she spent with him, the more she could see that he did not fit in here—from his habits to his clothes, right down to the horrible music he listened to. Yet, he liked it here.

Just as she needed his help to learn how to find a job in the cities, he needed her help to learn how to fit in with her people in Piney Meadows.

He stopped his car in front of Lois and Leonard's house and turned off the engine. As he opened his door, he paused and turned to her. "If you're tired, I can take you home. You don't need to help me clean the kitchen."

She shook her head. "I want to help. We must be fast, and finish before they get home. If we are not done, Lois will tell you to leave the kitchen and she will do all the work herself."

One eyebrow quirked. "Herself? What about Leonard?"

Leonard was a kind man, but he would not do women's work.

Chad certainly had much to learn, and she was going to be the one to teach him.

After they did the dishes.

10

Chad stopped typing as Anna walked into his office with yet another cup of coffee. He'd always been a heavy coffee drinker, but since he'd started here, his consumption had probably doubled. As he looked up and thanked her, he pushed the coaster away from his mouse pad, already accustomed to her routine.

Very gently, she set the mug down onto the coaster when it was an acceptable distance from his keyboard. Of course, he'd move it back when she left.

"You are smiling again," she said as she backed up a step.

After last night, it seemed he couldn't stop smiling. "Yeah. I can't believe this is real. It's even legal."

Anna's brows knotted. "Why would this not be legal? Ted can do whatever he wants with his house. He has wanted to sell it to you."

Chad felt his grin widen. Soon he would be the owner of his very own house, complete with his very own mortgage. He'd signed all the papers that Ted had brought with him at the airport. Since Chad had brought Anna along to give her a quick tour of the city before they headed back to Piney Meadows, she'd signed as a witness before Ted and Miranda needed to go into the boarding area.

On the way home he'd given Anna a quick tour of the downtown and the surrounding area, then headed back to Piney Meadows. They'd talked about the city for about half the trip, until Anna fell asleep, and he drove the rest of the way home in silence.

Home. This place was now his home. For the first three months, Chad would be paying Ted a very reasonable rent, and then after three months, after his probationary period at work was over, his rent turned into mortgage payments, with Ted holding the mortgage and no bank involved.

He stirred the coffee and looked back up at Anna, who had not moved from beside his desk. "Where I come from, when you get a mortgage from a person rather than the bank it's typically called a 'granny mortgage.' Usually it's a family member whose house is already paid for and they have enough disposable income to live comfortably, so they can afford to have the principle tied up while payments are made."

"But that is the way of everyone here. Most of the time it is family who will help with the house and it is always people who live here who do the building, so the cost is very reasonable."

He knew a few people back in Minneapolis who had subcontracted their own homes, although businesses, not friends and family, were hired to do the construction. In the end, every one of them had come up with more difficulties and costs than expected and said they'd never do it again. "That's really good, but I can't believe that Ted wouldn't need the money from this house to buy another house in Seattle. Although I don't know if the price he gave me on this house would even cover his down payment for a house in Seattle. Or Minneapolis, either." As often as he could, he intended to double up on his payments, both to give Ted some extra money and to get it paid off sooner.

In some ways, he was going to miss the big city for all the amenities, but last night, signing the legal documents, everything changed. As he fell asleep he'd felt a contentment he'd never known before. Soon the home in which he now lived would be his castle, and in that castle, he was safe. Safe from lies, deceit, and the one-upmanship that had become so much a part of his daily life he didn't know how miserable he'd been until he found himself at a distance, looking back.

Realistically, he would never be rich, but he could be comfortable. His salary here was lower, but his living expenses were less than half of what they'd been in Minneapolis. The mortgage payments for an entire house and a huge yard were significantly lower than what he'd been paying for rent. Also, he'd be saving a small fortune on the cost of gas, especially if he continued to walk to work and back with Anna.

He'd even thought of taking the insurance off the car and leaving it parked for a few months, but that seemed a little too extreme.

Still, with or without the car, he could be happy with this laid-back lifestyle.

Anna joined her hands in front of her tummy. "I wonder when they will come back for a visit."

"I don't know. I think whenever Ted can get some time off work they plan to go somewhere exciting for a real honeymoon. I saw both of them picking up brochures for Hawaii at the airport. When he thought we weren't watching, I saw him kissing Miranda behind his hat." Even now, the thought amused him. It wasn't as if no one would know what they were doing, using Ted's hat to hide from prying eyes as he kissed his new bride. Stuff like that didn't matter in the middle of a busy airport. In fact, he'd seen a lot of things over the years at the airport that should have been done in private. But he'd learned quickly that Piney Meadows was a very reserved community of very old-fashioned values and would never approve of couples kissing in public, even married couples.

Anna nodded. "I saw them, too. I must return to my work." Without any further comment she turned and disappeared through his office door and back to her desk.

Chad continued typing but had to stop when he needed more information to calculate some expenses. He stood, and leaning over his monitor, he looked through his office door at Anna, who was sitting at her desk, diligently typing.

She'd been trying so hard to improve her typing, he didn't want to disturb her. Instead of calling for her to get the figures he needed, he walked to the filing cabinet and pulled open the drawer.

As he reached for the file he needed, a sniffle sounded behind him.

He spun around. "Anna? What's wrong? Are you crying?"

She sniffled, then reached for a tissue to blow her nose. "It is nothing. I am fine."

"Are you sure? Are you hurt?"

She shook her head.

He waited for her to say more, but she didn't. She just kept typing.

"Okay. I'm going back into my office now." But he didn't move; instead he continued to watch her.

She nodded and resumed typing without turning.

With Brittany, he'd learned the hard way—when she said she didn't want to talk about something, she really did. But with Anna, everything she said, she really meant. His gut burned to ask her what was wrong, but his brain said to listen to her words, so he went back to his own office as he'd said.

He'd barely finished his report when Anna returned. No evidence of tears marred her face. It was almost as if he'd imagined it, but he knew he hadn't.

"Now you have signed papers to make you the owner of the house, does it mean you intend to become a permanent resident of Piney Meadows?"

He leaned back in the chair and folded his arms across his chest. This kind of lead-up to a conversation sounded ominous, and he wasn't sure he was ready for it. He didn't want to come down from the high he was currently feeling. He hadn't felt this way in a long time, and he wasn't ready for it to end. "Yes," he muttered and waited.

She cleared her throat. "Please forgive me for saying this, but even more than Miranda, your ways are of the cities."

He stiffened and frowned. "That's right. I've only been outside of Minneapolis a couple of times." Just like she'd only been outside of Piney Meadows a couple of times, and one of those times had been yesterday, with him.

"Then you will need to learn more about our people and living in Piney Meadows. You have been very kind to help me improve my typing. I would like to help you settle in to living in Piney Meadows."

He sat back and considered Anna's offer, and what she was really saying. Until Sunday, he'd been busy concentrating on his new job and enjoying the peace at night. He hadn't really thought about day-to-day living once the snow melted and he would be interacting more with the people in this community. He didn't know what they normally did when they could go outside without worrying about freezing to death.

Once, Anna had mentioned fishing. He'd never been fishing in his life. He went to the market to buy fresh fish with their innards scooped out and ready to season and throw on the barbecue. Every day, he realized a little more just how rural and isolated this community was. At the wedding reception he'd talked as much as he could to as many people as he could. He didn't know how it happened, but by the end of the evening, he'd found himself surrounded by single women.

He'd done his best to be polite, but he hadn't managed to escape to join the circle of men on the other side of the room.

Yesterday, at the church service, the enormity of his new situation had finally hit home. He'd realized he truly was one city mouse in a field of country mice. Monday to Friday, here at the factory he was the boss, and everyone respected him as such. But on the weekend, he was supposed to be just another resident of Piney Meadows, and he felt lost. Even though many had tried to include him in their conversations, he couldn't relate to very much of what had been said.

In order to make this gentle community his home, he needed to learn their ways, with or without cable television, and participate in the lifestyle. After all, their lifestyle drew him to this place.

He leaned forward and folded his hands on the desktop. "I'm going to take you up on it, but I don't think you realize how much you're offering. I've got a lot to learn, both about living the rural life and about your Mennonite ways. If you can guide me through this, then I truly want to repay the favor. Instead of just helping you with your typing, I'm offering to tutor you through some online business courses. It will mean a couple of evenings a week and will have to be here at the office, where we can access the Internet and have two computers logged in at the same time."

Her brows knotted, and he could see she was thinking very seriously about both his offer and what he needed from her.

"Ja. I think that would be of good benefit for both of us."

He extended one hand to shake on their agreement, but all she did was stare at it, like shaking hands was a foreign concept.

He retracted his hand and again crossed his arms over his chest.

Of course. Here she was a woman in a man's world. She wasn't going to shake hands with a man to seal the deal. He had her word, and her word was enough.

He'd already learned something.

"I'll find a good starter course to get you going, and we'll go from there."

"And I will help you meet people next Sunday, when everything is back to normal."

The need to shake hands burned in him, but he didn't move. "Great. Now let's get back to work."

❧

Anna looked down at Chad's Bible, which lay between them on the pew. He'd told her that he'd had it for years, yet when the congregation turned to the verses to follow along with Pastor Loewen's sermon, she hadn't seen any writing in the margins.

None. Not a single note. From the condition of the cover, she could see that his Bible was not new, yet the pages were pristine, with hardly a wrinkle or crumpled page. Most of all, not a page had handwriting or notes of any kind.

She'd never seen anything like it.

Yet, he did know where the books were, even if he did find verses faster in the New Testament than in the Old.

He sang well and he appeared to know most of the hymns; however, she also knew that he had taken guitar lessons and could read music.

After Pastor's closing prayer, most of the congregation rose to begin exiting the sanctuary. Instead of rising at the same time, Chad rested one hand on hers to keep her seated with him.

"Let's wait for a minute. On the way into the sanctuary, I noticed a lot of people watching me. Let's give the place a chance to empty out a bit."

Anna nodded. "Ja. I noticed the same thing." She could only imagine how much more people would have stared at him if she hadn't made him go back into his house when he came to pick her up this morning. All the men wore black suits on Sunday, with a white shirt and a dark tie. This morning Chad had arrived at her house wearing a gray suit. Beneath it, he wore a dark purple vest and lighter tone of purple shirt, and his tie was the same dark purple as the vest, but the fabric was shiny.

She'd sent him home to change.

Now that the service was over, it was time to stand and chat with the other church members, and perhaps some would invite them to their home for lunch.

After most of the congregation had exited, Chad stood and they made their way into the lobby.

She already knew that many of the single women wanted to meet him, but for today, the priority was to introduce him to the other men.

She nudged him, and taking her up on her nonverbal hint, he lowered his head, allowing her to speak softly. "We are going to find Leonard, and I will ask him to take you to the men."

He stiffened. "Why can't you introduce me around?"

"That is for Leonard to do, not me."

He looked around, his eyes locking on each of the groups of women and men, but said nothing.

"I will join one of the groups of ladies, and Leonard will take you to meet the men whom you have not yet met."

"I guess it would be too much to ask for everyone to wear name tags."

Anna looked up into his face, unable to tell if he was joking. She had a feeling he wasn't.

"Seriously, everyone knows my name before I tell them, but I've met so many people today, I'll never remember even half of them."

"That is okay. Not everyone expects you to remember. I will help you when I am with you. There is Leonard. Let us go."

As she guided him toward Leonard, he stiffened his posture, and his demeanor changed to the same way he presented himself at work when meeting someone he'd never met before. He smiled and shook Leonard's hand, gave her a quick glance over his shoulder, winked, then turned and let Leonard lead him to the group of men.

Anna stood, frozen, as she watched him introduce himself and shake hands with everyone in the group, smiling and making eye contact with everyone individually as he repeated their names.

He would be fine.

Yet still, a small piece of her heart went out to him. Only she knew how nervous he really was, beneath his charming smile.

11

As Anna worked on her current online assignment, Chad finished typing his e-mail, then started to reread it before sending it.

It was time. As the calendar had flipped to April, he'd worked the agreed three months of his probationary period and passed with flying colors. Now, not only was he officially and fully the general manager working under a full contract for Bart, but according to his contract with Ted, he also now owned the house, versus renting it.

No longer on probation, he had just hired a PI to find Brittany.

Counting on his fingers, if he was counting right and if she hadn't lied to him, again, he had until August to find her. All his online searches and phone calls had come up with nothing. The lack of proximity hadn't hampered his search. She intentionally didn't want him to find her. But he would, even if it took a professional to do it.

With his finger poised to hit the button to send the e-mail, out of the corner of his eye he saw his coaster shift to the right. That could only mean one thing.

He straightened, turned, and smiled up at Anna as she lowered a steaming mug onto the protective surface.

"You really don't have to do that, you know. I'm perfectly capable of getting my own coffee."

She shrugged her shoulders. "I know that, but I want to do this. I want to be a good secretary, which is my job."

Chad shook his head. "No, I told you, your official title is administrative assistant and it's how you have to refer to yourself. You must realize your worth around here. A couple of generations ago, the bulk of a secretary's time was spent typing, but those days are gone. Formal letters are no longer the primary source of communication, and execs all type their own e-mails. Your primary function is to assist me in what I need to do to keep this place running and growing and making a profit. You need to type proficiently, but it's not your primary job function."

Her cheeks turned the most adorable shade of pink. "That is a good thing, because you type much faster than I do. I do not think I will ever be able to type as fast."

"You might. You've improved significantly in just a few months. In a few more, who knows how fast you'll be?"

"Not fast enough, but I will continue to work on it."

His computer beeped, signaling a new e-mail message. "Odd. Who's working on Saturday?"

"You are." Anna wrung her hands. "You need to not work on the weekends, but you are working because you are here with me."

"Not really. I'm also doing a lot of personal stuff, with a little work mixed in." He clicked the button. "See? This one isn't business. It's personal. It's from Brian." He read while Anna stepped to the side politely, averting her eyes from Brian's words. He chuckled as he read. "The guys are going snowshoeing again. He said with the snow already melting, but today being a little colder, this might be the last time this year we can go."

"Are you going to go? I think you should. I will be fine by myself."

He looked outside. It had snowed again last night, but the cold was hanging in enough so it hadn't melted yet. With the spring melt already starting, the days of biting cold were gone, and the temperature today had dipped to just a little below freezing. Perfect for snowshoeing, and even more perfect for sharing some good hot chocolate afterward with his new friends. "Are you sure?"

"Of course. You spend too much time on Saturdays with me here. Go and have some fun."

He grinned. "If you would have asked me six months ago, I never would have said that walking around in the snow would be fun." But then, it wasn't all for fun. It was great exercise, and much cheaper than going to the gym. He'd found out the hard way that snowshoeing was much more difficult than it looked—even though he wasn't slogging through thigh-deep snow, he was walking on top of it. However, once up on the snowshoes, when he actually started trying to walk, the first thing he did was fall flat on his face. As the day wore on, he couldn't count the many times he'd fallen, and for days he couldn't believe how sore and bruised his ankles were. It had been hard work to keep up with the other guys and maintain the longer strides needed not to step on the frames of the snowshoes. Nor could he believe how many times he kept kicking himself in the ankles by not keeping his feet spread apart enough as he walked. Now, months later, he could keep up with the rest of them. And, he had great muscles in his legs.

Once he'd tried ice fishing. None of them had caught anything, but they promised to take him fishing again when the ice melted and they could simply sit on the rocks on the shore and catch enough fish to make a meal in just a couple of hours.

While he wanted to go, part of him wanted to stay with Anna. Over the past three months he'd come to know her, and he enjoyed spending time with her. Being at the office on the weekend was much different than during the week. With no one around, he saw her sense of humor and her warm heart. She would never fool around during working hours, but today, as she did every Saturday and evenings at the office after everyone else went home, she allowed herself some lighter moments.

She had an adorable little laugh. She didn't laugh enough. He wanted that to change.

This was also the only time he could spend with her without another person present. He would have liked to spend some quiet time during the evenings with her, but on the one evening a week that no Bible study or activity was planned, she wouldn't go to his house without another person there. Back in Minneapolis, it wouldn't matter. Here, it did, so he would abide by their ways. Once he'd even asked Brian to come over and be a third party, but Brian had laughed and said he'd been that route before. At first he had no idea what Brian meant, but the more he thought about it, he realized that Brian and Ted were good friends. Brian had probably been a third body for Ted and Miranda, and he didn't want to do so again.

Therefore, the only time Chad could spend alone with Anna was Saturday afternoons, at the office.

She smiled again. "Go. Soon the snow will be gone, and then the other men will be too busy for such things."

He hesitated. "That's exactly what I'm afraid of. Snowshoeing is fun, but on a limited timeframe. Once everyone can get back to what they normally do for the productive part of the year, I'm going to be left behind in the dirt. They've already started talking about preparing the farms and the animals and the planting, and I don't know anything about stuff like that. They tease me about being a city boy, but they're right. I don't know anything about farms. I've never been on a farm, and that's probably not going to change. I'm needed here. My loyalty and time are glued to the factory. I've got a lot of people here depending on this place for their jobs."

"Do not worry. I will think of something else to help you learn the ways of our people. Now go have fun with your friends."

Her words made up his mind. She'd been instrumental in getting him involved with the other single men his age, and he appreciated her help in her continual efforts to incorporate him into the community more than he could say. But on the other hand, when the men got too busy on Saturdays, as he knew would soon happen, then he would get Anna all to himself, and he could hardly wait.

༄

Holding the box very carefully, Anna stood behind William and Brian and her brooda David while they waited for Chad to answer the door. She had been watching the calendar very carefully, and today, the timing was right. At first, she wasn't sure this would be a good idea, but she remembered his request about needing something to help him understand the ways of the other men who didn't work at the factory.

The door opened. Chad stood before them wearing jeans and a T-shirt, his feet bare, his hair wet.

Her cheeks began to burn, despite the cool wind.

"What are you all doing here? Come on in."

"We have brought you something."

He looked curiously at the box David carried, then at the smaller box she carried. "Where would you like to go with, uh . . . those?"

All four men turned to her, but only three of them knew she carried the box with the most important contents.

"Into the kitchen. We must set up quickly."

"Set up?" Chad made eye contact with each of them, then looked back at her. "What are you talking about?"

"A couple of weeks ago you were saying you cannot go to the farm, so we have brought the farm to you."

Before he could question her, she stepped toward him and opened the cover of the box so he could see inside.

He looked down. "There's a couple of chicks in there."

"Many people here who do not live on farms have chicken coops in their backyards and you can do this, too. I have only brought you two chicks because you have not done this before. They are already two weeks old and past the critical stage, so they will be easy for you to care for until you can put them outside."

He looked out the window at his backyard. "There's still a couple of feet of snow out there. It's only started to melt."

Anna giggled. "They cannot go outside yet. They are too young. They must be kept under the heat lamp for two more weeks, and then they still must be kept warm. They can go outside during the daytime when they are six weeks old. Then when they are eight weeks old, which will be June, you will leave them outside."

He looked at the box David carried. "Heat lamp?"

William pulled a piece of paper out of his back pocket and spread it out on the kitchen table. "Here are the instructions on what to do with them as they grow. We will show you the first time, then you can do it yourself. It is very simple."

Brian grinned and rubbed one hand over his stomach. "If you are lucky you will have two hens, and you will get fresh eggs."

Chad stared at the chicks. "What do you mean, if I'm lucky? Do you mean you can't tell?"

Anna shook her head. "Nein. It is impossible to tell if they are hens or roosters until they are much older. You will tell when they either crow or lay an egg."

"Let me guess. If it crows, it's a rooster. If it lays an egg, it's a hen."

"Ja." She lowered herself to her knees, set the box on the floor, and reached in to pick up one of the chicks. Cradling it in her palm, she stroked the fuzzy reddish down.

He stared at the chick. "Why is it that color? I thought chicks were yellow."

She smiled. "These are Rhode Island Reds. They will be a dark reddish brown when they mature." Cupping it with both hands, she held it out to Chad for him to see. "They are very fragile right now and must be handled very gently, and you must keep them warm. They are very easy to feed. Just put the mix I have brought in a bowl for them. They will eat when they are hungry, so you do not need to have a schedule. Just keep it full and they will be fine. We have brought chick starter and some hay."

"Are they going to be noisy?" He glanced out the door, then back at the chick. "Will they wake me up?"

She lowered the chick back into the box. "No, they will not make noise now. They will peep a bit during the daytime, but they will sleep at night. Rhode Island Reds are an easy chicken to have. That is why I selected these for you."

Again, he looked outside.

Brian snickered. "Do not worry. We will help you build a small chicken coop when the snow melts. Do you know how to hold a hammer?"

Chad's face tightened. "I'm not that bad. Of course I know how to hold a hammer."

"We are just making sure."

The men set up the heat lamp, anchoring it securely above the box, while Anna spread newspaper and some straw in the bottom. When everything was ready and the men backed up, she reached in again to pick up one of the chicks. "Come here," she said to Chad as she petted the little chick.

He sat on the floor beside her, while William, Brian, and David sat in the chairs around the table and watched.

"Hold out your hands."

When he did, she placed the chick in his palms. "I don't know if I can do this," he muttered as he slowly closed his fingers around it.

"You must treat them gently, but they will not break. When they are small like this, they enjoy it when you hold them, and they are still very soft. If you are nice to them and talk to them when they are little, then they will come to you when you call them at feeding time, when they are big."

"Really?"

While he studied the chick in his hands, Anna picked up the other one. "Ja. We used to have a chicken coop and it was up to Sarah and me to feed the chickens. We had many more than two. So if you have any questions, just ask me."

"Do you have chickens now?"

"Nein. A few years ago the snow collapsed our chicken coop, and we did not rebuild it."

"Well, I guess I'm going to have to build a nice strong coop so that doesn't happen to me, right? I'm sure I can get some plans online."

William nodded. "There are many different plans on the Internet. We were going to help you build a basic coop, but it would be good if you want to get some ideas to tell us the size and shape you want."

Anna returned the chick to the box, then plucked the other chick from Chad's hands, since he seemed too afraid to move while holding it, and put it in the box as well.

She stood, while Chad remained sitting on the floor, looking down into the box. "We must go. Get familiar with them, and I will see you in the morning for work."

12

Chad flipped through his Bible to the right chapter and pulled his pencil out of his pocket. Following along as Leonard read the verses out loud, he hoped that Leonard would soon stop reading and make his point, so he could start writing.

Any other time, Chad didn't mind just following along, but today the lines were starting to blur. He needed something to keep him awake.

Anna had started bringing him to Bible study meetings not long after she'd offered to help him get involved with the community. Here, reading the Bible and studying together went hand in hand with socializing with friends. Naturally, she'd brought him to Leonard and Lois Toews' home because they were the first couple he had met, and he quickly became comfortable with them. As Anna said, he'd come to know everyone who came here on Monday nights—and everyone came regularly, so therefore, he did, too. He'd made quite a few friends. He'd probably even learned something, too. Even if he hadn't, his perspective seemed to be changing. Some pretty rotten things happened to a lot of people in the Bible, something no other group he'd been to church with had ever pointed out.

After everything that had happened to him, this topic grabbed his interest.

If only he could keep his eyes open.

Just like Anna said, the chickens hardly made any noise, but he must have gotten up twenty times to check on them. Then, every time he ventured into the kitchen he'd sat on the floor for a while, watching them sleep, wondering what to do with them when they woke up.

He'd stayed awake half the night, watching a couple of completely conked-out baby chickens.

He'd predicted a number of things about living in a small, rural community, but nothing could have prepared him for having farm animals in his kitchen. Or that this was apparently normal here.

This place defined normal under a completely different set of rules.

He was coming to terms with the dichotomy of roles between the men and the women. At first he'd thought it was like living in the Dark Ages, and very unfair. But as he lived among them and worked with the men and women in the factory every day, he learned that the roles weren't as black-and-white as they appeared on the surface. At Leonard and Lois's home, Lois was every inch a housewife, and Leonard was the sole income earner, being the principal at the local school. After getting to know them as a couple, Chad had no doubt about who ruled the roost in the home and it wasn't the half wearing the pants in the family. Away from home, Leonard ran the town's high school with complete efficiency. No one questioned or disputed his authority or his judgment. His word ruled at the school, most often without consultation. But at home, everything done was an agreement between the two of them, and if Lois didn't agree on something, it didn't happen.

It worked for them, and they liked it that way. They were comfortable in their lifestyle, and very much in love with each other, even after being married for more years than Chad had been alive. They were happy with their routine and each other, and in the end, that was what really mattered.

Half listening to Leonard reading, Chad turned his head slightly to watch Anna as she very diligently followed along. He wondered if domesticity in her household would be a democracy with her husband as well. He actually couldn't see it being any other way. Unlike many of the women he'd met who lived here, Anna didn't hesitate to stand up for herself. At least she did with everyone except her father. Peter seemed like a fair and honest man, but everything in his world was black-and-white, including the way he felt about the position and duties of the women in his household, especially his daughters.

Because of that, Chad didn't mind helping Anna improve her skills in order for her to make her own way in life and become independent from her father. Yet, even though she wasn't happy under her father's strict regimen, from everything he'd seen in the four months he'd been living here, what she was planning was extreme. Not many people, male or female, did what she was planning to do. Those who had left the protective wing of Piney Meadows, and gone to college had done so with full emotional support from family and friends.

At the same time, from what he gleaned, most who did seek an education outside Piney Meadows, and then a career, didn't return.

He didn't want to see that happen with Anna.

As much as he was reaping the benefits of Anna's improved skills, he didn't want her to reach the point where she would follow her decision to leave and not come back.

"Why are you looking at me? Have you lost your place?"

In a flash, his eyes came into focus and he snapped out of his musings. He grinned at Anna. "I was just thinking." He grinned wider. "About you." About how one day soon, he'd forget she was his assistant and kiss her.

Her eyes met his, she paled, and then broke into a charming blush.

She lowered her head so that she looked like she was intently studying her Bible. "I have no idea why you would be thinking about me, but this is not the place. Stop it."

Oh, yeah. She had his number. He leaned closer to her, so no one in the room could hear his words. "I'm always amazed at how organized and tidy your notes are and how you color code everything in your Bible. Want to show me how you do that?"

She kept her head lowered. "That is not what you are thinking. Shhh. *Dü mottst horjche.* You must listen."

Since Leonard was still reading aloud, Chad didn't have to follow along to pay attention. He halfheartedly listened to Leonard reading, but he watched Anna.

"Pay attention," she whispered without raising her head.

He grinned even wider. "How did you know I was watching you?"

"I just knew."

Just like he knew she'd know. Working side by side every day and then spending most evenings together, even in a crowd setting, they were getting to know each other pretty well. And the more he got to know her, the more he was coming to like her. A lot. She was different from any woman he'd ever met, not just because of the quaintness of her upbringing or the simplicity of her ways. She was intelligent and resourceful and had a sweet and gentle heart. Most people he knew would be bitter if they felt trapped in a situation like hers—he was no shining example himself. But Anna always saw the good in people and was resourceful in every situation. If this had been at another point in his life, he would have asked her out on a date to see where the relationship went, and he had a feeling it would go well. One day, she'd make the right man a very happy husband, and he wondered what it would be like to be that man.

He felt his heart start to pound. He didn't know why he'd just had that kind of thought. He wasn't in any spot to think about a committed relationship—or any relationship. He'd been that route and been dumped when he'd really pressed for marriage. He'd thought it had been the right thing to do, given the situation.

He looked down at the pages of his Bible, wide-awake now. He forced his mind back on track and back to where he was. Since he'd lost the flow of the passage, he flipped back a page and read all the verses in the section Leonard was reading aloud, finishing at the same time as Leonard quieted.

Leonard raised his head for a few seconds to address everyone in the room. "Now, after seeing what those closest to Jesus did when times were not so easy, turn to Jeremiah 6:16 and read it with me."

Since it was an easy book to find, Chad found it at the same time as everyone else. "Thus saith the LORD, stand ye in the ways, and see, and ask for the old paths, where is the good way, and walk therein, and ye shall find rest for your souls."

Chad stared at the page. He didn't read much Old Testament, but it was like God had a message just for him. Not that Piney Meadows was that ancient, but it was a few decades behind the times. Still, the bottom line was that these people were good and their ways were good. Even though he still had a lot of things to work out here, with them, he was finding rest for his weary soul.

Maybe God really hadn't forgotten about him after all.

Maybe God wanted him to go back to the almost-ancient ways, complete with chickens and all else that went with it.

He listened to Leonard talk about standing at the different crossroads in life. Of course, Chad already knew he'd come to a major crossroad in his life and had made his decision. He'd looked at where he was and where he was destined to go if he continued living at his broken home, working for his rotten boss, and he'd taken another path. He'd walked off his job and headed north. This was where he'd ended up.

Out of the corner of his eye, he saw Anna staring at him but saying nothing. Instead of meeting her eyes, he lowered his head and reread the verse.

He didn't have a highlighter or an assortment of colored pens like Anna, so he underlined the verse with his pencil, drew some arrows and stars around it, and then dog-eared the page before he turned to the new verse Leonard directed everyone to find.

When the lesson was at an end, he remained silent during the discussion. This had hit too close to his heart, and he wasn't ready to discuss it.

After the closing prayer, he joined the men while the women, including Anna, fussed with tea and brought out some delicious homemade muffins. He was getting to like tea, and he was going to get fat partaking of all the goodies he kept eating everywhere he went. This time, because he had to get home to his chickens, he was the first to get up to leave. Since they'd walked there together, Anna also prepared to leave with him. The second the door closed behind them, Anna gave him a look he was coming to know quite well. She might as well have had a neon question mark hovering over her head.

"I don't want to talk about it," he grumbled. "Let's just go home."

He wasn't surprised that she seemed to read his bad mood, and she kept silent as they walked. He didn't know how she did it, but just her presence made him feel better. By the time they reached her front door, he was more on track.

Except he wanted to kiss her.

Apparently, Anna had no such thoughts. She stepped forward and reached for the doorknob. As she pulled the door open, she turned to look at him over her shoulder. "*Goode nacht.* Good night. I will see you tomorrow morning for work."

She stepped inside, and the door closed in his face.

13

I've taken the liberty of signing you up for an online course. I also ordered some new accounting software, and together we're going to learn how to use it to the company's best advantage."

Anna's fingers froze over the keys. "I do not understand. Is there something inadequate about the way William has been doing his job?" During the last few weeks, William had spent a lot of time in Chad's office and most of the time had come out frustrated.

Chad shook his head. "Not at all. But things around here are about to change. I want you to get the forms and terminate his employment."

Anna's heart spiraled down into her shoes. "You have fired William?"

Chad propped himself up, half sitting on the corner of her desk. "Only technically. I've laid him off as an employee, and I'm contracting his new company to do the same accounting work. He wanted to cut down to two or three days a week so he could contract out to a couple of other businesses besides his sisters', so we're going to have him do the same here. We've been working together to get his business started up. It's been a little frustrating with all the government forms and regulations, but now he only has to do the final steps and it's done. This will be better for him, but it means that we're going to have to do more of the work ourselves because he's going to need more time with others."

Inwardly, Anna cringed. She didn't mind adding to her job, but Chad was already overworked. On Saturdays, when she came in to practice her typing lessons, Chad hadn't been playing computer games like he said he'd planned. He'd been working. Now he would need to do more. "Are you angry about this?"

"Of course not. This company should be using accounting software anyway, so this just forces us to catch up with it a little sooner than I'd planned. Besides, you can think of this as one more valuable job skill to add to your resumé."

"What about William? Will he not also have to learn to use the software?"

"No. He covered all the most common programs in college. All he'll need to do is catch up on the updates. For us, it will be slower while we're learning, but it will be faster once we know how to use it properly."

He grinned and waggled his eyebrows. "This means we'll have to spend more time together."

Anna could only stare back at him. She didn't know how much more time they could spend together. Besides being together all day at work, they spent most evenings in each others' company. At first, she'd only meant to be with him until he became familiar with more people, but somehow the separation she'd planned never happened.

He tapped his fingers on her desktop. "Before I forget, I need more food for Blinkie and Waddles."

"Who? *Waut sajst dü?* What are you saying?"

"There's only a little chicken food left in the bag. Where do I buy more?"

"You have named your chicks?"

He nodded. "I had to call them something, and I needed to pick something androgynous because we still can't tell gender."

Anna frowned. "It is not a good idea to name them."

"Too late. You told me to talk to them so they would come when it's time to feed them after I put them outside. If I'm going to talk to them, I have to call them something besides Chick One and Chick Two."

"I suppose I did say that." However, she hadn't meant for him to name them. She'd only meant for them to become accustomed to the sound of his voice.

"They've already started to hop out of the box, just like you said they'd do when they got to four weeks old. I need to tell them to get back in the box."

She shook her head. "They are chickens. They will not do that."

He shrugged his shoulders. "Probably not, but it gives me something to talk about with them. By the way, I won't be here at the office next Saturday. I bought all the supplies and we're going to build the chicken coop since all the snow finally melted."

"Ja. William told me about the plan you chose. You did not need to pay money for instructions. William and Brian and David could have built you a fine chicken coop without plans."

"I know, but I found one I really liked."

Before she could tell him that the three of them had built many fine chicken coops by themselves, he pulled a piece of paper out of his back pocket and flattened it out on the desktop.

The coop, which was elevated and accessible by a large ramp for the chickens, had been designed to look like a house, complete with windows, doors, and awnings. The enclosure was large enough for a tall man to stand inside without ducking and was covered by a sturdy roof, which included a fake chimney atop of the chicken's shelter. "This does not look like a chicken coop. This looks like a playhouse."

All traces of humor dropped from his face. "I want them to be comfortable, and it's got to look good. I'm going to paint it the same color as my house. I found some paint in the basement, as well as a pile of shingles in the storage shed. It's going to look like a miniature version of the big house."

"What have William and Brian and David said about this?"

"They kind of laughed, but after they calmed down they liked the idea of it being the same as the house. Brian said he's going to take pictures when we're done."

"You do not need to go to so much work for two chickens. All you need is to keep them protected from dogs, the weather, and wild animals."

He folded his arms across his chest and stiffened his back. "If I'm going to do this, I'm going to do it right. I want them to be happy in their new home."

Fortunately, the phone rang, saving her from having to tell him that all he had to do was keep them safe and well-fed. As she talked to a customer, Chad returned to his office and they both continued with their work.

Regardless of what she thought of building such an outlandish chicken coop, she knew it would be worth the entertainment watching them build it. After all, she was next door and would be able to watch through the kitchen window, and no one would know.

Chad stuck his finger in his mouth, partly to ease the sting from hitting it with the hammer but mostly to stop the string of bad words that he wanted to say.

"Have you changed your mind about this five-star chicken hotel, and now we can build a more sensible coop, City Boy?" Brian asked around a mouthful of nails as he attached one of the walls to the floor of the designer chicken coop.

Despite Brian's teasing, it didn't look like a hotel—he doubted that Brian had ever seen a real five-star hotel, for people or chickens. However, Blinkie and Waddles were certainly getting a luxury condo. "I'm not bleeding. I'm fine," he muttered around his finger, pulling it out of his mouth and shaking his hand in the air to get some feeling back. "It's just that it's been a long time since I've had to build something. It'll get easier." He held his recovered finger in the air, looked at the kitchen window of the Janzens' house next door, waved, and then grinned when the curtains moved.

He knew who had been watching. And because she was watching, he wished he were better at this handyman stuff. Part of living here and fitting in unfortunately meant he needed to be good with tools, and he wasn't. He found it easier to swap out a hard drive and add RAM than to nail two pieces of wood together, but that was going to change. It just wasn't going to happen in one day.

As he did what he could, taking ten times longer than his friends, he wondered how Blinkie and Waddles were going to like their new home. He'd bought the plans from a website specializing in homes for city chickens, meaning they had to look good as well as be functional.

It would still be another month before he could leave them outside, but soon, on the warm days, he could come home during his lunch break and put them outside, then be back home to put them back in the house before the evening chill.

Anna had told him they would need to be eight to ten weeks old before he could leave them out all night, but the deciding factor would be how cold it got at night. It was also a worry that predatory animals would see his chickens as a tasty midnight snack, so he'd purchased the best grade of chicken wire money could buy instead of the chicken wire that the plans had recommended.

But already, he wasn't sure he wanted to leave them outside all night. When they got to be adults, he didn't know what time they would fall asleep. For now, they went to sleep about an hour before sunset, which seemed late for the little critters. They started getting tired not long after supper. So on the evenings when he didn't go out, he'd been taking them and putting a towel in his lap to keep them warm, while he curled up with a good book. He'd found himself petting them as they nodded off to sleep. Even though they had already lost their down and the feathers were coming in, they were still soft, as long as he petted them in the right direction. They also seemed to like it. They even made funny little whistling sounds as he stroked them, or at least they did until they fell asleep.

He'd also noticed that since they could now hop out of their box in the kitchen, Waddles came to him whenever he sat down in the chair he used when he was reading, almost like she was expecting him to pick her up. He didn't know for sure that Waddles was a she, but he liked to think an animal that liked cuddling so much had to be female. As Anna said, he'd know for sure when the time came and Waddles either crowed or laid an egg. He was really hoping for an egg.

Blinkie wasn't so quick to jump up when Chad sat in his favorite chair, but when Waddles made it into his lap, Blinkie wasn't far behind. While Waddles always waited to let Chad pick her up, Blinkie liked to jump up on his leg. He didn't want a chicken walking up his leg and digging through his pants with its toenails, so he always picked Blinkie up, too.

"Quit dreaming and start hammering, City Boy!"

The intrusion of Brian calling to him got his mind back to where it should have been in the first place—not on his chickens, but on the task of building them a safe and secure home. "I was just wondering if I should wire this so I could put a heater in it." Besides, he was much better at wiring than he was at hammering.

"Waut sajst dü?" William stopped, his hammer poised in midair. "Certainly not. There will be hay, and hay can catch fire. You do not want to do that."

Chad shuddered at the thought of putting his chickens in danger. He would simply find another way to keep them warm at night.

Once more, the curtains next door moved.

He grinned. He didn't know why she was watching. He was only glad that she was.

Since he definitely had her interest, he was going to have to figure out what to do with it.

14

$\mathcal{A}$nna paused from her data entry and turned her head to look into Chad's office. Fortunately, he was concentrating on something, so he didn't notice her watching him, allowing her to continue to watch him as he typed.

Ever since they had started using the new accounting program he'd moved both her desk and William's. Now, when his office door wasn't closed, Chad and William could look at each other while they talked without either of them needing to get up. Then, when William wasn't there, he could do the same with her.

She didn't know why they couldn't just pick up the phone, or why he thought it necessary for them to look at each other when they talked. However, since he was the boss, she had to abide by his wishes, and this was his specific request.

He'd said that balancing the phone on his shoulder while he typed and talked was awkward, but Anna had looked in the office supply catalogue earlier this morning. She'd seen a cradle people could put on the phone to balance it comfortably. She didn't know why Chad didn't want to do that, although it was rather unsightly when not in use. She'd also seen head-sets to make phone calls hands-free, but neither of them spent enough time on the phone to make the expense worthwhile. Therefore, without William there, she and Chad now sat in direct line of each other's sight if either of them turned away from their computers.

Yet she liked the idea of watching him as he worked. Being a handsome man, he was easy to watch, but since she'd come to know him better she found many of his habits amusing. When he was thinking hard, he tapped his pen to his temple, and when frustrated, he smacked that pen into his open palm. When he thought she wasn't looking, he moved his coffee cup closer to his keyboard, then moved it back to an acceptable distance before he called her into his office.

Sometimes he smiled as he read something on his computer, and she found herself smiling, too.

This also meant he could watch her when she didn't know he was watching, and she didn't like that idea. She had nothing to be ashamed of. She worked hard and always did her best. To do less lacked honor. She just didn't like being watched.

As guilt crept up on her for doing to him what she didn't like him doing to her, she returned her concentration to her work. She managed to tune him out with the clacking of the keys as she typed until the phone rang. She put the call through and began to type when Chad's office door closed.

Her fingers froze over the keyboard. The only reason Chad ever closed his office door was when he had visitors. Even though she never deliberately listened to his telephone calls, she could always hear some of his conversation, unintentionally, of course. Chad closing the door could only mean that he didn't want her to hear any of his part of the conversation.

It shouldn't have bothered her, but it did.

It reminded her how little she knew of his life prior to four months ago. For all the time they spent together, she knew very little about his life before the day he got as far as Piney Meadows and ran out of gas on Christmas Eve.

She told herself it didn't matter how much she knew, or didn't know, about Chad Jones. As soon as she knew enough to get a good enough job to support herself, she would leave Piney Meadows and Chad behind.

Strange how she didn't feel as excited about that plan as she did a few months ago.

Just as she started typing again, the door to Chad's office opened.

He stood in the doorway, looking like he'd just done battle with one of John Penner's stubborn, old cows, and lost.

"*Waut schot die?* What is the matter?"

He sighed, then sagged against the doorframe, letting it support his weight. "That was a guy I hired to find my ex-girlfriend after she left me. He reported he still hasn't, but he's got a few more things to try. I really thought he should have found her by now. I thought once she heard through mutual acquaintances that I'd moved out of town, she'd start getting sloppy. But she hasn't."

Anna didn't know much about his situation; he'd been very silent about his life before he moved to Piney Meadows. He said very little about the friends he'd left behind, and even less of his ex-girlfriend. She only knew they'd had a rough breakup. It wasn't hard to figure out that he had been hurt deeply. "Sloppy?"

He shrugged his shoulders. "She's being careful so I don't find her."

A chill coursed through her. She didn't think Chad was capable of doing something horrible to a woman, yet this woman would have to have a very good reason for making sure Chad couldn't find her. Anna had heard in the cities some men were physically violent with women they supposedly loved. She couldn't see Chad being that way. Despite his large size, he was a very gentle man. She'd seen him with his chickens when he didn't know she was watching. Last Saturday had been a warm spring day, and after they had finished building the Poultry Palace, as William had called it, he'd taken the chickens into his backyard to test it. She'd been very surprised to see that instead of running around the yard, the chickens followed him to the coop. Then, instead of nudging them inside and closing the door, he'd picked up both chickens, cradling them in his arms. Neither chicken had fought or squirmed to escape. Unless she had imagined it, they'd both leaned into him as he carried them inside the coop. Then he sat on the ground and released them. He'd remained seated within the fenced area while the chickens explored the pen, then walked up the ramp into the nesting area. After a few minutes, the chickens walked down the ramp, at which time he'd stood and walked back into the house, again with the chickens trailing behind him like baby ducks after their mother.

If he could be so gentle with chickens, she couldn't see him being any different with a woman he loved.

Yet, she really didn't know. It was probably not her place to ask, and part of her was afraid of the answer he might give, but she had to know.

She gulped. "Is she frightened of you?"

Chad shook his head without hesitation. "Of course not. There's something I need to work out with her, and she doesn't want to talk about it." He squeezed his eyes shut for a second, then inhaled deeply. When he opened his eyes, they became unfocused as he spoke. "But I have to." As soon as the words left his mouth, he stiffened, and she could see him closing up. It made her think that in a moment of weakness he'd said more than he wanted her to know. She didn't know why that hurt, only that it did.

He pushed himself away from the doorway, swiped his palms down the sides of his pants, then stood very straight. "I need a cup of coffee, and I need to go get it myself."

Anna watched as he returned to his office, picked up his cup, gulped down the last sip of what was left, turned, and left the room.

She would respect his need to be alone. She'd never seen such raw emotion in a man as she had for that split second. His moment of sorrow tore at her heart. She hated to see him in such a state. If he later came to her because he needed to talk more, she would listen as a friend.

But in the meantime, she needed to distract herself, not dwell on her boss, the man from the cities. She was here to work, and so she would.

～❦～

Chad's hands shook as he poured himself a new cup of coffee.

Thankfully, no one was in the room to see.

He shook his head, then sank into one of the empty chairs in the lonely room.

Of course, no one was here. It wasn't lunchtime. He'd never seen a group of people like this. When it was time to work, they worked. There was no goofing around and no slacking. Ever. No one was ever late, and no one ever tried to sneak home early. No one ever took off sick time when they weren't really sick. The expression "doing an honest day's work" took on a whole new meaning here.

He'd never met such honest and trustworthy people in his life.

Chad stared out the window, blankly watching a bird landing on a tree branch.

He was the least honest person here. Not with his actions or his work, but with his words.

Not that he was lying, but evading the truth was next to it.

He lowered the steaming mug to the table, rested his elbows on his knees, and buried his face in his hands.

He'd been honest with Anna about Brittany leaving him, but not entirely about why. In fact, every time the subject of his prior living arrangements came up, he'd avoided that, too.

None of these good, honest people knew that not only was Brittany his girlfriend, she was his fiancée and they'd been living together. The reason he had to move out of his apartment was because Brittany's name was on the lease. He'd moved in with her because her place had been larger than his when they decided to live together.

In hindsight, he now knew moving in with her had been a huge mistake. She'd used all her feminine wiles to draw him in, and it had worked. Now he wasn't sure he'd really been in love with her in the first place. Sure, he'd asked her to marry him, but if he had to be honest, it was more infatuation than the I-love-you-until-the-end-of-time kind of feelings he should have had. As the engagement drew out longer and longer, he'd started to have doubts about their future together. When he mentally stepped back to analyze their relationship, he learned he didn't love her enough to spend a lifetime together. In fact, in the last few months of their relationship he'd felt them drifting apart, and it should have hurt much more than it had. He'd been ready to end the engagement the next time she delayed setting a date.

Until he found the discarded pregnancy kit and saw the blue stripe. They'd always been careful with birth control, but apparently they'd been in that low percentage of failure, and now had to deal with a baby on the way. He didn't love her, but he did want to do the right thing. So he'd demanded she finally set a wedding date, and soon. She said she'd think about it.

That Friday, when he'd come home from work, Brittany, all of her stuff, and a lot of his, was gone.

Most men in his situation probably would have felt relieved, but he didn't. A life was in the process of creation, and he was the father. He was glad he knew Brittany well enough to know she'd never get an abortion. Regardless of the status of his relationship with the mother, he wanted to be a viable part of the life of that child—the child of his genes. He would not be an absentee or deadbeat dad. Of course, now that he had chosen to live so far away from Minneapolis, it wasn't as if he would be able to see his son or daughter every day, but he did not intend to be an every-second-weekend father. With the way these people were here, the way they valued family, hearth, and home, he probably could ask someone like Lois to babysit during the day while he was at work, and he could have his son or daughter live with him every second week and weekend. Brittany would have to put the baby into daycare when she went back to work, and there was no reason he couldn't do the same. Unlike a place Brittany could afford on a single salary, the house he had was certainly big enough to sustain a family of a wife and children, plus a dog, and the chickens.

Except nothing was the way it was supposed to be.

Here, there were no single fathers. There weren't even any single mothers. Everyone single lived with their parents until their wedding day. The one couple he'd heard about who got pregnant before they were married eloped and moved to Minneapolis because they couldn't face the community's disapproval, even though they did get married before the baby was born.

No one here would approve of the relationship he'd had with Brittany, especially since he and Brittany would never be married.

Chad lowered his hands, leaned back, let his head fall back on the top of the chair, and stared up at the ceiling tiles.

Obviously, Brittany didn't want him to be part of his child's life. Not only had she left him, she was hiding from him. Even a paid PI couldn't find her.

All he had to do was tell the agency to drop it, and he could go on with his life as if it had never happened. But he couldn't.

He was going to be a father. He'd created a life that was precious in the sight of God.

Chad squeezed his eyes shut. In many ways, he'd felt God finally giving him a break since he came here, but today, he'd felt God step back again, leaving him alone at a time when he needed God the most.

He'd seen the look on Anna's face. He knew he wasn't hiding his feelings well, and she knew something was wrong. As always, Anna was kind and gracious. He could see the kindness in her eyes, and he felt the warmth in her soul.

But he couldn't tell her what was tearing him apart inside.

He hadn't known her long, but they spent most of their time in each other's company. They walked to work together, spent the day together, and walked home together. Often he ate at her home with her entire family, and then they went out together to either a Bible study or a young adults evening.

Every day he saw her, he liked her a little more than the day before. He had a bad feeling he could even be falling in love with her. Real love. Not the way he felt with Brittany. The true, real thing.

In fact, life would be so much better if maybe she could fall a little in love with him, too.

Maybe it could happen. He'd seen the way she'd looked at him a few nights ago when he walked her to her door. He'd felt like kissing her good night, and he had a feeling she would have let him.

But first, he had to be honest with her and tell her that he was an expectant father.

When he did, in an instant, everything she felt about him would change, and he didn't want that to happen. He couldn't handle seeing the disapproval and disappointment in her expressive eyes.

Chad sucked in a deep breath, stood, picked up his mug, and began walking back to his office.

He didn't want to tell her, but he had to.

He just couldn't do it today.

As he passed her desk, he did his best to smile before he sat down and returned to his work. Here, he couldn't allow himself to wallow in his personal problems. He was going to be the best boss they could have, and he was going to work for them with the same dedication they gave to him. He was on the verge of getting a big contract for the company, and he was going to use everything in him to get it. He couldn't be the person these good people deserved, but he could be the manager they needed. And maybe, just maybe, God could honor that.

15

Remaining seated in the pew, Anna smiled. Chad complained loudly, and often, about the lack of computers and how no one had any home access to the Internet or e-mail, but it didn't stop or slow the flow of communication in Piney Meadows. Friday night at the ladies' meeting Anna had asked for prayer for Chad, and today, both before and after the worship service, he'd been continuously surrounded by people.

She hoped it would cheer him up. All week long, he hadn't been his usual self. She didn't know what was wrong, but whatever it was, he'd been uncharacteristically solemn, and even sad. But what really disturbed her was the change in his work habits. He was a diligent and hard worker, but suddenly he became almost obsessive. Even William noticed a change, which said a lot, because William was now only there a few hours a day, three days a week.

The only time Chad seemed relaxed was after lunch. For the past week, since it was now the middle of May and warmer outside, he had jogged home during the lunch break to put his chickens into their coop, so they could be outside for the warm part of the day. Because they were only six weeks old, he took them back into the house before the temperature started to cool for the evening. Anna had expected him to complain when she knew they would be hopping out of the box in the kitchen at night, yet he never did.

All week long, even though she'd kept herself available for the time he was ready to talk, it never happened. She could only conclude, since he became moody after the call from the detective who could not find his ex-girlfriend, that the change was related to him being single and alone because the detective couldn't locate Brittany. In preparation to pray for him, she had told the group as little as she possibly could without betraying his confidence. The best she'd been able to come up with was to ask for prayer for him because he was struggling with being alone.

As she continued to watch, the crowd around him thinned until all those who now surrounded Chad were the mothers of single young ladies. To the side, all the young ladies stood watching, anxiously waiting to see which invitation to lunch Chad would accept.

To Anna's dismay, her own mother was not in the group. However, her mama didn't need to vie for his attention. Typically, Chad joined them for supper two or three days a week. They were past the point where he needed an invitation, although he never came without one.

Until now, Chad had accepted invitations only from Leonard and Lois, whose daughters were no longer single, and from her own mama and papa, with both herself and her sesta Sarah still not spoken for. She'd sustained repeated resentment from the other ladies, even though she couldn't count the times she'd assured them neither she nor Sarah was seeking Chad's attention—at least not in that way.

Friday night, during the time for sharing prayer requests, when she'd asked the group to pray for Chad, she'd again confirmed her relationship was only as his secretary, or rather, as he insisted, his administrative assistant. Once she'd reassured them, again, the talk had started. Since he had now been living in Piney Meadows for six months, everyone had plenty of opportunity to observe him during the Sunday worship services and at both the regular and young adult Bible study group meetings. During the sharing time, Chad didn't say much, but he always listened, and watching him make his sloppy notes in his Bible had become very entertaining. When he first began attending there hadn't been a single note or highlight in his Bible. He'd explained that he'd never written in his Bible before because he thought it was not allowed. Even though he was not one of them, he had slowly gained almost everyone's approval and had become accepted as a Christian brother among them. Since there were more single ladies than single men, the mamas had now officially added him to the bachelor pool.

Of course, she'd heard all the talk from all the ladies, each wondering when he would begin accepting invitations and whose he would accept first.

Anna could tell the second he accepted. Joanna broke out into a wide smile, then covered her mouth with her hands, while all the young ladies near her visibly sagged. Yet, instead of looking at Joanna, Chad turned to her, smiled, and waved.

She couldn't believe he would do such a thing in front of the young lady to whose home he had accepted an invitation.

Unless . . . he really didn't know the reason for the invitation.

❧

Chad held his breath, gritted his teeth, and banged on Anna's front door. Out of the corner of his eye he saw the curtain move, followed by the sounds of female murmurings through the glass.

The door opened. Anna was standing in front, and behind her were Sarah and their mother.

He forced his best imitation of a smile, even though smiling was the last thing he felt like doing.

Looking over Anna's shoulder, he made eye contact first with Susan. "Excuse me, would you mind if I talked to Anna? Alone?"

Sarah and Susan quickly shuffled backward, while Anna stiffened. Obviously, his anger was as visible as he thought it was, but he didn't care.

Sweeping one hand through the air, he motioned toward the door as he backed up a step, trying to indicate his need for privacy, or at least as much privacy as was possible in their front yard. But he wasn't going to say what he had to say in front of her mother.

"What just happened?" he snapped, using every bit of strength within him not to shout. "At church, it was bad enough being surrounded by all those women I barely know, but after I got to Joanna and her parents' home, with the way they treated me and the questions they asked, it dawned on me what changed. It just became open season for bachelor hunting, and it appears I'm the number-one catch. This isn't what I signed up for. Your name came up in the conversation, so I'm asking you—what did you say about me?"

Her eyes widened. "I did not say much. I just asked for the ladies to pray for you because you seemed sad because you were alone."

Squeezing his eyes shut, Chad dragged one hand down his face. Every day that went by, he ached to tell her everything, to lay his burdens before her. But he couldn't. He'd talked again to the detective, then done some searching into the legalities of his rights to the baby. As it turned out, in this state, a mother was not legally obligated to put the name of the father on the baby's birth certificate. If that were a requirement he could trace the baby, but considering the circumstances, it was extremely unlikely. Friends had advised him to let it drop, since Brittany obviously didn't want him to find her.

But he couldn't do it. And such being the case, there was nothing he could do until the PI either found Brittany or didn't, which left Chad in limbo. His last option was to count off the nine months on his fingers, then do a search to see if he was listed as the father, which seemed unlikely based on Brittany's disappearing act. If he was not listed on the birth certificate, he would be totally off the hook.

The bottom line was that he didn't want to be off the hook. He wanted to be a real father to his son or daughter.

So until the baby was born, all he could do was wait and hope he got lucky or that Brittany changed her mind.

He cleared his throat and opened his eyes, making direct eye contact with Anna as he spoke. "I know you meant well, but please don't worry about me. I'm alone because I've chosen to be alone."

Her eyes widened even more, causing his heart to skip a beat. Really, he hadn't chosen to be alone, at least not intentionally. But now he needed to do the right and honorable thing, and he had no choice until he exhausted all options.

All he wanted was to find the one woman God would put in his path, but that woman hadn't been Brittany. He'd ignored what he'd thought at the time were small things, including feeling God nudging him away from Brittany. Then he'd let Brittany pull him away from God until he was at a place where he didn't know if God would take him back. He was in a place he couldn't escape, and he wouldn't know which way his life would go until August, at which time he'd have to make more big changes. Now, another complication had been added.

Anna.

She hadn't meant any harm by asking the ladies' group to pray for him—the opposite. She'd done what she'd thought in her heart was best for him. He also appreciated it, because he'd messed up so much that he couldn't blame God for not listening to his prayers, but Anna lived a pure and honest life, and God did hear her prayers. She had all the ladies praying for the perfect woman for him, although he had a sinking feeling every one of them in the small group Sunday morning would be praying it was her.

As nice as they were, he didn't want Joanna or Rachel or any of the other single ladies to be that answer, but he couldn't pray for what he wanted.

He'd prayed for Brittany to love him the same way he'd loved her, or at least how he thought he'd loved her. That hadn't happened.

He'd prayed, whether married or not, he would be there to share Brittany's pregnancy. It hadn't happened.

He'd prayed for his ex-boss, Gary, to treat him with the respect befitting his position. It hadn't happened.

He continued to pray that he could one day be a part of his baby's life. It didn't look like it was going to happen.

He was too afraid to pray that Anna would turn out to be the woman God had chosen for him.

If he did pray for that, he would get the same answer he'd gotten every other time he'd prayed for something he wanted.

The only thing going well in his life was his new job, if he didn't consider how he didn't fit in with his employees (he heard through the grapevine he'd made one of the women cry when he thought he was being nice by helping with the dishes). Or that he still stuck out like a lone city mouse in the midst of a field of country mice.

Anna cleared her throat. "What is wrong? Why are you not speaking?"

Rather than reply immediately, he reached forward and grasped her hands. At the feel of her soft skin, his voice lodged in his throat. In all this time, he'd never touched her, at least not intentionally.

More than just touching her hands, he wanted to step closer, to cup her cheeks in his palms, tilt her face up to his, and kiss her. Not just a simple peck, but to kiss her properly, right, and good and tell her he was falling in love with her.

Instead, he felt his fingers starting to tremble. He dropped her hands and backed up. "It's not important anymore. I guess I really don't have anything to say. I just wanted to see you."

Her brows knotted. "You have already seen me today, at church. You came with me and my family."

But he hadn't gone home with them. He'd gone with a woman he had no interest in.

What he wanted was for Anna to come home with him. Forever.

"Chad? You are looking strange, again. Are you ill? Would you like to sit down?"

He shook his head. "No. I think I'd just better go home. I'll see you at the usual time before work tomorrow."

16

$\mathcal{A}$nna sat on the bed in her bedroom, pressed the switch, and waited for Chad's laptop to boot up. He'd signed her up for some Internet courses and helped her download the resources, then he'd put everything onto his laptop so she could take it home to study and do her homework. She couldn't type proficiently while sitting on the bed with the computer, but she certainly could read, as long as she kept the laptop on top of a book so the blanket did not insulate it and make it overheat. He'd also shown her how to adjust some of the options to get more life out of the battery.

He wasn't very handy with tools and every time he tried to build something he hurt himself, but he was very good at computers.

The screen came up to enter his password, so she typed it in and watched as everything continued to load without the noises like the computers at the office.

She'd been very careful to turn off the sounds. Her mama had found out that she had borrowed Chad's laptop to help her with some courses, but they both agreed that her papa should not know that she had a computer in their home.

Part of her felt bad doing this, but she'd experienced a tremendous relief that her mama knew she was taking the courses and approved. At least her mama understood that in order to remain a viable business they had to keep up with modern technology. Of course, Chad had laughed when she'd told him. He'd said everything they used was at least ten years out of date, with the exception of his new accounting program. It wasn't even the latest version, due to the age of their computers. She'd noticed that Chad's laptop did run differently, and much quicker, than her computer at the office, which she found amazing for something so small.

While she waited for the icon to come onto the screen to open the program she needed to do her assignment, Anna stood and walked to the window.

From her bedroom, she had a perfect view of the portion of Chad's backyard that contained his chicken coop, or rather, the chicken hotel. Inside the fenced area, his two chickens strutted proudly. Since it was now June, she'd told him to leave the chickens in the coop permanently, except when he had to hose it out. Tonight was to be the first night he was going to leave them in the coop. It also meant he would no longer need to go home at lunchtime to take the chickens out of their box in the kitchen and put them outside.

She couldn't help smiling. He'd been so convinced it was still too cool in the mornings, but it wasn't, really. With the chickens spending the night in their warm nests, they would be fine in the cool of the morning.

Because of the quiet of the evening, she heard the hum of Chad's car as he came home from his shopping trip. Usually he took her mama with him when he went grocery shopping because it was easier to carry all the groceries home in his car, rather than making two or three trips with their wagon. Mutta had often said to Pape that they should get a car because the groceries seemed to be getting heavier over the years, but he would not hear of such a thing. So now, with her papa's permission, Chad always took her mama to the grocery store in his car when he went, even if she only needed a few items, like tonight.

Personally, she thought her mama had fun being in the car, but tonight she really hadn't needed anything.

At the sound of the door, Sarah scurried to the kitchen to help mama, so Anna stayed in her bedroom with Chad's computer.

She was almost ready to return to her desk to read her new lesson when Chad's back door squeaked open.

Remaining at the window, she watched him. It was at this time he'd always taken his chickens into the house. Of course, today he would be leaving them outside, as per her instructions.

Knowing Chad, and the way he liked to talk to the chickens, he had come to wish them goodnight. She couldn't believe the conversations he had with them, and sometimes, they seemed to answer back.

Tonight, just like every previous night, as he approached the coop, the chickens scurried to the gate. Also just like all the previous nights, when he opened the door to the coop he squatted down, petted them, and called them both by name. In response, they both clucked back to him, and if it wasn't her imagination, both sounded happy to see him, which was absurd.

To her complete shock, he backed up, and the chickens exited their enclosure. He closed the door and latched it, then walked toward the house, with the two chickens following right behind him. He looked over his shoulder and smiled at them, as if they were pet dogs. "Race you inside!" he called out and broke into a slow jog.

The two chickens stretched out their necks, extended their wings, and ran frantically behind him—as though they really feared he would leave them—all the way into the open back door.

The door closed, and all was silent.

She didn't know why he had taken the chickens into the house, so she waited for him to come back outside.

He didn't.

Anna sighed. She thought she'd been very clear in telling him to leave them outside all night. She couldn't believe that he'd misunderstood.

Tomorrow she would be sure to repeat her instructions. But for now, she needed to complete her homework.

Yet, as hard as she tried, even knowing she had a time limit to e-mail back her replies to the questions, she couldn't concentrate.

Chad had taken his chickens into the house. In June.

There was only one way to get back all her concentration and turn it to her homework—she needed to solve the problem that distracted her.

She closed the laptop and moved it to the side of her dresser where her papa wouldn't see it if he walked past her bedroom and looked inside the door. She really wanted to cover it, but after all Chad's warnings about not letting it overheat, she didn't want to do so unless she turned it off.

Once assured it was out of sight from someone walking past her door, she hurried outside and knocked on Chad's door.

He answered with a book tucked under one arm and a chicken tucked under the other.

Anna extended one hand toward the chicken whom she was pretty sure was Waddles.

She paused at her own thoughts, exasperated with herself for being able to tell them apart and for thinking of the chicken by name.

"*Waut dast dü?* What are you doing?" she asked, waving one hand in the air toward Waddles. "I have told you to put them outside. That is why you have built them such a lavish chicken coop. To put them outside. Yet here you are, bringing them into the house with you again."

He grinned, and his eyes twinkled.

Something in Anna's chest felt strange. She gulped, then looked at the chicken instead of him.

"I was going to finish my book, and it's become a habit to have them sitting in my lap at night. It felt wrong sitting down to read without them. I brought them back in so I can finish my book. Besides, they like it. Want to come in?" He grinned wider. "I just put the kettle on to make a pot of tea."

She backed up a step. Even though they spent much time without anyone else present when they were at the office, this was different. This was his home, and she would not go into his home unescorted. She certainly could not sit and drink tea with him in his living room, like she would with one of her friends.

"I cannot come into your house. Besides, I was going to start my homework, but I became distracted watching you take your chickens into the house."

His smile dropped. "You saw us?"

"Ja. My bedroom window is in the back of the house. From the kitchen, I can see your whole yard, but from my bedroom, I can only see the corner with the chicken coop."

His cheeks darkened. "Oh."

"It is best to put the chickens into the coop overnight by now."

"Well . . . maybe tomorrow . . ." As he spoke, he hugged Waddles a little closer. Waddles cooed and settled into his arm even more.

Anna sighed. "It is warm enough now to put them out. They are protected, and they will be comfortable in the hay." Yet, even as she spoke, she knew she was fighting a losing battle. From the way he was hugging the one chicken—plus the other had now appeared and was leaning against his ankle— she could see he had no intention of putting them outside for the night. However, within a few weeks the heat of the summer would be upon them, and soon they would definitely be outside all night. If he didn't feel the chickens were safe from predators, she could almost see him taking a sleeping bag and staying in the chicken hotel with them. It was certainly cozy enough.

She turned around. "I must get back to my homework. I will see you tomorrow morning at the usual time."

⌘

Chad watched her walk across the grass and then disappear back into her own house just as the kettle whistled.

Since he could no longer see her, he backed up and closed the door, but he was in no hurry to get back to the kitchen. He'd really wanted her to stay.

He lowered Waddles to the floor, then walked into the kitchen and started making his tea.

He couldn't believe it. Here he was, making himself a pot of tea for the evening. Not popping open a beer. Nor did he have the television blasting with the latest ball game or newest episode of *NCIS*. He'd had Matt ship the television, but with no cable, he hadn't bothered to hook it up. Nicely packed, it was in the basement, covered by some spare sheets.

Instead, he was making tea for himself. Then he was going to settle into a soft chair and read a book with his chickens.

His friends wouldn't have believed it. Six months ago, he wouldn't have believed it, yet here he was, and the whole routine felt natural and comfortable—except he did wonder about the latest squabble between Leroy Jethro Gibbs and Tony DiNozzo.

After dropping the teabag into the teapot, he stared blankly at it without putting on the lid.

More than anything, he couldn't believe how disappointed he felt that Anna had turned down his invitation. Not that she'd ever come into the house before, but this time, she'd seemed adamant. The words had no sooner left his mouth inviting her in when she'd stepped backward and done a quick retreat.

If that didn't give him a hint, then he was a slow learner.

Yet, she didn't dislike him. In fact, he thought she did like him, quite a bit. However, she was truly a product of her culture, and despite the fact that she wanted to leave it for greener grass, she was still faithful to her values and the ways she had been raised.

Instead of making him feel rejected, it made him admire her. It didn't mean he was conceited or full of his own ego to know that, in general, ladies liked him. He'd never had difficulty attracting a lady's attention, once he set his mind to it. Even Brittany, despite the bad turns in their relationship, had been attracted to him when he turned on the charm.

But Anna wasn't falling for it. Quite the opposite: whenever he turned it on, she turned and ran. Just like today.

He sighed and put the lid on the teapot.

He'd never felt this way about a woman before. Not even Brittany. He'd thought he'd been in love with her, but the more he got to know her, the more everything fell apart. It wasn't a relationship to last until a fiftieth wedding anniversary. He wanted a good, happy marriage like his parents had.

Come to think of it, they hadn't approved of him moving in with Brittany, although they hadn't said anything specific, because in today's society, living together before marriage was pretty ordinary. But then, so many of the couples he knew who lived together never got married, even though they stayed together.

It made him think. They loved each other enough to live together but not enough to actually get married.

If he hadn't moved in with Brittany, it was very likely he wouldn't be where he was right now.

But he couldn't complain. For the first time in years, he felt content, when he could push aside the pending issues.

He truly could live like this.

Chad closed his eyes to try to see into the future. Of course, he couldn't, but he could see what he wanted, and that was to have Anna, here, with him, living together in the order in which God wanted it. It meant a courtship; not too long, of course, and then marriage, followed by children and the classic storybook happily ever after.

He opened his eyes and walked to the kitchen window, where he could see Anna's parents' house next door. He hadn't known her long in terms of months, but he spent more time with Anna in a week than he had with Brittany in a month, or more. He knew her both at work and at play. Attending Bible study meetings with her, he knew her values. Talking with her every day on the way to and from work, where they were in the middle of both worlds, he knew her heart. He didn't believe in love at first sight, but his first sight had been at Christmas—she'd been the voice and face of an angel then, and she certainly was that now. If he could believe in signs, this one flashed in bright neon.

He hadn't paid attention then, but he was paying attention now. And the sign was telling him Anna was the woman he'd prayed for, whom God had put in his path. Even though he hadn't prayed for years and he'd only started praying again recently, God had been listening after all. A recent Bible study meeting had talked about God's timing and how God's timing was seldom the same as a person's, and when the timing was right, God would make it clear.

If this was what God was telling him now, Chad was convinced.

Now if only he could figure out how to convince Anna.

17

$\mathcal{A}$nna stood at the entrance to Chad's office. Normally she would just walk in, but today it felt wrong to do so.

Saying nothing, she stood, watching him work. His desk was a total mess, piled with so many papers in random piles. A plate containing a half-eaten sandwich balanced precariously atop a stack of papers, and naturally, his coffee mug sat too close to his keyboard.

She could tell the second he noticed her standing there. He raised his mug, took a sip of his coffee, then set the mug where it should have been in the first place.

"Yes? Did you need something?"

"Ja. I need to talk to you."

Chad's brows knotted. "This feels serious. What's wrong?"

Anna clasped her hands together but couldn't help moving her fingers out of nervousness. "There is talk about you not being pleased with the work everyone is doing. There is so much work to be done, yet you have told people to go home."

"That's because it's the end of the first shift. Everyone was still working, so I told everyone who's been here eight hours to pack up and go."

She'd seen him go into the factory at the end of the first shift to send everyone home. Lately, he had sent her home at the end of her shift as well, while he said he had stayed to catch up on a few projects. Whenever he said this, she knew that he wouldn't just stay for a few minutes—it would be hours. She'd seen him arrive home with barely enough time to eat something and accompany her to whatever activity they had planned for the evening. She knew the extra hours he was working. Yet, he didn't allow anyone else to work extra time to complete their work. "Why do you send them home? They are not finished. They have too much to do with the rush order for our new customer."

"There isn't too much to do that it can't be done in their regular shifts. I've caught them before, staying past the end of their shift to continue working. It's a rush order, but if everyone works hard, which I know they will, it'll be done on time. I don't want anyone working overtime. I want them going home to their families."

Anna had told everyone that Chad would not understand, and she was right. Chad was the only one who worked overtime. Even though he never submitted a payroll form to be paid for it, it didn't negate the fact that he was working long past his agreed time. No one understood why he often worked late yet did not allow the same from anyone else. "They fear you are displeased and have asked me to talk to you."

Chad's head tilted. "Why would I be displeased? Have they done something wrong? What don't I know about?"

"There is nothing you do not know. But they do not wish to go home. They wish to stay until they are done with what they are doing."

"No. No overtime."

Anna's stomach clenched. "But they do not wish to be paid overtime with their paychecks. They only wish to get everything completed ahead of the deadline."

He ran his fingers through his hair, which she noticed was starting to look a bit shaggy. "Since I've been here, we haven't missed a single deadline. And from what I've seen, in all the files I've checked—and I've checked a lot—we've never missed a deadline. Ever. There's no need to work crazy hours. I set the completion date with reasonable production timelines. So did Ted, and so did Bart." He paused, then leaned back in his chair and crossed his arms over his chest. "My old boss would work everyone into an early grave to meet unreasonable deadlines. I won't do that to these people. Sales aren't hurting by setting reasonable runs, and if they were, I'd have to think twice if that's the kind of customers we want. They pay for quality, and they're not going to get it if everyone is overworked or overstressed."

"But you do not understand. Everyone knows this is an important order, so they want to work hard to have it completed ahead of schedule. Then if something goes wrong, they will still be on time with it." She cleared her throat and looked directly into his eyes as she spoke. "This is the way it is done. They want to work hard, but you are not allowing it."

"Of course, I'm allowing it. I expect it. But when everyone's eight hours are up, I expect them to go home."

She wrung her hands again. "But that is not our way. We will work hard until the job is done, and we will be happy because we have done it well." Anna watched all the emotions play in his face as he considered her words. One thought at a time, she could see him lose his rigor, until he slumped, plunked his elbows on his desk, and buried his face in his hands.

He shook his head as he spoke, without dropping his hands. "Every time you say 'that is not our way' I know I've done something else wrong. All I want to do is be fair and show everyone how much I appreciate them." He dropped his hands and looked at her, his eyes like those of a beaten puppy. "I know so many people who are so overworked. The overtime pay doesn't make them happy. Instead, with more money from more overtime, all that happens is that they only want more stuff. It just becomes a vicious cycle. I know a lot of people say they love their jobs, but when a person's life is nearly over and they're thinking about what they've done over the years, no one ever says they wish they'd spent more time at work. More people say they sacrificed too much time for their job and didn't spend enough time with their families." He waved one hand in the air, toward the window. "That's what I want to do here. Give these people a balance between work and spending all the time they can with the people who love them."

The pain in his eyes told her that the opposite had happened to him. "I know you said your old boss was not good and made everyone work too hard and did not pay them rightly for it. We all know you are not like that. You are a good man; you want what is best for everyone."

At her words, his eyes widened and he sagged even more. "Yeah. I want what's best both for the business and for everyone who works hard to make it successful. Sometimes the balance between the two is hard to find."

Anna nodded. "It is not hard here. Everyone wants to do a good job. Because when one person succeeds, we all succeed."

Chad sighed. "Okay. Tell everyone on both shifts that I'm calling a meeting in ten minutes. I'll offer everyone a trade. It would be nice to get this order shipped ahead of schedule. Reputation means everything in most businesses. I'll okay everyone to work up to two hours of overtime a day, and in exchange, I want them to agree to take equal time off when

we're between jobs. That's called banked time off. Do you
think they would agree to that?"

She couldn't help smiling. "I think that would be a wonderful idea. I will tell them to prepare for a meeting in ten
minutes."

Before he could say more, she turned and nearly ran to
where everyone from the first shift was waiting for her.
Immediately she found Harold, the supervisor. "I talked to
him, as you wanted, and he is coming. I think he is going
to have some very good news for all of us." She wouldn't say
more in her excitement and ran to tell the second shift the
same thing.

In exactly eight minutes, the staff assembled in the lunchroom, ready when Chad walked in.

She noticed he'd combed his hair.

He outlined the same plan he'd told her, except in more
detail. He then asked for a show of hands for all who agreed,
and of course, everyone did. She knew everyone wanted to
work hard and do their best, and it would be exciting to be
rewarded with equal time off with full pay.

As the room quieted, Chad turned his head and looked
toward her, causing all to do the same thing.

Anna felt her cheeks burn to have every person there watching her at once.

As Chad spoke, everyone continued to watch her. "In order
to be fair, everyone needs to keep track of their extra time, and
every day, before you leave, please write your name and the
time you left on a piece of paper and put it in an envelope I'm
going to tape near the door. If you leave on time, I still need
you to leave a note. In . . . uh . . . the cities . . . we'd be doing
this with a punch clock, which is a machine that stamps the
time on a card you insert into a slot. Everyone would put their
card into it when they arrived and then again when they left,

and this is how most employers keep track of a person's time in a factory like this. They do that every day, for as long as they work at that job."

He stopped to let all of them imagine the process. All Anna could think about was how needing to do such a thing displayed a complete lack of trust between people and the company they worked for. But if this was the way it was done in the cities, then she would accept it, and now that she knew, she would not be surprised when asked to do so. When she finished her work for the day, she would stay a few extra minutes and check the Internet for more information.

When the murmurs stopped, Chad continued. "I'm not going to buy a punch clock, but I'll buy time cards so no mistakes are made. We'll only use them when we have a rush order and we might need to work extra time. At the end of the week we'll give all the cards to Anna, she'll record everyone's extra hours, and she'll be the one to coordinate when everyone wants to take their days off. Remember, we can't have too many people taking the same day off, or this won't work. If you agree to this, please raise your hands."

Again, all hands raised.

Chad nodded. "We'll start this new system tomorrow. If you have any questions or need more information, please ask me."

Chad poured himself a cup of coffee and then sat at one of the tables to answer questions and explain his system in more detail. Instead of going back to her desk, Anna sat beside him so she could hear all the details about this wonderful new idea. When everyone was gone, she accompanied him back to the office. He wheeled his chair to her desk, and they sat side by side while he designed a spreadsheet and entered the code for the formulas to add everyone's times automatically.

"I'll order some timecards from the office supply store, but it will be a few days before they get here. Until that happens, we'll have to make our own. Do you want to go home, or do you want to stay and help me?"

"I want to stay. Show me what to do."

They made a form and printed one for everyone on the sturdiest paper she could find, then left the cards at a table beside the door.

Chad swiped his hands down the sides of his pants. "I want you to write down the extra time you took today to prepare for this. I don't want you doing this for free."

"But you work many extra hours for free. I hope that you have been keeping track of your own extra time in this same way, so that you can also take time off."

He shrugged his shoulders. "Of course not. I'm the boss. Now pack up your stuff and let's go home."

༄

For the first time since he'd met her, Anna chattered. The entire walk home, she talked nonstop about how happy everyone was with his new plan and how innovative it was.

He couldn't believe a group of people could be so excited about banked overtime. Personally, Chad had never been excited about it because even though Gary always promised equal time off, whenever anyone asked for the time off, Gary replied that it wasn't good for the company—or, in other words, him—and the time off was denied. Whenever anyone asked to be paid for it, Gary quickly reminded everyone that the agreement had been for equal time off only, not pay at time-and-a-half.

When Chad received his last paycheck, Gary hadn't paid out any of his banked overtime, even on termination of his employment. They had no punch clock at the office. The only record of banked overtime was on paper, on written requests.

Chad had kept a file in his desk, but he hadn't thought to take it with him when he impulsively quit. He had no doubt that Gary had destroyed it when going through his desk. He'd never taken a copy home, and Chad wasn't going to fight him for it because it was a battle he would never win, even though what Gary had done was against the law.

Chad would never do such a thing to these good people here. In fact, when they completed this order, Chad planned to ask Bart if he could give everyone a small bonus for their hard work and dedication, and he had no doubt Bart would agree, even though it technically came right out of Bart's pocket as the only shareholder.

Anna finally stopped her chatter when they arrived at her door. Instead of giving him a quick nod and disappearing before he could get a word in, she turned to him and smiled.

The stars in her eyes nearly blinded him.

Just like in a book, where the hero of the story falls madly in love with the heroine at first sight, his heart pounded and his head swam. In his mind, he pictured her leaning forward, resting her hands on his shoulders, raising herself up on her tiptoes, and kissing him hard and passionately. They would declare their love for each other, all the problems would melt away, the hero would propose, the heroine would swoon and answer affirmatively, and the book would be over, with a happily-ever-after ending.

But then, reality intruded.

He'd really been reading too many sappy books lately.

She smiled and looked down at her clasped hands. "You are such a good man, Chad. We are very blessed to have you running the factory."

A good man.

His heart sank. He wanted, needed, to be so much more to her. He really felt God had put Anna in his path for a reason, and he wanted the reason to be because one day soon she would marry him.

But for now, if good was all he was, he would take it. There were so many worse things—at least being "good" had the potential for more.

He could work at being better.

However, here, he didn't know what to do. Back at home, he would buy a woman flowers and small gifts and jewelry and pour on the charm. Here, such behavior seemed inappropriate. The problem was, he didn't know what was appropriate.

"Uh . . . well . . . thanks," he muttered, because he probably should say something, he just didn't know *what*.

However, now that he'd made some friends here, he did have other men available whom he could ask what was appropriate to attract a woman's attentions.

He considered his options.

Of his closest friends, he couldn't ask David; David was her brother. Back in Minneapolis, Chad had once asked a friend if he would mind if he dated his sister. That day, Chad went home with a black eye. And he didn't get the girl.

He couldn't ask William. Even though word had it that their parents planned to match William and Anna as a couple, he now knew that they were just friends, and friends were all they would ever be. Still, since they were friends, Chad didn't think William was the appropriate person to ask.

That left Brian, who, of all the men he'd ever met, was the most clueless about women. Still Brian would know what people did around here, and that was what mattered.

Whatever Brian said, Chad would make it happen.

"Goode nacht, Chad. I will see you tomorrow morning."

"Yeah. Good night."

Just as it did every day, the door closed in his face.

18

*B*rian wiped his hands on a rag and shoved the rag into his back pocket. "*Goondach.* Good morning. I see you have finally brought your car in for an oil change. It is past time for this."

Standing beside his car, Chad perused Brian's shop. From the outside, it looked just like any other gas station with a garage attached, except for the height of the garage. Up until recently it had been mostly empty every time he'd been by, which hadn't been often. Now some kind of large farm machine took the place of what, in any other auto shop he'd been to, normally would have been a car.

He probably should have wondered how it got here, but in this place, people took no notice of a combine ambling down Main Street.

Chad stroked the hood of his car gently, then turned back to Brian. "I guess I'm overdue for an oil change if you're looking at months, although I certainly haven't put many miles on her since I got here. You're a fully registered licensed mechanic, right? I'll need to keep the receipt in case I ever need to get anything done under warranty. By the way, I've been meaning to ask, how does one do a warranty on a combine? Instead of miles, do they count it by the bushel?"

"*En schnoddanas.* Smart aleck," Brian muttered under his breath, but Chad still heard him.

Thinking of writing down the mileage for the oil change, Chad smiled. Since he walked to work, to church, and most regular weekly activities, and the only large grocery store in town was less than a mile away, he didn't do much driving. He'd put more miles on the car the weekend he went to Minneapolis to pack up his apartment than in the rest of the six months he'd been living here. In the dead of winter, there were times he didn't start the car for over a week. Now that it was nearly summer, it hadn't changed. The only regular use of his car was to take Anna's mother grocery shopping. He just no longer needed to scrape the windows to do it.

Brian opened the driver's door and flicked the lever to release the hood latch, but instead of walking to the front of the car, Brian slid inside to sit behind the steering wheel. He ran his hands over the hard plastic and looked up at Chad. "This is a very nice car. I have been waiting for you to bring it in for a tune-up so I may check how it runs. Maybe I will take it for a test drive."

The thought of anyone here driving his car nearly caused Chad to break out into a cold sweat. Brian was one of the few people who actually owned a vehicle—an older pickup truck—but Chad had never seen it running. It seemed permanently parked behind Brian's garage and looked like it hadn't moved for a very long time. Like everyone else in town, Brian walked wherever he went.

Chad forced himself to smile. "You just want to drive my car so you can impress the chicks."

Brian frowned, and his brows knotted. "I do not have chickens. I do not know why you think a car would impress chickens. I hope you do not put your chickens in your car. I think it would frighten them."

"No, not chicken, *chicks.* Girl chicks. As in, impress the ladies. Do you have a lady you haven't told me about who you'd like to impress?"

Brian grinned. "No, there is no lady I wish to impress. I just wish to drive your car."

Chad sucked in a deep breath. There probably wouldn't be a better time. He couldn't have asked for a better lead-up. "In, uh, the cities, having a car like mine usually impresses the ladies. But it's different here. If there were a lady you wished to impress, what would you do to catch her attention?"

Brian shrugged his shoulders. "I would probably tell her that her cooking is even better than my mama's."

Maybe that would work on some of the young ladies, but Chad couldn't see that working with Anna. Whenever he went to Anna's house for supper, Anna's mother did most of the cooking while Anna and Sarah helped. He didn't think Anna really took much joy in cooking. He probably enjoyed cooking more than she did, probably because for him, it was optional; but for her, it was an expected duty. In fact, he wanted to learn how to cook some of the great meals they made for him, but he never felt welcome in their kitchen, so he never had an opportunity to look over Susan's shoulder or ask questions about her style and ingredients. Mostly, this was a cultural line he didn't want to cross. He could enjoy all the time he wanted in his own kitchen, but here, men barely poured their own water because it meant going into the kitchen. If he wanted to fit in, he had to follow their rules and abide by their customs.

Men didn't belong in the kitchen. Just like women didn't belong . . . he had to stop and think. He had no idea where women didn't belong. His first thought was that here, women didn't belong under the hood of a car, but so few people had cars, it didn't apply. Being under the hood of a car didn't even apply to most of the men.

"Hey, City Boy. *Waut denkje dü*? What are you thinking? Would you like to impress one of the mamas?" He grinned. "Are you not getting enough invitations?"

He'd actually been getting too many invitations. After the first, when he realized the strings attached, he turned them all down. Still, the mamas kept asking. "No. I don't want to impress one of the mamas. I want to impress one of the ladies." He'd already impressed Susan, and he hadn't been meaning to. The problem was that he couldn't seem to impress Susan's daughter.

Brian nodded. "Will you tell me who has caught your attention? Is it Rachel?"

Chad needed a few seconds to remember Rachel's face. "No. It's Anna."

Brian's smile widened. "Ah, Anna. She is very pretty. She is also a very good helper."

Chad clenched his fists, and his whole body stiffened.

Brian shook his head. "But she is not a good cook; she likes to read instead. I have heard that in the kitchen, she becomes distracted. What would you like to know about Anna?"

Chad felt himself relax. "I know what I'd do if I was trying to get her interest and we were on my own turf, but everything I do here turns out to be wrong."

"Ja. I have heard that you were washing dishes at work." Brian rolled his eyes.

Chad stiffened and rammed his hands into his pockets. "You mean you heard about that?"

"I think that everyone in town has heard about that. Also, you go home at lunchtime to put your chickens in the coop. And, you talk to them. I hope they do not talk back to you."

Actually, they did. If that was bad, then he didn't want to know what everyone would think if someone found out he'd been working on training Waddles and Blinkie. Not that they could ever be trained like dogs. He knew he would never be able to litterbox train them like cats, but so far, he'd had moderate success in teaching them to come when he called their names. They certainly knew the words "go get my book" meant sitting in his lap on the recliner. They also knew that "bedtime" meant go into the kitchen and settle down in their box. He suspected they also knew the meaning of "chicken hotel." He'd caught himself saying it just like all his friends and realized he said it often because Waddles and Blinkie knew it meant time to go make a trip to the coop.

Chad cleared his throat. "Never mind the chickens. I need to know what I can do to get Anna's attention. I want her to see me as more than just her boss."

"I do not know. Anna is very different from her sesta. I thought Sarah would be good for me, but it was not so. I know what Sarah likes, but I do not know what Anna likes."

Keeping his hands in his pockets, Chad turned around to look at Brian as he spoke. "Then what in general do men do around here when they seek a lady's affections?"

Brian jerked his head back, as if this was a foreign concept for him. Actually, he'd heard enough about Brian's reputation around women, or lack thereof, to know it really might be a foreign concept. He also knew the ladies outnumbered the men, so men didn't have to try too hard. Most often, the lady had already started sending out signals. Even flares.

Anna had not been sending signals. Just the opposite, she seemed rather gun-shy.

"Often the young men will take ladies for a root beer float at the soda shop. But it is for those younger than we are."

"If she likes that, maybe I can make my own root beer floats for the two of us."

Brian's eyes brightened. "That is what Ted did for Miranda. One day at choir practice, he came in with everything needed to make root beer floats. But he did not just make one for himself and Miranda. He made one for everyone in the choir. They were very good." Brian grinned and rested one hand over his stomach. "I was hoping there was going to be some leftover ice cream, but there was not. Ted made one float for everyone."

"But I need to do something that will impress Anna, not everyone in the church."

"Ja, but think about this. Miranda married Ted. He must have done something right."

"Root beer floats, huh?" He'd never made floats before, but unlike any of the men here, he knew his way around the kitchen and he was a very good cook. He obviously wasn't winning Anna's heart through his technical prowess, so maybe it was time to change tactics. Floats were easy. Too easy.

He turned to Brian. "You've just given me a great idea. I've got some shopping to do, so take your time with my car, and if you want to take a drive through town, knock yourself out."

Brian turned very serious. "I do not wish to hurt myself or damage your car. I just wish to have some fun driving it. I do not wish to get knocked out."

"That's just an expression. I'll be back in about an hour. I've got some shopping to do."

Chad raised his fist to knock on Anna's front door but froze with his knuckles inches from the wood surface. Part of him felt excited about his plan, but part of him was as nervous as a teenager about to embark on his first date, which made no sense. He was a grown man with two years of college and four more in the workforce. He'd just been on the wrong end of the breakup of a two-year relationship.

He'd never been a love-'em-and-leave-'em kind of guy, but he'd been out with enough women that he knew that in general, the ladies were attracted to him.

Except here, the usual rules didn't apply.

Only in Piney Meadows had he felt it important to ask an adult woman's mother permission to take her out for the evening. Of course, he hadn't called it a date. If he had, he doubted Anna would have agreed to go with him.

He sucked in a deep breath and knocked. This really wasn't a date.

The door opened. Anna stood in the doorway, frowning, while her mother stood behind Anna, her hands clasped, grinning like the cat who ate the canary.

"*Hab ein gootde tiet!* Have a good time!" Susan chorused and nudged Anna forward. The second Anna's feet crossed the threshold, the door closed.

"*Waut jeit aun hia?* What is going on here?" Anna grumbled as she stepped forward, so the door wasn't pressing against her backside. "Mama would not tell me what you have planned, except that I should bring a sweater."

Chad grinned and jerked his head toward his car, which was parked out on the driveway instead of inside the garage. "I think she's just excited because we're not walking, we're driving."

"Driving? Where are you taking me?"

His grin widened. "I'm taking you on a picnic to Cass Lake."

"A picnic? Who is going to be there?"

"Just you and me. This is a picnic for two."

Her brows knotted. "That does not make sense."

It would have made sense if he'd added the word he'd purposely left out. It was a going to be a *romantic* picnic for two, if everything went right. If things didn't go the way he wanted, then it would just be a friendly outing for the two of them—no harm, no foul—and that wouldn't be so bad either.

"Don't worry about it. I thought this would be fun, a chance to get away."

"Get away from what?"

If he were back in Minneapolis, he would have said it was a chance to get away from the hustle and bustle and enjoy some quiet time. But here, it was pretty much always quiet. "I don't know. I just wanted to do something different. To relax."

Her eyes narrowed, she glared at him for a few seconds, and then she looked at his car and back to him. "If we are to have a picnic, then we had better go back into the house and I will prepare a supper to take with us."

He shook his head. "No. Everything is already in the car."

She turned to stare at the car. "But I did not see Mama preparing a supper for us."

"She didn't. I put everything together." While Brian had been changing the oil in his car, Chad had gone on a shopping trip, then gone home and spent all afternoon cooking. "We're going to have a picnic at Cass Lake. Then we can go for a walk, and I'll have you back home right after the sunset." He forced himself to smile at his words, like it was a good thing. Only here would a date be over so early. Since it was June and soon to be the longest day of the year, it meant he'd have her home at the "late" time of 9:00 p.m. In Minneapolis, a date would only be just getting started around that time. Instead, he'd have her home before sunset so she could go to bed nice and early in order to get plenty of rest before church on Sunday morning.

Today, he was changing the game—and changing the rules. Going out of the town, away from work, church, and any place else they'd ever been together, seemed like a good place to just be himself and not her boss or the manager of the biggest employer in town. It would be just the two of them—a man and a woman getting to know each other a little better. Maybe introduce a little romance, and see where the future could go.

Then when they were back home with the usual routine, hopefully, enough would change so it could continue.

He motioned toward the car. "Come on. Let's go."

19

*A*nna stiffened, crossed her arms, turned to stare at Chad's car, and then looked back at him. He only shrugged his shoulders and grinned.

She couldn't figure out what he was thinking. Surely he wanted something, although she didn't know what. If he wanted a good meal he was going to be very disappointed with whatever he'd done for a picnic dinner for two, compared to what Mama had cooked. She'd made *en heenaborde met bubbat* for supper, which was one of his favorite meals.

Yet since he'd spoken to Mama, surely he knew what she'd made. During their time in the kitchen today to prepare ahead, she'd almost felt like they had been cooking with Chad in mind. She'd even said so, but her mama hadn't told her Chad was coming until they heard his knock on the door. Then Mama had nearly pushed her to the door and told her to open it, which hadn't made any sense until she saw Chad standing there.

Going to his car without Mama's cooking didn't make sense. He was even going to miss the *Syrutstlatz* cake they'd made for tomorrow's dessert after they came home from church. Even though no one in the family could touch it before Sunday, Mama would sneak a piece to Chad, because she always did.

She didn't know what he had planned, but he would be very disappointed when she told him what he'd left behind. She had no idea what he could possibly have prepared. All she could think of was what Ted, as another single man living alone, would have done.

She'd never had cheese and crackers for supper before, but there was always a first time for everything.

Since supper was not going to be included in their outing, she tried to figure out another reason for his strange plan.

It wasn't possible he wanted to talk about the new overtime plans at work. They'd already set up all the procedures, and everyone was very excited. More than that, since his arrival in Piney Meadows, Chad had always been very adamant that all talk of business remain at work, during working hours. The minute the door closed behind them as they left every day, their conversation always changed to other things. He always held firm with no exception.

The most likely conversation he would want to have in private would probably be another request to find another activity to help him become more familiar with the ways of her people. While everyone at the factory seemed to like him and he'd been doing fine at the Bible study meetings, he had dropped out of the young adult group. He'd told her that too many of the young ladies were looking at him as husband material, and he didn't want to mislead any of them or their mamas.

Even though most of his interaction with her people was in church on Sundays, almost everyone knew him better than he knew them. Word of Chad's chicken coop had spread quickly. Many people had come to her home on the pretext of talking to her mama or papa when all they'd wanted was to peek over the fence to see the infamous chicken hotel. At first Anna had cringed and wanted to reprimand people for ridiculing him for building such an extravagant structure for two chickens. But then, with the only exception being Rachel's mama, instead of being amused at Chad's expense, everyone actually liked it. Oddly, the person who liked it the most was elderly Mr. Reinhart. He snapped at everyone to mind their words and told each person how he saw much potential in Chad and to give "City Boy" time to adapt and prove himself. Naturally, everyone always minded Mr. Reinhart. After all, no one wanted to feel the rebuke of his cane.

Thinking of elderly Mr. Reinhart's words brought her mind back to Chad's chicken coop. She'd seen him put the chickens in it every night, and despite his worries, they settled in quickly. Every night, not long after she tucked herself into bed, she only heard one small bit of rustling, and then for the rest of the night, all was silent until he went into the coop the next morning to feed them.

She didn't know why he did that. Chickens were self-regulating and didn't need their food monitored or to be fed at intervals. They simply ate the amount they needed when they needed it. Yet every morning, Chad was there, picking them up and talking to them.

One day she would speak to him about that, but this was not the time.

She didn't know what he needed to talk to her about, but she could certainly listen, especially since he had gone to so much trouble. It was obviously something he couldn't talk to her about at work.

Once again, Anna glanced toward his car. Unlike her mama, she hadn't been in it often, but she could understand her mama's fascination with it. Riding in Chad's car was fun, except for the time he'd played some horrible music. "This is fine. Let us go. I suppose I will not need my purse if we are only going for a walk at Cass Lake."

"And a picnic supper."

She sighed. "Ja." Mama would have plenty of food in the fridge for her to eat when she got home. Of course the evening would not be over, because Mama would invite Chad in to eat, and he never turned down Mama's cooking.

Like he did every time she got in his car, he held the door open for her as she slid into the seat, and then he made sure she had her seatbelt buckled, as if she were incapable of clicking it together herself. In some ways it annoyed her, but another part of her liked his concern.

While he walked around the car to get in, a piece of paper lying on the dash with a badly drawn map complete with land-marks and mileage caught her attention.

She smiled. It was a map of how to get to Cass Lake.

As soon as the car started moving, Anna picked up the map. "I could have given you directions. Anyone could have given you directions. But this looks like Brian's bad handwriting." A smudge of grease on the edge of the paper also gave away its origin.

"Yes. This was Brian's idea. I trust him because I've never been there."

"Cass Lake is beautiful. In the summer, there is good fish-ing, and in the winter, it is good skating."

"Skating? Why didn't anyone ask me to go skating?"

The memory of his struggles the first time he tried to walk in snowshoes flashed through her mind's eye. "I would think it is because everyone was too afraid that you would break your leg or hurt yourself. Or maybe no one has skates in your size they could have loaned to you."

His cheeks turned a delightful shade of pink. "My feet aren't that big."

She'd seen his boots beside all the others when they went to Bible study meetings. When they went to someone's home in the winter, everyone brought extra shoes or slippers and left their boots on a mat beside the door. Chad's boots were the largest by at least two sizes. "You are tall, so it is natural that you will have large feet. But I think after helping you with the snowshoes, everyone wanted to be cautious. It does not hurt to fall on snow, but it does hurt to fall on ice. No one would like it if you were injured. I am sorry, I did not mean to hurt your feelings."

Chad shrugged his shoulders. "It's okay. But since I know now, I'd like to try skating. I've never done it before."

"You have not? How can this be?"

"I don't know. I guess when I grew up I spent more time in the winter in a warm living room playing video games than outside in the cold. But if I can do snowshoes, I can do skates."

She wasn't going to tell him that balancing on skates was harder than it looked and it would take him a while to build up the strength in his ankles, just as it had taken him a while to build up the muscles in his legs to keep up with the rest of the men on snowshoes.

Anna pointed forward, to the side of the road. "Be careful. There is a moose. It should not walk onto the road, but you must be careful."

"I see it," he muttered as he slowed his speed. "My camera is on the floor behind my seat. Can you reach it and get a picture of him as we go past?"

"Ja, I have taken pictures with Brian's camera. I think I can do that." She turned and reached behind the seat, but instead of touching a camera, she felt a large shape. She squirmed to look behind the seat. "You have your guitar down there."

"It's not mine. I've only got an electric guitar. This one is an acoustic and it's Brian's. He let me borrow it for the night."

"Why have you brought a guitar?"

"I thought we might sing together. You have such a beautiful voice. I remember you singing the part of the angel at the Christmas play the first night I got here. Why don't you sing like that in church? You're so quiet I barely hear you on Sundays."

Anna felt her cheeks grow warm. "If I sing loud at church, then sometimes people close to me stop their own songs of worship and watch me. That is not right or good that I would overpower them. I will not distract people who have come to worship for themselves in God's house."

"Now I'm really glad I brought the guitar. You can sing as loud as you want, and I'll bet the birds and animals will stop what they're doing and sing along with you."

Before Chad had come to a full stop, Anna found the camera and snapped a picture of the moose. "You are a crazy person," she muttered, wanting to reproach him, but at the same time, she did miss singing loud and clear on Sundays. After Christmas, the church had meant to start a choir, but with both Miranda and Ted gone no one had volunteered to take on the job of leadership.

He followed her directions instead of Brian's map. She showed him where to turn and the best place to park the car. "There is the path. We can walk to the lake from here."

After he opened the door and escorted her out, Chad stepped back. Instead of opening the trunk, he extended one arm toward the path's entrance. "This is it? It looks like it's only single file."

"Ja. For much of the way there is no path except for the one leading to the area where people can swim without getting tangled in seaweeds." It appeared Brian hadn't told him a walk around Cass Lake meant exactly that—walking around the lake, at the shoreline, single file. "We will probably work up quite an appetite after walking around the lake, and then we can eat the picnic you have brought."

He ran his fingers through his hair. "Actually, there's more to it than that. I brought the small barbecue I used to have on my balcony."

"You have brought a barbecue? Is that not a lot of work?"

"Not really. I thought it would be fun, barbecuing for two out here in the middle of nowhere. Nothing I brought is heavy, but it looks like it's going to take two trips."

"I will help carry things."

Chad shook his head. "No. This is my treat for you, and I'm doing all the work."

"That makes no sense. However, if there is much to carry, there is no one here except us. We can have our meal here, where the ground is level, and when we are done, we can go walk around the lake."

At first she thought he was going to argue with her, but he only shrugged his shoulders. "Sure. I guess there's no reason why not. It will also be harder lugging everything back to the car uphill. We'll eat up here, but I want to check out the lake first."

Anna looked down the hill to the lake. "That would be good. Also, the sunset is always very beautiful over the lake. We can watch it for a short time, as long as we leave with enough time to get back to the car before it is dark."

"Sunset over the lake? Brian never told me about that."

"That is strange. Brian has a camera and he enjoys taking photographs."

She waited while Chad walked to the car and opened the back door. He removed the guitar from behind the seat, slung the strap over his shoulder, hung the camera around his neck, picked up a book, and turned toward her. "Lead the way."

She led him down the path to the lake, making sure to go slow to account for the extra height of the guitar over his head, as he had to duck beneath the lower branches. Once at the shore, they stood and looked out over the calm lake. In the distance, birds chirped and ducks quacked, accompanied by the rustle of leaves in the wind. The only movement was a slight ripple of waves, and every once in a while, a fish broke the surface of the water to catch a bug.

"Brian was right. This is so peaceful."

"Ja. Today is a busy day for everyone on the farms—that is why it is so quiet. Tomorrow, after church, many will be here fishing and swimming."

He snickered. "I hope not in the same place."

Anna pointed across the lake. "Everyone goes to fish over there. Everyone says it is a secret spot. But since everyone knows about the same spot, it is not a very good secret."

"You said everyone is busy on the farms today. I know a lot of the people who work at the factory only work a few days there and the rest of the days on their farms. But there are many who work five days a week. Are you saying on Saturday, most of them go work on the farms, too?"

"Ja. They will be helping their friends. But no one will work on Sunday."

"I found that out the hard way. I don't mean about working at the factory, I mean everywhere else. Even the restaurant is closed on Sunday."

"Of course."

"Back in Minneapolis, all retail stores and restaurants are open and in full operation on Sundays. In fact, it's their busiest day. Many factories run 24–7. Nothing shuts down, ever, except maybe on Thanksgiving and Christmas. Of course, the hospitals and police work Thanksgiving and Christmas, too, but on reduced staff. Sundays are business as usual. I think I'm used to it here with everything shutting down every Sunday, but it took a while."

Anna couldn't imagine working Sundays. She turned to Chad. "When I find a job in the cities, will they expect me to work on the Sabbath?"

"It depends. Most offices, no. But if there is a crisis, yes. The Lord's Day doesn't mean the same thing there as it does here. Many Christian people work Sunday as a normal day because they have to or they won't have a job. They choose to take another day as their Sabbath. But for the most part, Sunday as the Sabbath day has completely lost its meaning."

She couldn't imagine that. If getting a good job might mean working on the Lord's Day, Anna had some very serious praying to do.

Chad slung the guitar off his shoulder, carefully set it on a fallen log, found a safe place to rest his camera, and opened the book to a page he had marked.

"You have brought a hymnal."

"Yes. Ted left it for me. All the hymns are chorded for guitar in this one. He said Miranda did it for him. He left it behind for me because she has a full selection of chorded hymnbooks at home, including this one." He played the introduction for "Blessed Assurance, Jesus Is Mine," one of her favorite hymns, then stopped and looked up at her. "I don't have any of these memorized, which is why I brought it. Besides, the hymns have a lot of words. Would you like to sing with me?"

The only times she'd sung outside, it had always been with a group and they'd gone caroling, of course without an instrument. It had only been a few years ago that they had started using a guitar in church, when Ted returned from college. Even though it felt less reverent singing with a guitar than with a piano, she enjoyed the sound. "I would like that, but only if you sing with me. I do not wish to sing alone."

"That was my plan."

He played the last line again as the introduction, and they began to sing. When they got to the chorus, Chad changed from singing unison to a harmony line that was so beautiful she nearly lost her concentration and stopped. At the last verse they sang the chorus a little slower, which seemed to emphasize the words, bringing the meaning closer to her heart. As Chad played a few more chords to close the hymn, she watched his hands, then looked up to his face while he continued to read the chords from the book. Her eyes started to burn and she struggled not to cry, which made no sense, because she had sung this same hymn more times than she could count, and this had never happened to her before. As he played the last chord, he closed his eyes, sighed, and smiled. While she watched, he raised his head, opened his eyes, and, still smiling, turned to her.

The second they made eye contact, his eyes widened and his smile dropped. "Is something wrong? Are you okay?"

Anna nodded, then shook her head. She wanted to say she was fine, but she was too afraid. If she tried to speak, her voice would crack, and then she really would start to cry and there would be no stopping it.

Completely serious now, Chad quickly shrugged the guitar strap off his shoulder, gently set the guitar down, and reached toward her, resting his hands on her shoulders. Very slowly, he lifted one hand and, using his thumb, brushed one tear off her cheek. "I know. That was really something, wasn't it?"

"Ja," she choked out, barely able to speak, knowing she couldn't say more.

His eyes softened, and his hand returned to her shoulder. Very gently, he pulled her toward him while leaning forward to meet her in the middle. As he shuffled his bottom closer to her, his hands slid to her back. Because it felt so good, she leaned into his chest and tucked her head beneath his chin. His hands slid further down her back, his fingers splayed, and his grip tightened, pressing her firmly into his chest; but not so firmly that if she tried to push herself away, he wouldn't let her. Slowly, he rested his cheek against her hair. She felt the expansion of his chest as he sighed, and then his embrace tightened as he released his breath.

Anna closed her eyes and leaned into him, enjoying his warmth and the steady beat of his heart. William had hugged her a few times, but it didn't feel like this.

Not able to help herself, Anna slowly ran her hands to the center of his back and gave him a gentle squeeze. For a brief second, he stiffened slightly, and then his heart started beating a little faster. He gave her a tiny squeeze, then released her, forcing her to lower her arms and sit straight.

The second they were no longer touching, Chad reached for the guitar, picked it up, and stood. "We should get back to the car. I wanted to cook supper, and if we're going to be finished before the sun sets, I have to start now."

She looked at her watch. The sun wouldn't be setting for hours, but then she had no idea of his plans. While part of her wanted to sing another hymn with him, part of her needed to move. "Ja, we probably should start to make our supper," she said as she pushed herself up off the log.

By the time she was standing, he already had the guitar slung on his back, the camera hanging from his neck, and the hymnal tucked under his arm.

"When I said I was cooking, I meant it. All you're going to do is watch and talk to me as I cook, then eat what I made."

Anna looked at him, his face stern, allowing no room for argument. All she could do was nod, then follow him back to the car.

20

$\mathcal{A}$s he ducked beneath the low-hanging branches, mentally Chad kicked himself around the block and halfway down the next one as he slogged through the path back up to his car.

He didn't know how something that felt so right could at the same time feel so wrong.

Anna felt so perfect in his arms. He'd almost nestled in a little more to kiss the top of her head when she gave him that little squeeze that nearly made him come undone.

He couldn't believe it. Just that small, innocent action sent his brain into a tailspin. It had been all he could do not to stop everything he was doing and kiss her senseless.

Except the senseless one was him. He knew a little about her history, but more about the history of the society in which she lived. Because of the lifestyle here, he wasn't even sure if she'd ever kissed a man before, but he doubted it. If she had, it would have been only a kiss of friendship or fondness, not a kiss of heart-pounding passion.

He'd done so much more than that. He was going to be a father. She was a complete innocent, and he . . . wasn't. He had no business touching her, and he especially had no business kissing her, without telling her the whole story of his sordid past. She really knew nothing of the man she'd just allowed to hold her.

From the depths of his soul he wanted to tell her everything, but now when he had the perfect opportunity all set up, all his plans fell apart like his first car. He hadn't even kissed her, and his brain was completely rattled. He couldn't blame the pounding of his heart on the walk up the hill. Just the thought of Anna holding him and responding to his touch made it beat even faster. He'd been fooling himself when he planned this evening, telling himself that he would be satisfied with a few small kisses. Touching her, holding her, he realized what he really wanted was to kiss her with all the passion in his soul and tell her how much he loved her—and he wanted to hear her say the same.

And then he wanted to ask if she'd marry him.

But he wasn't going to do that. She had no idea of all the baggage he would bring with him into a relationship, including what was going to be an ugly custody battle. In her eyes, he was only her boss—a poor hapless city boy still reeling from being recently jilted, having a hard time adjusting to laid-back, rural life. All he'd meant to do today was start to show her a small sample of how special he thought she was. He was hopeful that, by the time he told her about his potential son or daughter on the way, she'd love him enough to stand with him in whatever battle he would face. He'd nearly jumped way ahead to the last page. Fortunately, he'd come to his senses before he'd blown any chance he could have. He'd brought Anna here to surprise her and treat her like someone special, and that was all he was going to do.

Once they arrived back at his car, he pulled out the soft fuzzy picnic blanket he'd bought and spread it on the ground for Anna. When he stepped back to allow her to sit, she turned to him and started to open her mouth, but when she made eye contact with him, she quickly closed her mouth and sank down. Afraid his voice wouldn't come out the way he wanted, he simply smiled, then returned to the car to unload everything he'd brought and set up his portable barbecue.

After he hooked up the propane cylinder and turned the barbecue on to let it heat up, he hauled the cooler out of the car and set everything out within easy reach.

"What is all this? What have you brought?"

Back into his game, he grinned. "My own secret recipe potato salad, deviled eggs, Caesar salad; and when the barbecue is ready, I'm going to make the best hamburgers you've ever tasted in your life. Then for dessert, we're going to have double chocolate brownies and end everything with my special lemon iced tea."

"All this, for just the two of us?"

He cleared his throat. "Ja."

Her mouth opened, but no sound came out. Her eyes widened, she covered her mouth with her hands, and she burst out laughing.

He'd thought he'd do better at the accent, but even though he hadn't, seeing her laugh sent a wave of relief through him. "Maybe I won't try that again, if I did it so bad."

She waved one hand in the air as her laughter calmed. "I would like to say it was a good try, but you did sound very funny."

Chad felt his cheeks flame. So much for his efforts to be taken seriously. He'd picked up a few words and phrases of the German language, but if he couldn't even say "yes" in German and be taken seriously, he wasn't going to attempt anything else. Admittedly, most of the phrases he'd learned centered around food, but just like a teenager, he'd gone online and found the phrase he'd really wanted to say to her—*Ich leewe die*—I love you.

Not today but hopefully in the not too distant future, he could use it. And by the day he said it, he'd have practiced the accent.

"Never mind," he grumbled. "I'm going to start cooking. If you get your bun all fixed up the way you want it, I'll do the rest."

As he started cooking the beef patties, Anna began opening the containers he'd brought, and spooned portions onto both plates. "Did you really prepare all this food? Or are you teasing me?"

He shook his head. "I'm not teasing. I really made everything myself. If you doubt me, just ask Frank Neufeld, at the store. I bought everything this morning. Even the eggs. Speaking of eggs, I have to ask. When will Waddles and Blinkie start laying eggs? They're just over two months old, and they're getting pretty big."

Anna smiled, causing him to nearly drop one of the burgers he'd been in the process of flipping. "Hens will not lay until they are five or six months old, and your two chickens still have much growing to do. I am sorry. For now, you must simply feed them and keep them healthy."

"Don't be sorry. I'm having a lot of fun with them."

"I have never thought of chickens as fun, but I am glad you are enjoying them." She paused to close the containers, then raised her head again. "I cannot believe you have made this by yourself."

"I did, but I probably shouldn't be admitting it. You can keep a secret, can't you?"

"Ja, I can. Even though this is very odd. Of course, since you live alone, you must do much of your own cooking, but this is not what I expected."

"I enjoy cooking. I always have. I wish your mama would show me how to make those *Glums wareneki*, but she always kicks me out of the kitchen."

She stared at him like she thought he was kidding.

"I also make great shrimp curry. You've probably never had curry, have you?"

"Nein, I have not."

"Then you'll have to come over to my place for supper one night. I'd bring some for lunch, but it can have a strong smell. It's not bad, but it's not like anything anyone here would ever cook, so people would ask what it was and where it came from. It would probably be best to keep it at home. I'll invite Brian over, too. I know he likes to try different things, and he'd keep a secret for a free meal."

Anna shook her head. "I am not sure of that. I remember the first time Miranda made a new kind of chicken dish called Shake 'N Bake. No one here had ever heard of it. But when Miranda made it for Ted and Brian, Brian told everyone how delicious it was, and now it is a regular item at Frank's store. Brian would mean well, but I believe he would accidentally say something. He is very enthusiastic when it comes to food he likes."

"You're probably right. Now I'm going to have to think about it. I don't want to do anything to rock the boat any more than I already have. I had a hard enough time redeeming myself after helping the ladies do the dishes that one day."

"Then we will only do this, and I will not say more."

It was too bad he couldn't cook curried shrimp on a barbecue. Although, he probably wouldn't be able to get shrimp in Piney Meadows anyway. Or curry powder. He'd already used up almost all he'd brought when he moved. "The burgers are ready. Can you please hand me a plate?"

He set the burgers onto the plate, closed the lid to the barbecue to let it burn itself clean for a few minutes, and then joined Anna on the blanket. He led with a short prayer of thanks, then waited for her to take her first bite.

At her first taste of the burger, her eyes opened wide. "This is *zehr gut*. Very good." Instead of taking a second bite, she took a taste of his potato salad. "This, too. Zehr gut." Next, she nibbled one of the deviled eggs with his secret ingredient, a pinch of curry.

"These are also zehr gut. I have never tasted deviled eggs like this."

"And you likely never will again, except for mine."

"Will you tell me how you have made these? I wish to take this the next time I attend the knitting group lunch on the weekend."

"Nope. I won't tell you. But I'll make a batch for you."

"*Du deist mie spos?* Are you making fun of me?"

He grinned. "Nope. I'm very serious. If you want to find out my secret ingredient, you'll have to marry me first." He hadn't meant to blurt it out, but now that the words were said, he couldn't take them back.

He cringed, waiting for a tongue-lashing. Instead, the corners of Anna's mouth quivered, and she broke out into a full-bellied laugh. "That is what all the mamas say when they are trying to find a husband for their daughters. That in order to get good food like they are eating, they will have to marry their daughters." She covered her mouth with one hand but didn't stop giggling.

Personally, he didn't know what was so funny. Back in Minneapolis, his talents in the kitchen made him a desirable commodity among the women. To everyone except Brittany, apparently. But here in Piney Meadows, just like so many things, it only made him odd.

When Anna finally noticed he wasn't laughing with her, her laughter faded. "I am sorry. I am not laughing because you like to cook. I think you are very brave for admitting such a thing. I was laughing because most women would not know what to do with a man in their kitchen."

He wanted to ask if she would know what to do with him in the kitchen but thought it best not to push his luck. For now, she appreciated his cooking—at least while they were in the middle of nowhere eating it—and most of all, she didn't say that she would never allow him in her kitchen. He decided it best to leave it alone.

Chad checked his watch. "We don't want to take too long to eat. I want to go back to the lake and take pictures when the sun starts to set. We have to make sure we leave enough time to get back through the path before it becomes too dark to see."

"Of course, you are right."

They ate the rest of their meal in companionable silence. The lack of conversation emphasized to him how right this was—they felt so comfortable with each other that it wasn't necessary to fill every minute with meaningless conversation The silence said so much more than words could.

They hurried to pack everything in the car so they wouldn't have to do it in the dark, in case they didn't beat the setting sun on their way back up the path. As they prepared to leave to go back to the lake, Anna scanned the area. "I think we are leaving the area clean. I do not see any crumbs on the ground, so the bears should not come while we are away."

All Chad's motions froze. "Bears?"

"Ja. We do not want them to come while we are gone. It would not be good if they were between us and the car."

"What bears?"

"The brown bears. We should not have to worry; we only need to remain cautious. You make a lot of noise when going through the bush, so that would send them away unless they are going to their den to sleep for the night."

"There are bears here?"

She stopped moving, planted her fists on her hips, and glared at him. "Of course there are bears here. No one builds them a nice bear hotel in which to sleep. Where do you think they live?"

"I don't know." He made a lame laugh. "The zoo or something. I hadn't thought about it, but you're right. We are just borrowing this spot from the wild animals." He glanced around, paying more attention to what might be lurking in the bush just out of sight, suddenly feeling far less relaxed in this beautiful patch of wilderness than he had a few minutes ago. "What else lives here that has fur and big teeth?"

"I suppose the only other animal we need to be cautious about would be cougars. Bobcats and coyotes will not usually attack people, they eat smaller animals."

He had been warned coyotes were the worst for coming into town to try to eat everyone's chickens at night, but he hadn't thought about where they lived when they weren't hunting for domestic chickens.

"What about wolves? Are they here, too?"

"Ja, but I have never seen one. They do not come near the town."

Suddenly, Chad didn't feel so complacent about making a trip to the lake in the near-dusk. "You know, maybe we should just go back home." To the "metropolis" of Piney Meadows. Where there were people. And good, solid buildings.

Anna grinned. "We will be fine. We just cannot take too long. I will race you to the lake."

Before he had a chance to try to convince her otherwise, Anna turned and sprinted down the path, giving him no choice but to follow.

The sunset had better be worth it.

21

$\mathcal{A}$nna stood in the doorway of Chad's office, watching him type. For some reason, she seemed to find herself doing this often, whenever she needed to talk to him about something and didn't know how to start the conversation.

As usual, after about a minute, he noticed her standing there, not doing anything but watching him. He stopped typing, not so discreetly slid his coffee mug further away from his keyboard, and turned to her. "Yes?"

"Two boxes have arrived for you. They are in shipping."

His eyes lit up, and he broke into a smile so bright she nearly had to blink. "Fantastic!"

"I see you were expecting them. The documents list them as two bicycles."

He stood. "That's correct."

"Why do you need two bicycles?"

"I don't. One is for you."

She stepped back. "But I already own a bicycle."

"Which I've never seen you ride. So I got a bike for you, the girl's version of what I got for myself, and we can do some real biking. We'll start off by riding to work every day. I see a lot of people here take their bikes to work, and now we can do the same. Then, on the weekends, we can head for the hills and have an adventure."

"I do not think that would be good."

Chad stood and waved one arm in the direction of the spot where all the people who had ridden bicycles had parked them. "Not with that kind of bike. I got us a couple of five-speed mountain bikes."

"Five speeds? Why would a bicycle need to go five speeds?"

His grin widened. "These bikes have gears. Depending on the surface or the steepness of a hill, you change the gear ratio to match your cadence to make your peddling easier or more efficient and a nicer ride. You'll see." He walked around her toward the hallway to the warehouse, then stopped. "Are you coming?"

She followed him to the shipping area, where in the short time since she'd been there to sign for his packages, the men had opened both boxes and were already assembling the bicycles.

"Thanks, guys," Chad said as he watched. "Did the other stuff come, too?"

"Ja." Frank nodded. "They came yesterday, and we put them aside for you. Two baskets, two headlights, and two helmets."

"Great. You'll give me a call when they're ready?"

"Ja. I have never seen a bicycle like this before."

"If you want, go ahead and take it for a test drive."

Frank nodded again. "I think I would like to do that."

Chad turned to the group of men, some of whom were openly examining the gears on the bicycles, while others were reading the instructions. "If anyone wants to take it for a ride around the block, go ahead. The instructions for changing gears are in the manual." He turned to Anna. "Do you mind if any of the ladies here take your bike for a test drive? I thought you might want to be the first to give it a test. Just tell me when you're going, so I can answer the phone if it rings."

Anna shook her head. "I do not know how to change gears. I will not be good at this."

"I'll show you, you'll do it a few times, and then it will just be natural. It's not hard."

"I think I will do that then." Given the opportunity, it would be better for her to learn to use the gears without Chad watching—then she wouldn't look so foolish in his eyes. She didn't know why she felt it important, but she did. "Also, I do not mind if any of the ladies want to try out this bicycle." Although Anna did think it not right that everyone was enthusiastically building the bicycles instead of doing their regular work, when they were on the program to bank their overtime. However, obviously Chad had allowed them to assemble the bicycles and encouraged everyone to go for a short ride, so she said nothing. But then, knowing her people, they would all work extra hours and not write it down to make up for the time they took to build and ride the new bicycles.

Leaving everyone to their temporary project, she walked back to the office with Chad. "I have received an invitation for the two of us on Thursday evening to go to Henry Friesen's farm. He has invited everyone to come watch and celebrate his new chicken plucker."

If she weren't mistaken, Chad's steps slowed and then he resumed his speed. "Chicken plucker?"

"He has a new chicken plucker—the fastest he has ever seen—and he wants everyone to see. I thought that this would be a good opportunity to visit one of the farms, because many people will be going."

"To celebrate the new chicken plucker . . ."

"Would you like to go?"

He turned to watch her face as they walked side by side. "I suppose this is a good time to meet people who don't work at the factory away from church activities. Am I supposed to bring anything?"

"*Oba nü.* Of course not. All the ladies will bring all the food. We will have a small celebration, and then everyone will go home."

"Since this is on a farm, then do we ride our new bikes or take the car?"

"Everyone will be on bicycles except Pastor Jake and Kathleen."

"Then we'll use our new bikes, too. But for now, it's time to get back to work."

❧

Anna had hit the save button on Chad's laptop computer and just started to read the next portion of her assignment when her mama stepped inside her bedroom. "The telephone, it is for you."

For today, since her papa wasn't home, Anna didn't need to make sure the computer was out of sight when she left her bedroom. "Who is calling for me?"

"It is Rebecca. She sounded very strange. I hope nothing is wrong."

Anna quickened her pace. "Rebecca. Hello. Is something the matter?"

Rebecca spoke so fast her words nearly blurred together. "It is Chad. He is on his bicycle, and he has just ridden past my house."

Anna smiled. "Yes. He is enjoying his new bicycle. He is very enthusiastic about it." So enthusiastic, it was as if he were a young boy just getting his first adult-size bicycle, able to go faster for the first time, as boys liked to do.

"Anna, he is riding around with his chickens. One of them is in the basket, the other is perched on the handlebars."

Visions of Rebecca's street passed through her mind. The only reason he could have his chickens with him was if something was wrong, and he was taking them to Zebediah's veterinary clinic. But that was on the other side of Piney Meadows from Rebecca's parents' home, and since it was evening, the clinic was closed. "He must be lost. Or maybe his is trying to find Zebediah's house." Surely he had his cell phone in his pocket. As soon as she hung up with Rebecca, she would phone him and give him directions.

"Nein. He does not look lost at all. He was smiling. Wait. He is in front of my house again." Anna heard a shuffle, like Rebecca was trying to stretch the cord from the phone while she looked out the window. "He is switching the chickens. He has taken the one from the basket and put it on the handlebars, and now he is putting the chicken that was on the handlebars into the basket." Anna's grip on the phone tightened as Rebecca gasped. "The chickens are jumping! No, only one is jumping. It is jumping back into the basket, and now the one from the basket is jumping back onto the handlebars. Chad is now moving again. He is not going toward the clinic. He is going the other way. He is going to Brian's gas station. Why is he taking his chickens to Brian?"

"*Ick pliewe daut nijch!* I do not believe this! Brian's parents have chickens, but Brian does not know about them." Anna began to run her fingers through her hair, then froze with her fingers still on top of her head. This was something she saw Chad do when he was frustrated, and she seemed to be picking up his bad habits. She would now be careful of where she left her coffee mug on her desk.

"Anna! I see them! Now Brian is riding his bicycle, and the two of them are going down the street. *Mein seit!* Oh dear! Brian is riding without his hands touching the handlebars. He is sticking his arms out to the sides and clucking like a chicken. Chad is now going faster. Brian has put his hands down and now he is catching up to Chad. The two of them are now not in front of my house anymore. They are continuing down the street. I do not know where they are going."

"Chad must have asked Brian how to get to Zebediah's home, and Brian is now taking him there." She didn't know anything was wrong with his chickens, but the possibility made her feel strangely sad. Even though they were only chickens, Chad had been very careful with everything they needed. Most people didn't treat their dogs as well as Chad treated his chickens. If something happened and one or both of them died, it would be quite a shame, considering all the work he put into them. "I do not need to phone him anymore, Brian will take him to Zebediah's house. I do not know if Zebediah has ever been asked to look at chickens after he has closed his clinic, but I know he will not mind. Everyone knows that Chad is working very hard to care for his chickens. I will phone you back later when I find out more."

As Anna hung up, she sighed, then walked to the kitchen window and stared at Chad's empty chicken coop. The chickens had seemed healthy and active last night when he'd put them into the coop, and they seemed fine now if they were jumping between the handlebars and the basket as Rebecca had just told her. She hoped the only reason Chad would be taking his chickens to Zebediah was to get their wings clipped, although that would be a strange thing to do in the evening, as it wasn't an emergency but maintenance. She probably should have shown him how to do that, but she'd completely forgotten.

Instead of going back to her homework, she continued to stare at the empty chicken coop. Despite his strange ways, she felt an odd fondness for Chad. He was a very hard worker and had made some very good decisions for the factory. Already Bart had noticed increased business and increased productivity. As people who worked at the factory became more familiar with him, everyone worked very hard for him, and they seemed to like him, even though he was not one of them. He was very kind-hearted, both to the people who worked for him and to his chickens.

Thinking of chickens, Anna smiled. She couldn't imagine what would go through Chad's mind when he saw the thousands of chickens at Henry's farm, when he was going through so much work to care for only two. Maybe, since they were going to be right on the farm, not only could he buy a few dozen eggs to make his delicious deviled eggs, he could also buy a couple of freshly butchered roasters. Since he liked to cook, he should have no trouble.

But that was going to be tomorrow. For today, she had to make sure she got all her homework done; because tomorrow evening, she would be at Henry's farm.

⋙⋘

"You look like you're doing just fine with the gears. Didn't I tell you it would change the way you rode a bike?"

Just because he seemed to suggest it, Anna thought she wanted to go a little faster, so she switched gears as Chad had shown her, since they were on a flat, even road. "Ja. This is a very nice way to ride a bike. It is easier to peddle, for sure."

"The point is to find your optimal cadence, which is that speed of peddling that's just right for you. Instead of peddling faster or slower, switch gears and make the bike work for you, instead of you working for the bike."

"I think I understand what you are saying. This will take time and practice for me. But it is very strange to be wearing a helmet while I am riding. No one else I know does this."

"You know the rules. No helmet, no bicycle. No exceptions." He turned to her; one hand released the handlebar, and he knocked on top of his own helmet. "If something happens, I don't want to be shoveling your brains off the side of the road."

The thought was so disgusting that she didn't want to reply.

She glanced at Chad while he rode beside her. For both of them, the helmets he had bought exactly matched the colors of the bicycles. He'd called it a fashion statement. Then when she said she didn't need to have fashion, he said he would take her bicycle apart and send it back to the store if she ever rode without the helmet.

For this, she took him very seriously. Besides, even without his graphic description of possible head injuries, she would have worn the helmet with only his request. It hadn't taken long, and she'd very much come to like riding this new kind of bicycle.

As they continued down the road to get to Henry's farm, Anna smiled as she watched Chad on his bicycle. He was much more agile on the bicycle than he had been on the snowshoes. After only a few days, he started doing tricks and riding for short distances on one tire. She'd even seen him balance on just the front tire, something she'd never seen a person do. "You are very good at riding your bicycle. How do you do those things?"

He grinned, pulled on the handlebars, and jerked backward so he once again balanced on the rear tire for a few dozen yards and then bumped back down. "This is nothing. I used to do stunt riding on a BMX when I was younger. I paid for my first year of college winning competitions and through sponsorships. Then I had to get serious and study, so the bike got parked, and the next generation took over with bigger and better stunts. I don't regret giving it up. It was fun while it lasted."

Earlier, while they were in the town, he'd ridden his bike on the narrow curb, hopped the bike down, and kept going without losing his balance, yet he couldn't hammer a nail in straight. She would never understand that, except to know that God gave different people different gifts, and sometimes they only made sense in God's greater perspective. "You must have had a very fancy bicycle to do that, yet you have bought a new bicycle for yourself. Why is this?"

"I sold the BMX I used for the stunts a long time ago. I had another good bike—not for stunts, but just for regular riding—but someone stole it. Rather than buy a new one and store it all winter, I decided to wait until spring, and I'm glad I did. A bike wouldn't have fit into my car. It was easier to buy a new one and have it shipped."

"If this is the kind of bicycle you are used to, I can see why you did not buy one from Frank's store. He would never have anything like this. I have never seen a bicycle with gears."

"After everyone in the factory took our bikes for a little test run, I have a feeling that Frank's going to be placing an order for some."

Even though the bicycles they rode were probably fairly expensive, she thought he was right. Not only were these bicycles more comfortable to ride, they were also faster, with less effort. Although most people wouldn't be riding their bicycles like Chad and doing tricks and spins and flips or even riding on one tire. And, because he was not riding smoothly, she doubted he would buy eggs today—they would never stay in his basket. However, she intended to buy eggs. She had a craving for deviled eggs, even without Chad's secret ingredient.

"This is fun. Let us go faster."

"You're on. Gear down, and let's go."

Taking advantage of the gears on the bicycles, she'd never gone so fast for so far. Even though they'd left home to allow the same time as usual, they had passed many people on the way to Henry's farm and arrived very early.

"Since we are here before everyone, let me show you Henry's chickens." She took the basket of *Roll Kuchen* she'd brought and set it on the table beside the back door. Then instead of walking, she got back on her bicycle and led Chad across the field to the barn.

Once inside, Chad's eyes widened like a child looking at a Christmas tree for the first time.

"There are many chickens, are there not?"

He sucked in a deep breath, then coughed. "Yeah. I couldn't have imagined this. There's got to be over a thousand chickens. I guess they can't hose out a barn like a backyard coop. It stinks in here." Anna clenched her lower lip with her teeth to keep herself from snickering. The smell of Henry's chicken barn was nothing compared to a cow barn. Even worse was George Rempel's pig barn.

Chad began to squat down to touch one of the many chickens strutting around them, but as he reached out, the chickens scattered. Remaining hunkered down, he rested his elbows on his knees. "They don't seem very tame."

"*Oba nü*. This is a farm. Get up. Let us go. Everyone should be here by now."

They hopped back on the bikes and rode back to the yard where people were gathering. They laid the bikes on the grass with the rest and set their helmets down resting on their bicycles. As they walked to join the crowd, Anna pulled her prayer cap out of her purse and put it on, hoping she had it straight and none of her hair was sticking out.

Chad leaned down to speak softly in her ear. "Which one is the new chicken plucker?"

Anna turned to him. "Which one? I do not understand your question. The chicken plucker is over there. See it? It is red."

"The barrel? What kind of chicken plucker is that?"

Anna crossed her arms. "It is Henry's new design. He has made some improvements over his last one, and he says this one is much better."

"Oh."

She watched him look at Hannah and then back to the chicken plucker. "Please tell me that you did not think we were talking about a person."

"Well, yeah, I did."

"It would take much too long for a person to pluck a chicken. They must pluck hundreds in a day."

He shrugged his shoulders. "I never thought about it like that. I really was expecting a person. An older lady, actually. Kind of like her."

"That is Hannah. Henry's wife."

Henry joined the crowd and motioned them all closer to the chicken plucker. "I would like everyone to look inside, to see how I have changed the spikes to different heights."

Anna nudged Chad's arm. "Come, you must look. Later, when everyone is talking about how it works, you need to know what they are talking about. I have seen this before, in his previous design."

She led him to the barrel and watched as he leaned forward to look inside, as instructed.

His face tightened and he stepped back. "I don't understand."

"You will when you see it in motion."

"Motion?"

Hank from the furniture factory appeared beside Chad. He nudged Chad forward, closer to the barrel of the chicken plucker. "We have all seen this before, you are the only one who has not. So I think you should have the closest view."

All around them nodded and stepped aside for Chad to move forward. Soon, everyone pushed closer to make room for Hannah as she approached with a headless chicken, holding it by the legs, upside down.

With everyone pressed together so more people could see, Anna felt herself get even more squished up beside Chad. When Hannah held the chicken over the barrel, she felt Chad stiffen. Henry started turning a handle, and the barrel started spinning; Hannah turned on the hose, began to spray water into the plucker, and dropped the chicken inside.

"No . . ." Chad murmured.

Instead of watching the machine work, Anna looked up to watch Chad. His entire body went ramrod stiff, and his breathing became shallow. He watched for a few rotations as the chicken banged around inside, bumping against all the spikes. Chad's eyes suddenly squeezed shut. His face paled, and with every thump of the chicken banging around inside the plucker, his face continued to lose color.

Pressed up against him, she felt him sway.

She'd never seen a man faint and didn't want this to be the first time.

She grabbed his hand, pulled, and stepped back through the crowd. "Chad, step back. Come with me."

He gave no resistance as she pulled him away. He opened his eyes, blinked, and looked at her, his eyes completely lacking focus.

"Thirty-two seconds!" Henry called out. "A new record!"

At Henry's voice, Chad looked up to see Henry holding up the limp, headless, featherless chicken, dangling it by one naked wing.

Chad's face turned almost white. His body lurched. He gagged and raised one hand to cover his mouth, then swayed.

"Quickly, sit down. Lean on me."

She wrapped her arms around him, but she couldn't support his weight. She barely kept him from falling as he sank to the ground in under a second, taking nearly all her strength to control his fall to guide him to a sitting position. Fortunately, he landed with his knees raised. He thunked his forehead to his knees, then lifted his arms to cover the back of his head. "I don't feel very good," he groaned into his knees. "I think I'm going to throw up."

Anna dropped to her knees and reached toward him, but froze before she touched him. She didn't know what to do, so she gently ran her fingers up and down his forearm. "Breathe deeply," she murmured. "Count with me. One . . . two . . . three . . ."

22

$\mathcal{A}$s Chad concentrated on his breathing, the tsunami in his stomach began to ebb to a rolling tidal wave and the ringing in his ears was reduced to a dull roar. Slowly, the white light behind his eyes morphed to a dancing kaleidoscope, the tunnel widened and then faded to the normal black of just having his eyes closed.

Slowly, the noise echoing through his head calmed to just the voices and movement of the crowd around him, and he became aware of the comforting motion of a hand on his arm, gently stroking back and forth.

He wondered how long, realistically, it would take before the ground would swallow him up.

"He is breathing better now," Anna's voice came from beside him. "I will stay with him. Go eat, we will come later." Her hand moved. Then instead of on his arm, he felt Anna rubbing soothing circles on his back.

He couldn't believe it. He'd nearly fainted like a woman, except he'd never seen or actually heard of a woman fainting in the last century. He'd also come within a hair's breadth of losing his lunch. It would not have been a pretty sight.

In the distance, the voices became silent. Henry's voice rang out loud and clear, praying first for him and a quick recovery and then asking for a blessing for their meal. Chatter resumed, accompanied by the clicking of spoons and dishes.

"Chad? Are you going to be alright? I am so sorry. I had no idea. I have now realized that you have never seen such a thing before."

All he could think of was Waddles and Blinkie. They had the same color of feathers as the dead chicken dumped into the spike-laced barrel, while it still had feathers.

His stomach churned again.

He told himself that Waddles and Blinkie were fine. They were locked up, safe and sound, in their coop in the backyard.

They were going to get an extra share of chicken chow when he got home, plus a slice of apple, which was their favorite snack. And tonight, he wasn't going to make them run around the living room and do their little dance before he picked them up to do his reading. Tonight, they were going to get some extra lap time before he put them outside and then sneaked them back into the house after Anna's bedroom light went out.

"I'll never eat chicken again," he muttered, only half joking. "Is anyone still watching?"

"No. Everyone is getting food. Some of the mamas look at you every once in a while, but they are leaving you alone until you are ready to get up."

"I can't believe this is happening," he mumbled, still not raising his head from his knees. Even though he'd have to get up at some point, for now it was easier to deal with looking like a wuss if he couldn't see anyone watching him and feeling sorry for him. "I'm first-aid certified. I've attended to injuries. Real injuries. Broken arms and broken legs and blood. Even a skull injury, when I worked at the half-pipe."

"I know you are not good with tools, but I do not understand how working with half of a pipe could be dangerous."

"No." He shook his head without raising his forehead off his knees. "That's what they call the track, the structure where you do freestyle BMX biking, with the flips and the jumps. They call it that because of the shape. It's curved, like half a pipe, cut lengthwise, but on a gargantuan level. You go down one side of the curve to gain momentum and then you launch up the other side, flip yourself on the bike when you clear the edge, somersault with it, spin it, or whatever you're going to do, then come down, gliding down the curve instead of landing flat, so you don't fall. Extreme sports can be dangerous, and accidents happen often. I've attended to a couple of bad injuries—I used to supervise my local half-pipe as a summer job. I was the only one certified with first-aid training until the ambulance got there when someone hurt themselves. I've seen some really awful stuff, but nothing like this has ever happened to me before."

"Then you are a hero with people who need you, but not so much with animals. It is different."

Probably because the animal was already dead.

His stomach lurched again. He bit his lower lip so he wouldn't groan out loud. If there were ever a time he wished he had his car, this was it.

"Are you feeling better now? Can you stand?"

Even though he didn't get up, he raised his head to look at Anna, blinking until his eyes adjusted once again to the bright daylight. "This is pretty embarrassing."

"Do not worry so much. Everyone is only happy you are not hurt. I will understand if you do not wish to eat, but it is probably a good thing for you to have something to drink."

Taking her at her word, Chad cautiously pushed himself to his feet and sucked in a deep breath to clear his head. He didn't feel as unsteady as he thought he would, so he slowly made his way to the crowd, ready to take his lumps.

Brian was the first to approach him. Strangely, he hadn't seen Brian arrive, but then there were a lot of people here, and he'd quickly been escorted to the front of the crowd to be closest to the event of the day.

Brian rested one hand on his shoulder and guided him away from the crowd, and most important, away from the food table. "Well, City Boy, I have just heard this is your first time to be on a farm. This may not have been the best introduction to what happens to chickens before they become our supper."

"That's okay. I've heard that sometimes life's best lessons are learned the hard way."

Brian pulled him farther away from the crowd, many of whom kept glancing over at him. "You were asking me about ways to catch the attention of the ladies. I think you have found a good way, but you should not do this again."

Chad lowered his head. He'd never been so embarrassed in his whole life, and he'd done a lot of dumb things. "I don't plan to," he muttered. "Believe me, I didn't do this on purpose."

Brian jerked his head toward a circle of ladies. "They are all waiting for you to be alone, so they may ask how you are."

"But it's not any one of them I wanted to be interested. It's Anna."

Anna, who'd steadied him as he sank to the ground like a wet noodle in a rainstorm.

Chad squeezed his eyes shut. Could this get any worse?

Brian poked him in the ribs. "Stand straight. Here comes Rebecca." Brian's voice lowered. "And she is bringing Anna with her."

Rebecca gave Brian a quick smile of greeting as the ladies joined them, and then she approached Chad, rested one hand on his forearm, and looked up at him, directly into his eyes.

Chad forced himself to smile. He wondered if this was the Mennonite equivalent of a woman batting her eyelashes.

Rebecca smiled. "I saw you the other day riding past my house on your bicycle. I wanted to ask if your chickens were okay."

He paused, trying to think of why she might think there had been anything wrong with them. "They're fine. Why do you ask?"

Rebecca's head tilted. "Because you had your chickens in the basket on your bicycle. It looked like you were taking them to Zebediah's house and you were lost."

His brows knotted. "Whose house?"

"Zebediah's. The veterinarian. I thought there was something wrong with your chickens. It looked like you were going to his house. But Anna told me that you were probably only going to get their wings clipped."

He opened his mouth but snapped it shut before he spoke too fast, without thinking out his words first. He'd taken Waddles and Blinkie for a ride because he thought it would be fun for them, since they couldn't fly. He'd thought they would enjoy the motion of the bike. As it turned out, Blinkie enjoyed riding on the handlebars, but Waddles preferred to stay in the basket. The purpose of the trip had been to ask Brian a question, since Brian wasn't answering his phone. Then Brian had ended up going back to the house with him to help with the remote control door opener he'd installed on the chicken coop.

"Uh . . . no . . . I . . . Wings clipped? You mean like a parrot? I heard that you're supposed to clip a parrot's wings. I didn't know you were supposed to clip a chicken's wings."

Rebecca moved closer. "I can show you how to do it. Then you will not have to pay for a veterinarian's bill."

Anna sighed and glared at her friend. "I can show him. The chickens are right next door to me."

Rebecca turned to Anna. "But I have asked him, and you did not."

Anna turned directly to face Rebecca. "I gave him the chickens, so I am the one who should help him raise them."

Rebecca's eyes narrowed. "I am the one who saw him riding down the street with the chickens. If I had not called you, you would never have known."

If he wasn't mistaken, Rebecca had just called first dibs. Except he wasn't a prize to be claimed. Chad raised one finger in the air. "But I . . ."

Rebecca stepped closer to Anna. "You think you are so good because you have a job and are using a computer, but that does not mean you are better at everything."

Anna's mouth dropped open. "Waut sajst dü?"

Rebecca's face turned beet red. She clenched her jaw, turned, and ran off, joining the group of ladies by the coffee urn.

Anna planted her fists on her hips, blew out a breath of air, and then looked over her shoulder at Chad. Her eyes narrowed. "*Dit est dientschult*. This is your fault. See what you have done?" she snapped, then stomped to the group of ladies, following Rebecca.

Brian's eyes widened and his mouth dropped open. "What has just happened?"

"My friend, you just witnessed a catfight." Somehow, he'd found himself right in the middle, as the cause of it. He sighed. "And now I've got to go fix it."

First, he approached Rebecca, because he figured she'd be the easiest. Or rather, if he had to be honest with himself, because he didn't have as much to lose if he didn't handle it right.

As soon as he appeared beside Rebecca, the rest of the group excused themselves without words and filtered away.

"I'm sorry, Rebecca," he said softly. "I actually hadn't been on my way to the vet, but I do appreciate your offer. I have no plans to clip their wings. I did a little research on Rhode Island Reds and found out that they're a heavier chicken and don't really fly. I'm not worried about losing them, so I want to leave them in their natural state."

She looked up at him. "Then why did you have them with you? Where were you going with them?"

"I went to Brian's garage and back, that's all. I just thought I would take them with me." He knew that dogs liked the wind in their faces and stuck their heads out the window when riding in a car, so he thought a chicken, because it was a bird, would enjoy the feel of the movement from the bicycle, since they didn't really fly. He hadn't been worried about them hopping off the bike. After all, he wasn't going very fast, and most important, it wasn't like there were any cars on the road that would hit them if they decided to jump.

"I understand. But if you need any help with your chickens, you can ask me. I have had many chickens, and I would enjoy helping you with them."

He smiled. "I know you would, but I'm doing just fine. They're really easy to look after. Thank you for your offer. Now I've got to go talk to Anna."

Rebecca nodded, then lowered her gaze to stare at the ground. He wasn't sure if it was good or bad, but she seemed calm, so he chose to take it as good.

He left before that changed, going in search of Anna.

As he passed all the small groups of people talking, many people—some whom he knew, some not—asked if he was feeling better without being specific, for which he was grateful. It was going to be a long time before he lived this one down. He chatted for a short time with every group. After all, he really hadn't come to see the chicken plucker; he'd come to meet more people in a setting other than work- or church-related activities. When he passed by the last circle of people gathered, he turned around and checked to make sure he hadn't missed one. In the groups he'd stopped to chat with, he hadn't found Anna.

He didn't think she would be so angry she would leave without him, but just in case, he continued behind the house to check the bikes, to make sure her bike was still there. As he rounded the corner, a spot of pink sticking out from behind a large tree caught his eye.

He smiled. Anna had worn a pretty pink blouse today. Considering the plain and shapeless clothes the women here wore, by comparison he'd found it pretty and feminine, and he really liked it on her.

As he looked at her from the back, knowing she didn't see him, he contemplated the whole picture that was Anna. As a statement to her beliefs and her upbringing, just like the rest of the ladies present, she wore her stark white prayer cap, emphasizing her pure, sweet nature, and her firm conviction to her beliefs, yet showing she still functioned with the rest of the world. She was moving forward with the times, at least as much as one could do in Piney Meadows; she wore a store-bought pink blouse. While it was somewhat plain and not particularly eye-catching for anyone anywhere else, it was pretty in its modesty and was actually quite vivid compared to the usual bland and neutral colors the majority of the women wore.

And, unlike the older ladies, who wore loose, modest, mid-calf or ankle-length skirts for comfort on their bikes, Anna wore jeans, which truly heightened the difference between Anna and the rest of the women. They allowed her the freedom and dexterity to keep up with him on the bicycle today. And she had kept up, at least for speed. She hadn't done any tricks or fancy balancing on her bike, but he could see that the acceleration and speed she'd achieved had given her quite a thrill as they passed everyone else, doing at least triple their speed. He'd nearly hooted with excitement as Anna—smiling ear to ear, not bound by conformity or tradition, complete with her pink blouse and jeans—shot past all the other ladies on her purple bike with a matching helmet.

But for now, for this moment, none of that rebel spirit showed. Instead, judging from her posture and location, she looked like she wanted to be left alone.

He knew he would be intruding, but being in a place near enough to a crowd to be acceptable, yet far enough away to be private was exactly what he needed. Since she would never go into his house without another adult present, he never really had a chance to talk to her in private unless he wanted to compete for space with the local bears.

Fortunately, walking in the grass, his steps were silent as he approached her. Judging from the way she flinched when he stepped in front of her, she hadn't expected him to come looking.

She quickly lowered her head and stared at the ground.

He didn't know why she had sneaked away from the crowd, but at least she didn't seem angry. He didn't really know what to do, but he could deal with anything other than anger.

Chad stepped closer, reached forward, and brushed his fingers against her cheek. "I've been looking for you," he muttered softly. "I want you to know that any time I need help with Waddles and Blinkie, I'll always go to you first."

She didn't look up but kept staring at the ground. "It is okay."

Chad sucked in a deep breath. He didn't really understand women, and he understood the women here even less, but he couldn't leave this the way it was. Whatever was wrong, he needed to fix it, and he needed to fix it now.

"I don't want you to have an argument with your friend because of me."

She didn't raise her head, but she looked up, causing her eyes to go big and round. If it wasn't his imagination, they were bloodshot.

His stomach clenched. She'd been crying.

Maybe he was wrong. He could deal with anything except that.

But he couldn't leave her like this. He rubbed the pad of his thumb against her cheek and told himself to be strong. "What's wrong?"

"This is so strange. I do not know why I am angry with Rebecca, and now she is angry with me. She has done nothing. She has only offered to help you, and that is something good. I do not know why this makes me feel angry."

Chad's heart quickened. He didn't know much about women, but he did know a little about jealousy. For a brief moment, he'd thought Brian might be interested in Anna, and just the thought of the possibility had made him consider leaving Brian with a few bruises. It wasn't a very good Christian attitude, but it was how he felt.

If there was sudden tension between Anna and her friend, he didn't want to be the cause of it. But at the same time, it meant Anna felt something for him and she didn't want to share, or Rebecca's intrusion wouldn't cause her emotions to rise to the surface so fast.

A million thoughts zinged through his head, but none of them connected to any course of action. His heart beat faster at the concept that thinking of him pulled at her emotions— emotions she hadn't felt before—and knowing it made him want to yell and pound his chest like a gorilla.

Instead, Chad shuffled closer and raised his other hand, to cup her face in his palms and look into her eyes—eyes wide and full of wonder, and something else . . . was it anticipation or fear? Or maybe it was a bit of both. Those two emotions were certainly swirling and warring in his own brain right now.

He really didn't have the right to kiss her. He didn't even have the right to touch her.

Looking into her face, he tried to focus on just her eyes but couldn't. His gaze took in the whole picture, including the prayer cap.

He couldn't kiss her. Everything in her was purity, innocence . . . and inexperience. Falling in love with her was like tumbling off a cliff, following a sequence that, once started, had no turning back. He knew what he wanted, and he knew what he was getting.

But if Anna was starting to have feelings for him—and he hoped and prayed she was—she didn't know what she was getting. He hadn't been deliberately dishonest, but he hadn't told her the truth, either.

It wouldn't have bothered him a year ago, but after reading God's word like he had been, and trying to learn what God was telling him, many things had begun to stick with him that he hadn't thought about before. It wasn't exactly like God was speaking aloud from the sky, but Chad was sure getting the message.

To withhold the truth was as bad as lying.

His chest constricted at the thought. He didn't know how she would react when he told her, but they'd come to a point where he could no longer withhold his issues. The sum of his past—both good and bad—made him what he was today. And today, he was in love with Anna, and he couldn't go further in their relationship until she knew what she was getting.

To make things even more complicated, she was also his employee. It didn't matter that she'd been working there for years before him. He was still her boss.

He couldn't kiss her like he wanted, but he couldn't release her, either. Slowly, so he wouldn't frighten her, in order to maintain some scrap of control, he guided her head so her cheek pressed into his shoulder. One hand slid down to the center of her back, and he splayed the fingers of his other hand so he cupped the back of her head in his palm, feeling the smooth fabric of her prayer cap.

Chad squeezed his eyes shut. Her prayer cap. Here he was, wanting so badly to kiss her—not just a quick or friendly peck on her cheek, but the hot and passionate kiss of a lover.

He wondered if such thoughts would have him rot in hell for the rest of his days. But if he had to justify himself, he wanted more than to just be her lover. He wanted to be her husband.

He loved her, and he had it bad.

But in order to go forward he had to go back and make it right, and the first step in making anything right was to tell the truth.

His throat felt gravelly, so he cleared his throat to speak softly with his head beside her ear. "We have to talk, there's something about me you don't know, and I need to tell you. Just not here, okay?"

At his words, her body stiffened. He felt too tempted, wanting to kiss her to make it all go away. Since it would only make everything worse, he released her and backed up a step.

Anna looked up at him, her eyes full of unspoken questions. "From the look on your face, this is important, is it not?"

He swallowed hard. "Not important for this exact second, but for the big picture, yes, it's important."

Anna turned to stare at the bikes, then turned to the side of the house, where the crowd was around the corner. Anywhere but at him. "We should leave, then. Where would you like to say this important thing to me?"

He sighed. He would have preferred the privacy of his living room, but that wasn't going to happen. Still, he felt too raw to expose his soul in a semi-public place. "How about if we go into my backyard and we can sit on the back porch?" Open enough that her parents could see her through their kitchen window, but private enough so no one would hear their conversation. "I can also barbecue a couple of hamburgers for supper. Would that work for you?"

Her eyes lost focus, and he knew she was contemplating the process of going into his house, unescorted, in order to get to the backyard. If he had to, he'd take her around the side of the house, get her seated at the patio table where she could be in full view of her parents if they were in their kitchen, and he could run inside for a few minutes and find what they needed for supper.

"Ja," she said softly, almost hesitantly. "That is fine. Let us tell everyone we are leaving, and we will go."

They said their goodbyes quickly, and as they prepared to leave, he noticed a lot of not very subtle sympathetic glances. But if everyone thought his still feeling queasy was their reason for leaving, it was fine with him—and was a good enough excuse.

Unlike the trip to the farm, on the way home Chad felt none of the anticipation or rush to get to his destination. While being able to release the burdens that had been weighing him down for the last seven months would be a relief, at the same time, it terrified him to tell her.

Everything here was black-and-white; there was no gray and no middle ground. These good Mennonite people tried their best to live their lives the way they thought God meant them to. It was right, or it was wrong.

Outside this community, the way he'd lived was fine and normal, according to the ways of the world. But here, such a lifestyle was very wrong.

Before he moved here, even though he used to go to church most Sundays, he hadn't thought he was doing anything wrong. He'd wanted to get married, and if he was living in a married lifestyle without the license and government stamp, it didn't matter. Lots of people did it, and they were happy.

But here, living together without the legalities of a marriage certificate and the pastor's blessing was not in the "white" column.

The world could come up with a million reasons why modern people in today's society didn't really need marriage to live together happily ever after. Yet, if he and Brittany hadn't lived together like they were married, if they'd waited until they both knew what they wanted and made sure they wanted the same thing from each other, neither of them would be in the positions they were in now.

Wherever Brittany was, whatever she was doing, she was going through a lot of effort so he couldn't find her. She was going to be a single mother and it wouldn't be an easy life. Conversely, he was going through a lot to find her and make everything as right as he could. Except, it would never be right.

Maybe, just maybe, God had the right idea all along.

When they arrived at his home, before he had a chance to suggest she simply go around the house and wait for him in the backyard, she went straight inside, directly to the kitchen, right for the fridge, and removed everything they would need for barbecuing hamburgers. He gathered up the plates and utensils, and they made a beeline for the back door and the patio table. Anna immediately set to work arranging everything in the most expedient and efficient manner, just like the way she handled everything at the office. Before he knew it, all he had to do was light the flame to start cooking.

Chad's gut clenched as he pushed the button.

This was it. As the saying went, the rubber had just hit the road and he would either go down the highway or crash and burn.

Anna appeared beside him as he stood staring blankly at the flame licking the grill.

"While you are waiting for it to be right to start cooking, you can tell me what you need to say."

Chad swallowed hard, and looked at the two uncooked burger patties she'd set on the plate. He hoped and prayed that after he opened his heart and bared his soul, he'd still be cooking for two.

23

$\mathcal{A}$nna watched Chad staring at the two burgers on the plate.

She doubted he was really thinking hard about cooking something he'd obviously cooked many times before. Instead, she suspected he was trying to gather his thoughts, and his thoughts didn't seem like they were easy to catch.

For a long time she'd suspected something important to him had caused him deep hurts.

Part of her wanted to be able to help him, whatever it was, even if all she could do was listen. But another part of her feared his words. If he hadn't shared it after all this time, she didn't know what had changed, and why he felt an urgent need to say this now.

Just watching his inner pain, her soul ached for him. Whatever had hurt him, she wanted to make it better. She'd been praying for him for a long time—private prayers she hadn't shared with the ladies' group or her Sunday morning prayer group. At the same time as she'd prayed for him, she'd also prayed for direction over her own feelings for him, because she'd never felt the same way about another man as she did about Chad.

Now, added to the confusion was the fear that whatever he struggled with would change their relationship. Not that they had a relationship, really. However, even though he was her boss, there was something between them she couldn't define. They weren't friends, not like her friendship with William, but when she and Chad weren't together, unlike William, she thought about Chad far too much. Chad sighed deeply, and laid the burgers on the grill. "For so long I've tried to think of the best way to start this conversation, but any way to start this gently would be candy-coating it. I'm just going to be blunt and skip the rhetoric." He tapped the burgers with the flipper, sighed again, and continued to stare at the burgers. "While it's true that Brittany was my girlfriend, the relationship was more serious than that. We were engaged, and we were living together."

He paused, and she suspected he was giving her time to let his words sink in, so she contemplated the meaning of what he'd said.

Anna had heard of this, that in the cities, very often a couple lived together as man and wife before the wedding. But she'd also learned that often a man and woman never got married and continued to live together as if they were married, in all ways, except for the blessing of being under God's plan.

Suddenly, Anna couldn't face Chad as the meaning of his words sank in. Instead, she turned to the chicken coop, to Chad's chickens, who were making quite a ruckus at not being let out of the coop while Chad was in the backyard.

To give herself something to do, she walked to the chicken coop and reached to flip the latch to the gate and froze. It was a strange and complicated latch, something she had never seen before.

She didn't know how to open the door to the chicken coop, to let his chickens out.

Chad appeared beside her and pointed to a button. "Press here to open it."

She didn't know why he didn't have a simple hook-style latch like everyone else, but her mind was swimming too much with the thought of Chad living with a woman without being married to her.

And all that entailed.

Chad pushed the button, the door opened, and his two chickens ran out, strutting in circles around his feet and clucking their greeting. He squatted down and ran his fingers through their feathers, then stood. "Excuse me, but since I'm cooking, I'd better go wash my hands." He turned and strode into the house, and the chickens hurried to keep up with him, following him, and the door closed behind them.

Anna walked to the patio table and sank into one of the chairs. Of all the things he could have said, this was not something she could have expected.

Before she could think too much about the relationship he must have had with Brittany, Chad returned to the barbecue. As he flipped the burgers, the chickens walked past him to hunt for bugs and explore the yard.

"That's not the whole story." His voice lowered. "She kept postponing the wedding plans, and it didn't feel right. I was starting to reevaluate our relationship and what kind of future we'd have, and then I found out she was pregnant."

Anna's breath caught, and her stomach did a flip. When her friend Theresa found out she was pregnant, Theresa and Evan felt shamed. They hadn't told either of their parents or anyone in the church but instead had run away to the cities, where they got an apartment and got married. Evan found a job, and they were still there, struggling but happy together with their daughter.

She looked up at Chad. This time, instead of staring intently at his cooking burgers, he was staring back at her.

Anna cleared her throat. "What are you doing here? That would have been before Christmas. It is now summer. Why have you not married her?"

He sighed, turned his back to her, and began poking at the hamburgers on the grill. "She didn't exactly tell me she was pregnant. I found the kit, with a positive result, in the wastebasket in the bathroom. I told her I wanted to get married right away, a few days went by, and then when I got home from work that Friday, Brittany, everything she owned, and most of what I owned was gone. I haven't been able to find her. That fellow who phones me from Minneapolis once a month is a private detective. When I couldn't find her, I hired him. He hasn't been able to find her either, but he's still trying."

Anna's throat tightened.

Chad had lived as a married man, and he was a father.

"Does that mean you do not know where Brittany or the baby are?"

He shook his head, while still poking at the burgers. "That's right. Also, there actually isn't a baby yet, if I'm counting on my fingers properly, which I know I am, because I'm a business major. The baby is probably due sometime in August, and this is only June." He turned around, looked at her, raised one hand, and dragged his palm over his face. "I know I should have told you sooner, but there never seemed to be a good time."

Anna shook her head. "I still do not understand. Are you saying that instead of marrying you and giving the baby a father, she has run away? Why would a woman do this?"

Chad turned the grill off without removing the burgers to the plate. "I have no idea. Even though the relationship wasn't what it should have been, I still would have married her. Even if she won't marry me, I still want to do the right thing with support, and I want to get to know my son or daughter as a father and not as a deadbeat dad." He shook his head, then turned away. "But I can't. She didn't just move out. She went into hiding. I don't know why. I didn't do anything bad, I didn't hurt her or neglect her. I know I worked a lot, but I never ignored her. For some reason, we just seemed to drift apart. If it weren't for the baby on the way, we probably would have split up and moved on."

If it weren't for the baby on the way . . .

The words echoed in Anna's head.

But there was a baby on the way. He'd had that kind of relationship with Brittany. Without being married to her.

He sighed again. "We should probably eat, but I'm not really hungry anymore. I can get your burger ready, though. I kept them on the grill to keep them warm."

Anna pressed her hand to her stomach, which was at war with the rest of her body. "I am no longer hungry, either. I will put everything back in the fridge so nothing will spoil."

They both stood at the same time, but instead of turning to the table with the buns and condiments, Chad turned to her. "I'm so sorry. I don't know what to say. Everything is so mixed up right now. This isn't the way it's supposed to be."

Just looking at him tore her soul open. Short of the death of a loved one, she'd never seen such sorrow in a person's face. While part of her reeled at the magnitude of his transgression, she couldn't judge him. God didn't grade sins on a scale of one to ten. She was no different in God's sight.

"Have you prayed about this?"

"More than you could ever know."

"Then God will have an answer for you. It may not be the answer you want, but you will have one."

"You know, I honestly believe that. It's probably the only thing that's held me up in all this, as it gets closer to August."

She couldn't help herself; the sadness in his eyes was her undoing. She stepped toward him so that they were toe to toe and reached forward to grasp his hands. "You know I will pray for you," she whispered.

Before she knew what had happened, he pulled his hands out of hers, his arms were around her, and he pulled her in for a tight embrace. His arms pressed into her back, holding her close against his chest, and his cheek pressed against her temple. Yet, even though his grip was firm, she felt him tremble.

Knowing the relationship he'd had with Brittany and that he had created a child with her, she should have been repelled and pushed him away. Yet so many thoughts ran through her that she didn't know what to say or think. Regardless of what she thought or how she felt, she was in no position to judge him. She was not to compare sins as to which was the worst but only knew she was also a sinner, and she also fell short of God's glory. All she could do was love him as a brother and help him deal with his repentance, because she could certainly see his pain.

Despite what he had done, seeing his pain and knowing that he was honestly trying to meet his obligations and pay for his transgressions helped her deal with the shock.

"Have you told this to anyone else?" Even asking the question, she had a feeling she already knew his answer.

His arms shook, and he held her tighter. "No."

"Not even Pastor Jake?"

"No."

"Why not?" She wanted to look up at him, into his eyes at his reply, but he didn't loosen his grip.

"Because I wanted you to be the first person I told. I'm really afraid of what everyone is going to think. As far as transgressions, this is a dandy. It's also not something that's going to go away. When I find Brittany—and I will find her—I want joint custody. I'm going to have to ask people for help, because I really don't know what to do. But as they say, 'it takes two,' so I want to do my half."

Something inside Anna told her that Chad would make a good father—and a good husband, despite his, as he called it, transgression.

"You know you must tell Pastor Jake, and you also must say this in your testimony when you become a member here. You are planning on becoming a member at our church, are you not?"

He stiffened. "I can do that? But I'm not a Mennonite." He paused, his hands slid to her shoulders, and he gently pushed her away just far enough to look into her face but not release her. He grinned. "I really like those hats the men wear. Do you think I'd look good in one of those?"

At his joke about the men's hats, the tension started to drain from her body. "I do not know about you wearing a hat, but you can certainly become a member of Piney Meadows Full Gospel Mennonite Church. Have you been baptized?"

He nodded. "Yes, I have. Which is probably a good thing. It wasn't a Mennonite church, but I don't think that makes a difference. In the city, my church had what could best be described as an oversized portable hot tub that we filled up for baptism Sundays. Here, I'm thinking that you only baptize people in the summer, and you do it in the river."

Anna gasped. "Do you mean you baptize people in a bathtub?" She couldn't imagine such a thing.

"No, it's not a bathtub. Most city churches use a portable tub big enough for people to stand in for baptisms. Instead of a cold stream, it's filled with nice warm water." His grin widened, then faded. "I'm guessing I'd join by testimony, and my testimony would have to include some personal history, which includes that I'm about to become a single father, whether I know where the mother and baby are, or not."

She nodded. "That is correct. But also, it will be good to have people pray for you, and they cannot pray for you over something they do not know. This is a good way for them to know, so they see it told from your heart, not from listening to people talking." She didn't want to say gossip, but unfortunately, sometimes a few of their members took advantage of the prayer request circles to find out interesting personal information which otherwise would not have been their business.

He sighed. "This has been weighing on me for a long time. Ever since I got here, really. It's actually been a relief to talk to you about it, although I don't think I'm going to get such an understanding reaction from the whole congregation."

Even though Anna wanted to refute him, in this case, she couldn't. With Chad being the manager at the factory, everyone considered it a huge blessing to have him take over for Ted. Between his experience and ability, he'd made many improvements and significantly increased their client base. At church, the same opinion wasn't as prevalent. Most, but not all, of the people at church had accepted him with open arms as a regular attender. However, he hadn't yet asked to be a member. While Chad was a Christian brother, he was not born and raised a Mennonite, and despite his best efforts, especially after the incident earlier at the chicken farm, he didn't really fit into their community.

So far, everyone here and everyone in their church had been born here and had always been a part of Piney Meadows. Even though Miranda had not been, her birth and upbringing were still Mennonite. Chad was the first non-resident, non-Mennonite to become an active participant in their church.

Anna forced herself to smile. "After you speak to Pastor Jake about this, I am sure everything will be fine."

24

$\mathcal{I}$f it was acceptable to put on a poker face in a church, Chad hoped he'd been able to do exactly that.

When he was called to the front to give his testimony he received a warm response from the congregation as he began to speak. When he got to the part about where his church attendance started to drop off, a few of the people stiffened and a few nodded. But when he got to the part in his life about living with a woman without the marriage certificate, pretty much all the warm smiles disappeared.

As soon as he told them about being an expectant father, a number of people gasped and two women stood and started to walk out.

Elderly Mr. Rempel jumped to his feet. Or rather, he cleared his throat loudly as he shakily pushed himself up using the back of the pew in front of him for support. The person beside him raised one hand to offer support as Mr. Rempel turned toward the back and pointed to the exiting people with his cane, nearly hitting Emma Klassen in the head.

"*Mensche! Daut es nüach!* People! That is enough!" Mr. Rempel hollered through the church. The echo of his voice hung in the air as the people leaving stopped dead in their tracks. "Let he who is without sin cast the first stone! Do you not think it has taken great courage for him to say these things in front of us? He has made his peace with God. He does not need to make peace with us. It is up to us to accept him and pray with him and rejoice with him that he has joined with us as another of God's children."

Mr. Rempel turned around, handed his cane to his son George, and pointed a bony finger at Chad, standing stock-still at the front of the church, hanging onto the podium so tightly his fingers hurt and his knuckles had turned white. "Have you made your peace with God and given your heart to our Lord and Savior Jesus Christ, City Boy?"

Chad forced himself to breathe. Again the silence hung in the building while everyone stared at him. He squeezed his eyes shut and inhaled deeply.

He'd never had a worse sleepless night, including the night Brittany left him, and he hadn't ever been such a wreck in front of an audience, including at a business conference when he'd taken an opposing view against the keynote speaker in a debate in front of fourteen hundred people. He'd probably spent most of the night making peace with God. Again.

Over the last few years he'd had many arguments with God. Before arriving in Piney Meadows, he probably hadn't prayed at all for close to a year. Except for the new job, everything in his life felt like it had gone swirling down the toilet, and he'd been sure God had been taunting him. But slowly, he'd come to admit it wasn't God who had shut him out—it was he who had shut God out. He'd done so much he knew was wrong in God's eyes, but he'd not given anything any importance or significance. After all, it wasn't like he'd committed murder or stolen anything. He'd accepted Jesus Christ as his Lord and Savior years ago and that hadn't changed. But by being with these good people, by listening to their teaching and watching them in their daily lives, he'd opened his heart, and he had made peace with God, whether or not things turned out the way he wanted.

He opened his eyes, looking straight at Mr. Rempel. "Yes," he said, his voice barely above a whisper, yet he was sure that with the silence hanging in the church, he wasn't the only one holding his breath.

"*Gott es aula daut dü bruckst.* That is all that you need," Mr. Rempel called out, then sat.

While a few people continued to sit stone-faced with no change, most of them softened. Many smiled at him and nodded, which he took as signs of encouragement, and a few ladies started to sniffle. One of the ladies who had started to walk out started bawling.

Chad cleared his throat. "I don't know what else I can say. I've got a private detective trying to find Brittany, and when he finds her, I'm going to request joint custody. It's not the best arrangement, but it's the best I can do. I'd really appreciate everyone's prayers."

A few more ladies started sniffling.

Pastor Jake stood and left the pew while his wife, Kathleen, remained seated and blew her nose quite loudly.

Once beside him, Pastor Jake put one arm around Chad's shoulders and faced the congregation. "Let us now accept Chad Jones into our membership here at Piney Meadows Full Gospel Mennonite Church. Please join me in prayer over him."

Chad closed his eyes. As he listened to the pastor's prayers and murmurs of agreement from the congregation, he felt his throat tighten, and his eyes started to burn.

Since hopefully everyone there had their eyes closed, he quickly swiped at his eyes with his sleeve, preparing himself for the group's "amen."

"Welcome, Chad Jones! Now let us all turn to hymn number 447, and let us sing 'Who Is on the Lord's Side.'"

Pastor opened his hymnal to the page already bookmarked, held it so they could both see it, and began to sing. Having to concentrate on reading the music helped Chad to focus and compose himself, so by the time they'd finished and Pastor had given the closing prayer, he was okay to talk to people without blubbering like an idiot.

More people came to him than he'd expected, although a very noticeable absence was Anna's father. Without her parents, Anna had moved to sit beside Kathleen. Chad gladly accepted Pastor Jake's invitation to lunch, and he thought it quite interesting that Pastor Jake and Kathleen had automatically assumed Anna would be with him.

By the time everyone had filtered out, it was later than the usual end time for the service. Along with Anna, he helped Pastor and Kathleen tidy up the lobby and make sure all the hymnals were tucked neatly into the shelves on the backs of the pews, and waited while Pastor locked up the building. Two other couples had already arrived by the time they arrived at Pastor's house, comfortably sitting on chairs near the door and chatting.

One of the ladies, whose name he couldn't remember, smiled at him. "I see that you have walked here. I was hoping you would have your shiny red car, so that you could take us for a ride. I have heard of your car." Her voice lowered. "And I have seen it parked at Frank's store."

Chad bit back a grin. No matter where he went, his shiny car was quite visible. Even back in Minneapolis, the vivid red made it easy to find in most parking lots, at least the smaller ones. Here, in any parking area, it was impossible to miss. Besides the bright color, it was the only car in sight.

Her husband frowned and rested his palm on her forearm. "Mary, do not ask such a thing. Many people would like to ride in Chad's car, but he will not drive it unless it is a necessary thing."

Chad couldn't hold back his grin. Now he knew her name. He turned to Mary's husband, whose name he knew was Robert, then back to Mary. "I certainly don't mind when people need a ride. If you have something heavy to carry or are going a longer distance that you'd rather not walk, just give me a call."

She smiled at him. "Danke shoen. I will do that."

The other lady, whose name he knew was Catherine, looked at him from her seat. "Would it be acceptable if I can have a ride in your fine car as well? I have heard the seats are very soft."

Chad frowned. "Who did you hear that from?"

She shrugged her shoulders. "I do not remember."

"Sure, you can have a ride, too."

Anna's elbow poking him in the ribs made him turn. "I hope you realize that if you start giving rides in your car to a few people, you will have many more requests."

He shrugged his shoulders. "I don't mind. It's not like any-place around here is far to go." The farthest he'd been from home had been George Rempel's farm, and for that trip, they'd taken the bikes. Besides, it wasn't like he had a lot else to do. Piney Meadows wasn't exactly a hub of activity.

Anna leaned closer. "I am saying this because everyone finds your car very attractive. Especially the ladies."

The conversation he'd had with Brian about him wanting to drive the car flashed through his memory. With the ladies suddenly asking to be taken for a ride in his car, he wondered what exactly Brian had done with it on his alleged "test" drive while Chad was in the store doing his grocery shopping.

He stepped toward the door but stopped on the porch when Pastor Jake, frowning deeply, stopped. "This shiny red car of yours, it is causing quite a stir. As you know, I have a car and Ted had a car, but they do not look like your car."

In the back of his mind, Chad pictured both cars. Both were plain, basic, dull, and functional. The only other non-farm vehicle in town was Brian's beat-up pickup truck. The opposite of those vehicles, Chad's car was built for speed, looks, and impressing the women.

He hadn't meant for it to happen, but apparently, the car had done what it was designed to do. He'd known all along that his car was an oddity here, but now, looking at it from a different perspective, it was wrong for this community and especially wrong for the lifestyle here. It was flashy and sexy and went from zero to sixty in 5.8 seconds, while he doubted the pastor's car had ever made it to sixty in the ten years he'd owned it. He'd seen Pastor Jake drive. Little old ladies in Minneapolis drove faster and with more flare than Pastor Jake.

He had a feeling he was going to be getting a lot more use out of his car, just driving people around.

As he scanned both couples, who were still watching him, Chad thought back to giving his testimony. It had probably been the hardest thing he'd ever done, facing them while laying his soul bare for all to see. While he'd seen many faces and hearts close up, more had opened, and even though no one here approved of his past, he felt more accepted into their hearts in those few minutes than he had in the past six months he'd been here.

Up until now, except for Anna's mother, no one had asked him for a ride in his car, but now, as a new official member of their church, already he'd had two requests. With more people accepting him into their tight-knit community, he couldn't help thinking that he was going to be spending more on gas, especially since the price of gas had just gone up again.

In his mind, he pictured Brian changing the price per gallon on the sign at his gas station. It wasn't as if he couldn't afford a few dollars; he was just annoyed it was going to cost him more money.

Chad smiled. For the first time, he'd been annoyed rather than accepting that something was going to cost him more money. Maybe he really was starting to fit into this Mennonite community after all.

Kathleen opened the door and waved them all inside. "*Lote onns nenn gone en meddach äte.* Let us go in and have lunch. I had everything in the oven cooking while we were at church, and now everything is ready to eat. The table is already set. Let us go eat."

❧

"We need to go shopping."

Anna's fingers froze over her keyboard, and she stared at Chad, standing in the doorway of his office with one hand resting over his stomach.

"*Wuá romm sajst dü dit?* Why are you saying this? And why do you say this now?"

He extended his hand, showing a button in his palm. With his hand sticking out, it showed that the waistband of his pants was loose.

Quickly, Anna averted her eyes. "This is something I do not wish to see," she grumbled as she pushed herself to her feet. "I will go get a needle and a spool of thread from the factory."

"No, that's not what I need. What I need are some new pants. With all the great food everyone's been giving me, and the recipes I've picked up to make all my own favorites for myself, I've been putting on a pound or two a month, and I'm afraid it's caught up with me. All my pants are too tight. I think today's lunch pushed me over the point of no return." As if to emphasize his words, he made a fist, raised his hand to cover his mouth, and burped.

As Anna turned to look at him, his cheeks and his ears reddened. "Oops. Excuse me," he muttered. "Your mother's *Schmoor kohl* always does that to me."

Just because he'd made a point of it, Anna lowered her gaze to look at his belly. Since his shirt was neatly tucked into his pants nothing was exposed; therefore, she could contemplate the truth of his words. He was right in that he had gained some weight since he'd first arrived, but that was not a bad thing. When he'd first arrived he'd been far too thin, which he'd attributed to too many nights of working late and not eating supper, plus too much coffee to keep him wired, as he called it.

Anna, as well as all of the other unmarried ladies in Piney Meadows, had considered him very handsome even then. Now that he had filled out a little more, his good looks were an even greater conversation point during the ladies' group sessions.

"I am thinking you would like to go shopping now, rather than when we have done our work for the day."

He nodded. "You've got that right. Besides, if we go now, fewer people will see me with a button missing. This is kind of embarrassing."

"Not as embarrassing as if you had split the seam. Let us go."

As they walked to the store, which was only a few blocks from the factory, Anna couldn't help feeling that Chad was not walking at as fast a pace as usual. Just as she was ready to tell him to walk faster so they could get back to work in good time, he slowed even more.

"While we're away from the office, I need to talk to you about something."

Her stomach clenched. The tone of his voice told her that this was not going to be a conversation she was going to enjoy. "*Waut wursht dü mie saje?* What did you want to say to me?"

He cleared his throat. "I'm not really sure of how to say this, but I think I've been put back on the eligible-bachelors list, and I want to be taken off."

She wanted to say she had no idea what he meant, but suddenly many of the questions she'd been asked about him in the last few days made sense. "I have heard that you have had many requests to have rides in your car."

"That's right, and at first I didn't think anything of it, but after thinking of everyone who's asked, it's only single ladies. I'd expected the guys to be the ones to ask. Back in the city, when we had nothing to do on a Friday or Saturday night, me and a bunch of my friends would just hop in the car and go cruising. But here, the same rules don't apply."

"You would go cruising? How can this be? Minneapolis is landlocked. There are no cruise ships there."

"No, not boat cruising. We'd all throw in some money to split the gas and ride around the hot spots in town until the gas gauge went down, then we'd go home and call it a night. 'Cruising' in the car."

"Do you mean you would drive around, with no specific destination? Why would you do that?"

"Just for something to do. It's a guy thing. But not only is there nothing to see here, it's not the guys who are asking. It's the ladies."

Anna sucked in a deep breath. "Some of the ladies have asked if you will be needing help when you find Brittany and the baby." She didn't want to tell him, but knowing Chad was going to be a single father had regenerated interest in him as a potential husband. Many young ladies hoped that Chad would be looking for a wife to help him raise the baby, even if it wasn't full custody.

Chad stiffened as he walked, though he didn't walk any faster. "I know the reason for the sudden interest, and even though I'm going to need help, what they're all thinking isn't going to be how I'm going to do this. When I get married, it's going to be for love and love only. Not for daycare help." He stopped walking, forcing Anna to skid to a halt and turn around. "What about you, Anna? Do you want to get married?"

She gulped. Of course, she wanted to get married. And, like Chad, she would get married for love, not because her parents selected a man they liked and thought he would be a good addition to their family. Unfortunately, no man here affected her heart that way, although if Chad had been here sooner, she certainly would not be thinking the same way. Like all the other ladies, she couldn't help liking him. In fact, when she thought about him, she liked him far too much. All the odd things about him, things he would not change about himself, like his love for cooking and the strange way he cared for his chickens, made her like him so much more.

When she finished her online courses and found a place in Minneapolis to live, she would miss him. Greatly.

She turned, not able to look at him as she spoke. If she allowed it, she could easily fall in love with him, but it was not in her plan. "Yes, I will get married some day. But it will not be for a long time." It would not be fair to another man to carry a liking for Chad in her heart, so before she considered marriage, she would be gone from Piney Meadows and gone from Chad Jones. "Come, we must get to the store. I have much work to do."

He resumed walking, and this time he accelerated to his normal walking pace.

Once inside the store, she led him to the men's clothing. "Which is your size?" she asked with her hand hovering over the rack containing the pants.

Apparently, he didn't need her help. Without answering, he flipped through the rack, pulled a pair of pants, and held them up, examining both the front and back.

He frowned, draped them over one arm, flipped through the rack a second time, pulled out a different pair, also examined both sides, and draped that pair over his arm as well.

A third time, he did the same, but stopped when he saw there were only two styles in different colors, and he had one of each.

He swept his free hand in the air toward the rack. "Is this all there is?"

"Besides the jeans, yes. Does this surprise you? You go shopping often. I know you have been here before."

He lowered his hand. "Only once, and I rushed in and bought exactly what I needed, which was a coat, boots, and an emergency off-the-rack suit, and I was out of here in five minutes flat. Other than that, the only thing I shop for is groceries. Which is why I'm now buying new pants."

"This is all there is, unless you go to the next town. They have a larger store there, but that should not be necessary. I believe those will fit you just fine."

He held one pair up to his waist. "I've worn the same size for years, so I've never needed to try anything on, but I think I'd better do that. This isn't my usual style, and I'm not sure of these."

While he went into the men's changing room Anna walked to the sale rack of ladies' clothing and browsed through the blouses. Not that she needed anything, but when she started a job in the cities she'd need more than her current wardrobe of the same style of blue dresses that now filled her closet.

Just as she selected a pretty green blouse, Chad appeared beside her.

"If this is all they have here for men's pants, then I see why everyone always wears suspenders. Part of me is saying I don't have a choice, but another part of me is saying if I want to run with the crowd, this is the way to be. My only other choice would be wearing jeans or sweatpants to the office, and neither one of those is going to happen." He looked down to the blouse draped over her arm. "Do you like that one? Let me see it. Do you want it?"

She held it up to show him. "Yes. I am trying to buy one new item of clothing every payday. I am a few days early, but this will save me a trip later in the week."

He removed it from her hand and draped it over his arm, on top of the two pairs of pants. He also carried a small basket piled with smaller and sundry items, on top of which was a pair of suspenders. "Let's go pay for all this stuff and get back to work."

She allowed him to carry the blouse for her, but when they reached the till, he didn't separate the blouse from his own items.

"Nein," she said to the cashier from behind Chad. "That is not his. That is mine."

Chad peeked over his shoulder. "Nope. I'm going to buy that for you. My treat, since this is company time."

"Since this is company time, my time is already being paid for. I do not need you to do this."

"But I want to," he replied, then turned back to the cashier. "Keep going. That's on my bill."

"Thank you," she muttered, trying to be gracious rather than embarrassed. No man had ever bought her anything, much less an item of clothing, and she wasn't sure how to feel about it, since it wasn't her birthday or any other occasion.

When they arrived back at the factory, Chad went straight into his office, and the door closed. When it opened, he had changed into one of the new pairs of pants he'd purchased, complete with suspenders. He sucked in a deep breath, pressed both hands over his stomach, and grinned. "This sure feels better. Maybe this suspender thing isn't going to be so strange after all. It's actually pretty comfortable."

Instead of returning to his desk, he reached into the shopping bag he'd placed in one of his visitor's chairs and lifted out her new blouse and a small box. After she accepted the blouse from him, he held out his hand toward her, the small box cradled in his palm. "I bought this for you. I probably should have wrapped it, but I forgot to buy wrapping paper."

She stared at the small box. "I do not understand. What is this for?"

He grinned. "It's a gift."

"But it is not my birthday."

"I know that. But it's not a birthday gift. It's just a little something for no reason in particular. Just something to say I'm thinking of you. Take it."

She didn't know why he would want her to know he was thinking of her since she saw him every day anyway, but her hand trembled as she opened the lid of the box.

Anna gasped at the small gold heart hanging on a delicate gold chain nestled on a soft velvet liner.

"I hope you like it."

"It . . . it is beautiful! What is this for?"

"It's a heart, Anna. Figure it out. Here, let me put it on you."

All she could do was stare at it—she didn't trust her fingers to stop shaking to pick up the delicate piece of jewelry. Unable to move, she watched as Chad reached into the box and lifted it out.

"Put your chin down. Now hold still."

She lowered her chin and pressed it into her chest, while Chad slipped the chain around her throat and clipped the tiny fastener together behind her neck. "There. Done. Let's see what it looks like on you."

She couldn't help pressing her fingers to the small heart, which of course prevented him from seeing it.

All he did was smile. "Okay, break time's over. Let's get back to work."

25

"Mutta? What are you doing here?"

Her mama stood in front of her desk, wringing her hands and looking around the office. "I have come so that we may go shopping when you get off from work."

Anna's hands froze over her keyboard. There was no reason for her mama to come to the office just so they could walk to the store together. Not only that, she had never come into the factory before, ever. She'd never had a reason to.

Anna's stomach churned. Something was wrong.

She pushed herself out of her chair just as Chad came out of his office. "Mrs. Janzen? This is a pleasant surprise to see you. What can I do for you?"

"I have come for Anna, so that I would not miss her today. We will go shopping together."

His brows knotted. From Chad's expression Anna could see that he thought the exact same thing she had, and he was trying to make sense of it. Still sporting his stern expression, Chad stepped in front of her desk, beside her mama. "If you need to talk to Anna about something important, rather than going to a public place like the store, why don't you two make yourself comfortable in my office? I've got to talk to Frank about something anyway. I figure I'll be about half an hour. Is that enough time?"

Mama's eyes widened, and she glanced back and forth between Anna and Chad.

Anna stood. "I am sure that will be enough time. Danke shoen, Chad. Come, Mutta. This is a better place to speak privately."

Chad shuffled his feet. "Can I bring you two ladies some coffee?"

Mama's eyes widened. "Oh my!" she gasped. "Why would you do that?"

If she hadn't been so worried about what her mama needed to tell her so much she'd interrupted her at her job, Anna would have laughed. "Do not mind Chad, *Mutta*. He wants everyone to drink as much coffee as he does so he does not feel guilty about it."

As if realizing his gaffe, Chad hurried out, and his footsteps faded down the hall until all was silent.

"This way, Mutta."

Instead of sitting in Chad's chair behind his desk, Anna sat in one of the visitor chairs and motioned for her mama to sit in the other. "Why are you here? What is wrong?"

Her mama looked down and again wrung her hands. "It is your papa. He is very displeased. After you and Chad went to see Henry's new chicken plucker, he saw Chad with his arms around you while you were in his yard. It is a good thing I had seen that you had just arrived there and you were not in his house with him for more than a few minutes. But now that Chad has given his testimony that he has made a woman be with child when they are not married . . ." Her mama wrung her hands still more. "Your papa does not want you to be with Chad again, at all. Except he is your boss. I have tried to tell him that we should not make you quit this job that you enjoy so much. But it was not good." Her mama shook her head. "He says that you should stay at home like all the other girls your age, until you and William will become married."

Anna's heart froze, and a million thoughts zinged through her head. "Mutta, at that moment, Chad was in much distress. He had just told me the story of what he said in his testimony, but what he told me was how much he was hurt, how he wanted to marry her, but his fiancée not only ran away so he could not find her but also stole most of his furniture. I have never seen a person so sad, and he needed a hug. That is all it was."

Even though telling the recap of why Chad had embraced her brought back the sadness of his story, at the same time, Anna felt anger in her heart—not only had her parents watched her during a private time, they had also judged her and found her wanting when she had done nothing evil. She had done the opposite, showing comfort to a friend who needed someone to share his pain.

Yet at the same time, in addition to her anger, her thoughts swirled with confusion at calling Chad a friend. Of course they were friends, but the feelings she held for him were not like her feelings for William, who had been her friend since childhood. What she felt for Chad was different and changing every day. Even today, he had given her his office to use for as long as she needed it. Anna knew he only needed to speak to Frank for a minute. She also knew he was very busy and needed to be at his desk working or else he would have to stay late to get his work completed. Everything he did made her realize even more just how special he was.

"Are you sure this is only friendship? Your papa thinks there is much more, and with a man who has done what he has done, this would not be a good thing. We do not want him to take advantage of you as he has taken liberties with this other woman."

Anna clenched her teeth. She knew she had been feeling more than simple friendship for Chad, but again, her anger burned at her parents' accusation. "Mutta, it was not like that at all. Chad was very sad; his heart was breaking. He had wanted to get married, but she deserted him. He has been trying to find her and he wants to make it right. He has even hired a detective to help him."

Her mama turned to the window, not looking at Anna as she spoke. Because of this, Anna's heart sank, knowing she was not going to like what her mama was going to say.

"Your papa and I, we have decided that you will no longer be seeing Chad except for when you are at work. Also there will be no more long working hours for you. You are to leave at your assigned time. There especially will be no more working on Saturdays."

Anna jumped to her feet. "But I am not working on Saturdays. I am using the Internet to do the classes I have told you I am taking because I cannot go away to college. Chad is allowing me to do this, and he is helping me to learn and study."

Her mama turned to her. "That is why you can no longer do this. It is not good when there are just the two of you in the building."

"But he is a good man! I trust him!"

Her mama also stood. "Your papa has spoken. This is the way it will be. You will be home on time today."

"But there are so many things we do together, when there are other people with us, when it is not at work. Certainly Papa cannot forbid me to be in the same room with him when there are others with us. And certainly we can speak to each other outside when there are people watching."

Her mama bowed her head. "I do not disagree with you, but I cannot disagree with your papa."

Before she could think of a response that would still be respectful, her mama turned and walked out.

Anna sank into the chair and stared blankly out the window.

Her papa had always been a fair man. He'd always used wisdom and good judgment. But in this, he was wrong.

At a loss for what to do, her mind drained of thought and her body drained of energy. She was not good at cooking, and all her sewing looked like the work of a child. Once a house was clean, she would not do the work again until it was needed. Without this job, this is what she would be doing most of her days—staring at the trees outside, looking out the window, watching the leaves and flowers grow.

"Anna? What happened? What's wrong?"

She turned to Chad and looked up at him.

He sank into the chair beside her and cupped her hands in his. "I saw your mother leave, and she was crying as she walked. What's the matter?"

Feeling numb inside, she recapped the conversation, including her mama's words and her papa's ultimatum, then stared down at their joined hands. Before he'd come into the room, she'd felt so alone and defeated, but now, even though nothing had changed, Chad's presence and the comfort of his simple gesture made her feel that things weren't quite as bad.

"This is my fault. First we need to pray about this, and then you need to leave it with me." He gave her hands a gentle squeeze. "Most of all, don't do anything rash or without thinking real hard first."

She looked up into his eyes. "But what about you? Would you not say leaving your job as you did was a foolish thing?"

One side of his mouth twitched up. "Probably. But I had options. I have no doubt that I wouldn't have had any problem finding another job once I got back. But I really believe God wanted me here. Let's pray first, and then we'll trust that God also has a plan for you."

He led her in a short prayer, finishing just as the clock hit her regular finish time, without banking overtime.

"It's time for you to leave. Don't worry about falling behind, I'll help you. We'll work this out. Now pack up your stuff and go home. I'll see you later."

Chad carefully lifted the baking sheet out of the oven and set it on the stovetop. He'd just picked up the spatula when the doorbell rang.

He sucked in a deep breath and pressed his hands to his stomach to calm his nerves, then went to answer the door. He didn't know if Anna had spoken to her mother, but since arrangements for the evening had already been made, and since Brian was the one who actually went to her house to get her, she said she was still coming.

They'd both prayed that her mother could talk some sense into her father, and since they didn't have an answer either way, Anna said she would keep seeing him, as long as there was another adult present, or they were out in public. Technically, this wasn't really any different than what they'd already been doing, so he wasn't sure this was the right solution. All he could do was to continue on, and pray hard.

With Anna beside him, Brian stood at the door grinning like a cat who had just eaten a canary, probably because he was going to be eating something much better, at least in human terms.

Anna's eyes opened wide. "What is that I smell? What are you cooking?"

"A bunch of stuff, actually. Have a seat. I'll be right back." He hurried back into the kitchen and lifted the buns from the baking sheet onto the cooling rack, then returned to the living room to be with his guests.

He found Brian checking out his CDs, and Anna checking out the bookshelf.

As Anna turned around, a flicker of gold at her throat reflected the light.

He smiled. She was still wearing the necklace with the little gold heart that he'd given her a week ago. That had to be a good sign. Now, if she enjoyed his cooking, that would be another good one.

"Everything is ready. We should eat now, so we don't have to rush. I don't want to be late."

Brian made a sound almost like a snort. "We will not be late. If we take too long to eat what you have cooked us, we will simply take your car."

Anna groaned. "But we cannot. If we do, every woman there will ask him to take her for a ride."

Chad nearly groaned along with her. If they had been simply going to an adult Bible study meeting, there would be mostly married couples attending and most of the married women were not interested in his car. Or at least, not many dared to admit it in front of their husbands. However, the young adult group was different. Everyone attending, except for the leaders, was single, and the women outnumbered the men.

"I'm with Anna on this one, sorry," said Chad. "Besides, knowing you, you're going to gobble down supper and either be ready to run out the door to eat whatever snacks they'll have, or you'll want to roll over and fall asleep on the couch because of your full stomach."

Brian grinned and rubbed his stomach with one hand. "You may test me on this."

Chad rolled his eyes. One day, when Brian decided to start looking for a wife, the woman he chose had better like cooking, because she was destined to spend a lot of time in the kitchen feeding him. But then, Brian would truly appreciate everything she did, so he supposed that would make it even.

Fortunately for Chad, this meant Brian would never have his eye out for Anna. Unlike her mother, Anna was not a star in the kitchen, and in all likelihood, never would be. Therefore, he hoped that he could charm her with his cooking. It probably wasn't a typical way for a man to woo the woman of his dreams, but here, the usual rules didn't apply. Here, a woman didn't have to worry about her waistline to the point of starving herself. If a woman enjoyed food, it was normal to eat portions that could actually sustain life. Therefore, he'd decided to pull out all the stops, and hopefully, when he let Anna have it with everything he thought would open her heart to him, she wouldn't know what hit her, except for Cupid's arrow.

He pulled out a chair so she could sit down, then began removing the covers from all the serving dishes, which he had already set on the table.

"This is so strange," she said, not meeting his eyes as she spoke. "It should be me who is serving the meal and you who is sitting."

"My house, my rules. I'm not really serving, I'm just taking the lids off." As he spoke, he removed the last lid and piled all of them on the stovetop. "There. All ready." He sat and folded his hands on the table in front of him. "Brian, would you like to say the blessing?"

In less than a nanosecond, Brian closed his eyes and folded his hands in front of him on the tabletop. He gave an enthusiastic prayer of thanks for the food and their time together and immediately started helping himself.

"What is all this?" Anna asked, scanning all the food without yet taking anything.

"This is my granny's special meatloaf—the recipe has been handed down through the generations in my family, regardless of gender—accompanied by mashed potatoes with another of my special secret ingredients. I made the gravy myself—it's not from a mix. Next to it is a nice fresh salad, and tender steamed broccoli. On the side, here's some fresh bread. I cheated and used a bread making machine, because after all, I had to work today. Then for dessert, cinnamon buns, which unfortunately were made with baking powder, not good old-fashioned yeast, because the bread was in the machine all day and I didn't have time to make them the right way. I just thought I'd mention that the cheese sauce for the broccoli is, of course, my mother's special secret recipe that no one knows outside of our immediate family."

"I can barely believe that you have made all this. Just how many secret ingredients do you have?"

He grinned. "It's a secret."

Brian reached enthusiastically for the bowl of mashed potatoes. "I do not usually like secrets, but I am liking yours."

Hopefully, the plan would work. Today, Chad had put together this stately meal in order to have Anna over as his guest—first, so he could impress her with his cooking; but second and equally important, he needed to say he had something special planned. Today it would have been extremely awkward to eat at her home, with her parents, and especially her father.

Yesterday, he'd had quite a conversation with Peter. The man had no idea how stifled and unhappy his daughter was, and Chad hadn't told him. That wasn't his place. When Anna decided the time was right, then it was up to her to tell him.

Chad only hoped she wouldn't wait until the day her suitcases were packed and she had one foot out the door.

Actually, starting today, Chad's plan for Anna had changed. He'd already planned to try to convince her to stay, but now he planned to be more specific. He wanted her to stay with him.

He watched as she took her first nibble of his prized meatloaf. Her eyes widened, and she stopped chewing for just a second. "This is zehr gut. Amazing. Everything you have done is just right." Her eyes narrowed. "This is not from a package, like the Shake 'N Bake that Miranda used to make her famous chicken recipe, is it?"

"Nope. I slaved for hours over a hot stove to make this for you."

"You are teasing me. You have not been home from work that long."

He hadn't. But he'd had just enough time to throw the ingredients together and let the meatloaf bake for an hour while he got everything else together and ready within minutes of their arrival.

The trick today hadn't been any complicated cooking skill. It had been timing.

Just like he'd done his best on his timing to talk to Anna's father.

He'd gone yesterday, when all the ladies were at their women's Bible study meeting and he should have gone to the men's group meeting. Instead, he'd stood at his door, peeking through the curtains, watching and waiting for Anna and her mother to leave. Then, the second David left for the youth group meeting, Chad ran to their door to talk to Peter, before he left as well.

He wouldn't have called it a pleasant welcome, but considering Peter's thoughts, the man was gracious to have let him in. After all, Peter had thought Chad was going to tarnish his daughter.

Really, Peter had no idea of the inner strength of his lovely daughter. Anna's sweet and gentle spirit was truly her biggest asset, but at the same time, when she had a plan, everyone knew who was in charge.

All Chad could do was promise Peter he would honor his daughter, keep her safe—not just from the evil world out there, but from himself as well. And he'd do everything he could to make her happy.

Because if she was happy, maybe, hopefully, he could get her to stay in Piney Meadows with him.

So now, here he was, trying to show Anna the person he was—that he really wasn't a bad guy and could make her happy, if she'd just give him a chance. He could make her happier here, with him, than she'd be alone in Minneapolis. And maybe, just maybe, if she fell half as in love with him as he was with her, they would both be happier together.

How different his life would have been if he'd met Anna first, before he'd met Brittany.

"Chad? Why are you not eating your own food? Everything is zehr gut. Brian has already taken a second helping of everything, and you have not finished your first."

He put on his most charming smile and gazed what he hoped was lovingly into her eyes. In the background, he heard Brian choke. "I was distracted, thinking of what I'm going to make, just special for you, next time, that's even better than this."

All her movements froze. "Next time?"

He raised an eyebrow. "Oh, yeah. Next time. I plan to have a lot of next times." Before she could argue, he helped himself to more potatoes, putting more on her plate as well. He spooned a generous serving of gravy over both and winked.

Anna's eyes widened. She gasped and raised one hand to her throat, pressing her fingers into the tiny gold heart he'd given her.

His heart swelled. She was still wearing it.

All he had to do was to keep raising the bar.

26

$\mathcal{A}$nna looked out the kitchen window and shook her head.

Chad would never be a farmer. Saturday morning, Chad was outside, walking around the yard pulling weeds from the most disorganized mixture of flowers and vegetables she'd ever seen—only Chad could call it a garden. As he did his weeding, his chickens followed him. Every time he stopped to pull a weed, they would stop to see if any worms came up with it. And when Chad started walking again, they would start walking as well. Every once in a while, he'd stop, pick one up, give it a hug and ruffle its feathers, and put it back down. Then he'd do the same to the other chicken. If he followed his pattern, after one round through the yard he would go around to the side of the house and into the garage, the chickens would follow him, and he'd stop where he parked his bicycle. He would place one chicken in the basket and the other on the handlebars. He would then hit a switch to operate a small electric motor mounted at the top of the garage, which moved a chain to pull the garage door open. Why he needed a motor to open the garage, she would never know, but Chad did many odd things. Then he would be gone.

Rebecca hadn't been the only person to phone Anna to ask, in complete amazement, where Chad was going with his chickens, and she still didn't know. When she'd asked, he'd replied he was "just taking them for a ride," as if it made sense to do so.

Only to Chad.

Today, before he disappeared into the garage to take his chickens for a ride, Anna went into her yard, through the gate joining their two yards, and approached him.

He bent down to pick up Blinkie, gave Blinkie's feathers a few gentle strokes in the right direction, and then grinned at Anna. "Hey. Fancy meeting you here. I was just about to take them for a ride. Want to join us?"

She looked down at Waddles still on the ground, a little embarrassed that she could tell his chickens apart. "Only if you do not ask me to put a chicken on my bicycle. I would never be able to live with my friends if anyone saw me do such a thing." Yet, even as she spoke, she couldn't help admiring him. Not only was Chad making the best of caring for farm animals when he didn't know what he was doing, he was happy doing it. Like everything else, whatever he chose to do, he did with confidence and without apology.

"Sure. They're actually pretty comfortable doing it this way." He put his hand over Blinkie's head, as if to cover Blinkie's ears, and lowered his voice. "I don't think they're very smart. Once I get them used to doing something, I can't change it or they get confused. Once they learn something, they don't seem able to change. I also have to keep it pretty simple, or there's a high margin for error."

She looked first at Blinkie and then down at Waddles. "Actually, everyone is very amazed at what you are doing with them. I have told many people that when you tell them to get into their coop, most of the time, they do. I have not told them you also tell them to go into the house. They are getting big now. They do not belong in the house. They will make your house dirty."

Chad shook his head. "Nope. I bought them chicken diapers on eBay. It took a while for them to get used to it, but they're fine."

Anna froze, and she felt her mouth drop open. "Excuse me? What did you say? What did you buy for them?"

"Chicken diapers. They look a little strange, but they work, and that's what's important. Do you want to come with me for a short ride? If you do, I'm not going to go as fast as we usually go. I don't want Blinkie to fall off."

She wanted to ask why he didn't just put both chickens in the basket, but having any chickens in the basket was strange. "The basket was supposed to be for groceries, not your chickens."

He shook his head. "When I buy groceries, I take my car."

Anna went home to change into her jeans and get her bicycle and helmet. By the time she made it to the front, Chad and his chickens were ready and waiting.

As they rode through the town, nearly everyone they passed stopped and waved. If she wasn't mistaken, more people were outside than usual, almost like they expected him and were waiting for him to ride past. Yet a few people, when they saw him coming, turned and scurried into their homes.

Not one to disappoint, Chad waved at everyone who looked at him. Once, when he had slowed almost to a stop to say hello to Kathy Friesen from the factory, Blinkie stretched and extended her wings and clucked, almost like she was showing off.

Anna looked at Blinkie, surprised at herself that she'd begun to think of Blinkie as a hen. As the chickens were nearing five months old, soon they would be able to tell if Chad

had two hens, two roosters, or one of each. From Waddles's docile nature, Anna thought Waddles was probably a hen, but at this age, no one could be sure until they saw an egg. Blinkie was not as passive, making her almost sad that Blinkie might be a rooster—even though it was still possible that being a Rhode Island Red, Blinkie was simply more active and following the nature of the breed.

"Why are you looking at my chickens like that? Is something wrong?"

"No, they are fine. I was thinking that they are looking very good and very plump."

Chad's face paled. "Don't say they're plump. Don't say anything like that. They're going to lay eggs until they're old and gray."

"I do not think chickens go gray." Although, she really didn't know for sure. She'd never seen an old chicken. On the farms, and likewise in their backyard coops, no one let the chickens get old because then their meat would not be tender.

"I plan to find out if chickens go gray." He paused and knotted his brows. "Chickens don't go bald or anything when they get old, I hope. Anyway, let's turn around and go back now."

She turned and followed him home, and when he neared his house, he sped up. Both chickens leaned down and nosed into the wind, if a chicken could do such a thing. When he came to a stop, he put both on the ground. They shook out their feathers and strutted happily in circles, then followed Chad as he went into the garage with his bicycle.

After he parked his bicycle, he turned to her. "It's almost lunch time. How about I put Blinkie and Waddles into their coop and you and I go for a ride to the soda shop? I'd like to buy you a burger for lunch, but mostly, I'm in the mood for a milk shake. They make them with real milk and real ice cream there."

Anna crinkled her brows. "I do not understand. What else would you use to make a milk shake?"

Chad closed his eyes and shuddered. "You don't want to know. All the fast-food places—the ones you've never been to—don't use a drop of milk in their shakes. That's why they don't say 'milk shake' on the menu, just 'shake.' It's all whipped oil with lots of sugar and flavoring. There isn't a drop of milk in them."

"I think that sounds disgusting."

"They taste pretty good, until you stop and think of how they're made. It's why the shakes at the soda shop are so great. They make shakes the old-fashioned way, with real food product ingredients. I hear they use real fruit, too."

"Of course they do. But are you sure you want to go there? Mostly that is where the young people go. Young people who are fond of each other and use the soda shop as a public place to meet, where no one pays attention to anyone else."

He pressed his palms over his chest. "I'm just feeling young at heart right now." He walked closer to Anna and picked up her hands, keeping them firmly grasped in his own. "Please?"

She gulped. "I think my papa would not approve."

"You can't get much more of a public spot on a Saturday morning. There's nothing to disapprove of. But if you really don't feel right, then we can do something else."

Anna turned to look at her house, to her living room window, where she knew her papa would be—sitting on the couch reading.

Chad was correct in saying they would be doing nothing wrong, and they would be in the middle of a crowd. The soda shop was a very busy place on a hot Saturday. In fact, as the temperature continued to climb, being a hot July day, the thought of a smooth, cool milk shake sounded better and better. "Ja, it does sound like a good idea. I will tell my mama we are going, and I will be right back."

To purposely avoid her papa, Anna went around the house through the back door so she could talk to her mama in the kitchen and avoid contact with her papa in the living room.

Part of her felt wrong in doing this—it felt like she was sneaking around her papa in order to see Chad. But she was no longer a child—she was twenty-five years old and able to make her own decisions. She knew the reason her papa didn't want her spending too much time with Chad. As he was supposed to do, Chad had confessed his biggest sins to God in front of the congregation in his testimony, and now, everyone knew. Mr. Rempel was a very wise man. He had been correct in pointing out to all who suddenly became very judgmental of Chad that Chad had been very brave; he'd known he faced the risk of rejection for confessing such things.

While Anna had known that many in the congregation would look down at Chad for his sins, what was the most disappointing was her father's reaction. Papa had always been strict, and Anna had not been surprised at his reaction to Chad, but she'd been disappointed nonetheless. Like Mr. Rempel, she'd thought Chad had been very brave to confess his sins in church.

"Mutta, I am going to the soda shop with Chad. He would like to buy us milk shakes."

Not unexpectedly, her mama glanced toward the entrance to the living room, where her papa now sat in his favorite chair, reading. "You may go, but do not be too long, and if there are not many people there, you must come home."

Anna bit her lower lip to keep silent. In other words, if she didn't have lots of witnesses, she was to come home.

Rather than express her disagreement or show her disappointment in her mama's words, Anna turned without comment and returned to Chad's driveway. As soon as he saw her, he smiled, but his smile faded when she didn't smile back.

"What's wrong?"

Anna forced herself to smile. She knew he already struggled with the negative reactions and judgmental attitudes of many of the other people in their church after his testimony. She would not risk ruining this day by adding her parents to the list. "Nothing is wrong. I am thinking that instead of a milk shake, I would like a root beer float today. Would you like to race me there?"

For the first time in a long, long time, Chad laughed. "You're on. I think the loser should pay, because that's going to be you."

"Then this is a race." She scrambled onto the bike and took off before Chad yelled go. She knew she would not win, regardless of her head start, but she would have fun racing with him. Before riding with Chad, she had never raced on her bicycle. Only boys raced, yet Chad didn't seem to notice this.

As expected, Chad beat her. He also made her pay.

Since it was before lunch, there was only one other couple there who were already married, but Anna didn't care. Actually, it was better. This way, no prying eyes watched, and no curious ears listened to their conversation. She couldn't remember the last time she'd had so much fun.

When they were finished, instead of going home, Chad ordered two burgers with fries, and they returned to the table.

"What are you doing? This is strange."

"We're adults. We can eat dessert first."

"But I am not so hungry now."

He grinned. "That's okay. Whatever you leave, I'll eat."

Anna chose not to remind him that this was the reason he recently had to buy pants in a larger size.

They took far longer than usual to eat their meal. For their ride home, since their stomachs were full, they didn't fool around or try to ride fast. In fact, Anna had the feeling that Chad was riding even slower so he could make the trip last for a longer period of time.

As they neared his house, the squawking and squalling of one of his chickens disturbed the quiet of the hot summer day.

Chad's face tightened. "Something is wrong. They never make so much noise."

He tensed, lowered his head, and sped the rest of the way home. Anna did the same and somehow managed to not be too far behind him.

She ran into the yard behind Chad to see one of his chickens strutting in circles and bobbing its head, clucking and being very noisy.

He ran to the coop and pulled the door open and stepped inside. "Blinkie? What's wrong? Are you hurt?"

Anna ran behind him and grasped his arm. "Chad, wait. Nothing is wrong. This is very right. I think if you look in the nest boxes, you will find an egg. This is what chickens do when they lay an egg. This means that Blinkie is a hen, and you will have a good breakfast tomorrow."

He froze. "Really?"

"Ja. Let her be for now, do not pick her up. She is showing how proud she is that she has laid an egg."

"Whoo hoo!" Chad yelled. He spun, causing her to lose her grip. She backed up a step to give him room, but he stepped close to her, wrapped his arms around her, and squeezed. "Blinkie's a girl!" His arms dropped, but instead of stepping back, he reached up and cupped her face in his palms. His eyes shone with excitement. "I'm going to get eggs every day."

"Nein, a hen does not lay every day, but—"

The press of Chad's lips cut off Anna's words. Before she had time to close her eyes or think about what was happening, it was over.

But he didn't let her go or step back. His eyes widened, his entire face softened, and one corner of his mouth tilted up. She barely became aware of him tilting her chin up, just a little, but she was very aware of his mouth lowering to hers, this time very slowly.

His eyes drifted shut, and his thumbs brushed her cheeks, and he tilted his head.

Anna closed her eyes just as his lips touched hers. This time his kiss was slow, and the slowness of it made her heart race. She'd never felt anything as wonderful as the heat of Chad's kiss and the warmth of his touch.

Just as slowly, he broke their kiss, but instead of stepping away, he straightened a little and lowered his head to kiss her again. She closed her eyes, wanting this again like nothing she'd ever wanted in her life before. But instead of the press of his soft lips, she heard the smack and felt the padding of the helmet pressing into her forehead as the protruding front sections of their helmets collided.

He backed up and pulled his helmet off his head. "Sorry," he muttered. "Now if that wasn't a mood breaker."

The fog in her head began to clear as reality began to intrude.

Chad had just kissed her . . . and she'd kissed him right back . . .

She looked up, toward the kitchen window of her parents' house.

The curtain didn't move, which so far was a good sign.

She turned back to Chad and backed up a step. She'd been kissed before. Twice—both times by William. It had not been like that.

She backed up another step. "*Ekȳ mott ne tüsf gone.* I must go home. I will see you in church tomorrow."

Before she could escape, Chad stepped forward and wrapped his fingers around her arm. "No. Wait. Don't leave like this. I didn't mean to frighten you. Earlier this morning I called Brian and invited him over for supper, so he can pick you up and the three of us can have some fun this evening."

She stopped, and he released his grip. She shook her head. "You did not frighten me. But suddenly I feel I need some time to think and to go pray. I will talk to you later."

Before he could change her mind, or worse, kiss her again, Anna turned and ran home.

She would come back for her bicycle later.

27

Chad threw the peelings from the potatoes into the bucket for the compost so hard that a couple bounced out.

He couldn't believe he'd kissed her.

He stopped with his hands in the sink, grasped around the next handful of peelings, and then mentally shook his head. Of course he could believe it. He'd wanted to kiss her for months. What he couldn't believe was how he'd done it. He'd been planning and working up to the perfect romance-filled right moment.

Standing inside the smelly chicken coop with a squawking chicken bellowing and prancing around their feet hadn't been it.

But then, she had kissed him back.

Chad closed his eyes and sighed. She really had kissed him back.

The image of Anna with her eyes closed, her head tilted slightly back, lost in the moment, rushed through his head. At just the thought of her sweet face he wanted to kiss her again.

But, of course, he couldn't. Once it was over and she had come back to earth and thought about what they'd done, she'd hightailed it out of there like a scared rabbit. And now, living out here in the middle of nowhere, he could say he'd actually seen, in real life, what a scared rabbit really looked like.

Only one thing stopped him from running to her house and begging her on his knees to forgive him and forget about it.

He wanted to do it again.

And he was walking on thin ice with her father.

Okay, two things stopped him.

And the only time he could see her not in a crowd was when they were with Brian, a semiwilling third party.

So that was three things.

Since he didn't want to go on with a list to infinity, Chad grabbed the peelings and tossed them into the bucket, picked it up, and strode outside.

On his way to the compost box, he slowed as he passed Waddles and Blinkie in the coop. "Sorry, gals, not today," he called out, even though he still wasn't sure of the gal-ness of Waddles, and kept walking. Unfortunately today he hadn't cooked any of the peelings, and they looked disappointed they were missing a treat. Not knowing much about chickens, he'd used the Internet to find out what chickens liked for a snack to find to his horror that raw potato peels were toxic to chickens. The website source said they were okay if cooked, but today he hadn't had time, so they didn't get a snack.

As he dumped the peelings into the compost box behind the garden he looked over his shoulder at the kitchen window to Anna's parents' house.

In all things, God watched and knew what he was doing, but since God knew his thoughts, it didn't scare him. Instead, it strengthened him.

But Anna's father watching scared him spitless.

Chad sighed and let his arms fall limply to his sides. If he were a father with a daughter in a community like this, he didn't know if he would think much differently than Anna's father, although he hoped he wouldn't be so harshly judgmental. Yet, considering his own history, Chad couldn't entirely fault Anna's father for his feelings. Chad had bared his heart and soul in his testimony in front of the church, and he'd done it again on a more personal level when he'd sat and spoken with Peter alone that evening, meaning to confess his sins and be forgiven for them.

But Peter still didn't trust him. Probably Peter had forgiven him, in a Christian way, even though his sins weren't for Peter to forgive. The bottom line was that Peter didn't trust Chad with his daughter.

At the same time, knowing how tight this community was, being the only outsider, despite the welcome he'd received, he would never make it into that inner circle. No one would admit to it, but it was there. Up until now, it hadn't bothered him. Now it did, especially if he had to be there to win the heart of the girl of his dreams and earn from her father the right to court her. He'd also felt that "inner circle" more from other members of the community as well. Not that he was pushed out, he just wasn't in, and he never would be.

Chad turned and went inside the house to continue his meal preparations. Again, everything would be done in advance and not need any preparation or work until it was ready to serve.

For the tenth time, or maybe more, he looked up at the clock. Anna hadn't said she wouldn't come, so he had to think she would. Still his stomach wouldn't rest easy until the doorbell rang and he saw two people—Brian and Anna—outside versus just Brian and his empty stomach.

When the doorbell rang, he knew it was Anna outside. Brian never rang the doorbell—Brian always knocked.

Chad fought to make himself appear normal, instead of being so excited he felt like pumping his fist in the air and grunting like his favorite team had just scored a touchdown.

He sucked in a deep breath to calm himself, then opened the door. "Hi. Come on in. I'm almost ready."

He made one last check of his casserole and returned to the living room. However, instead of finding Brian picking through his CD collection, Chad found Brian and Anna sitting on the couch, engrossed in what looked like a very serious conversation.

The second they noticed him, conversation stopped.

"This looks serious," Chad muttered, not sure whether or not to join them.

Anna turned to him. "Before I left to come here, my mama and papa were together in the living room, and my mama asked what my plans were—if I wanted to continue working at the factory. But it was strange, the way she asked. She knows I would not want to stay home to do housework and do sewing. If I did not work and did not spend most of my time at home, what would I then do? I wondered if she knew of my plan to move to find a home and a job in the cities." She waved one hand in the air toward Brian. "I have just now told Brian my plan and how you are helping me. But I have not said anything of this to anyone else. Not even Rebecca."

Chad shook his head. "I certainly haven't said anything." Already, he was not looked upon favorably by Anna's father. Regardless of the fact that Anna had made her decision to leave Piney Meadows before he arrived, Chad knew he would get the blame anyway. "In fact, that was one thing I wanted to talk to you about." He opened his mouth, about to tell her how valuable she'd become to the company and that he wanted to give her a raise and that he wanted her to stay, but stopped before he spoke. If he asked her to stay, possibly she would think he wasn't supporting her in her efforts to leave, and then she would no longer trust him as she did now.

Anna's eyes widened. "What is it you want to say?"

He snapped his big mouth shut and shook his head. "Nothing that can't wait until we're back at the office on Monday." Where he'd tell her she needed to take more courses, which would hopefully keep her in Piney Meadows longer and give him more time to convince her to change her mind about leaving.

Chad rubbed his hands together. "I hope everyone's hungry, because I have another treat for supper today, with yet another of my secret ingredients."

Anna rolled her eyes, and Brian rubbed his stomach. "I am liking your secret ingredients."

Chad grinned. "There's always more where those came from. Let's go eat."

The evening passed quickly—too quickly—and before he realized the time, Anna and Brian left.

Chad didn't feel right letting Brian walk Anna home, but he had no excuse to do it himself when Brian was leaving at the same time and Anna lived only next door.

He barely had the sink full of hot water to wash the dishes when pounding echoed from his front door. Pounding meant Brian had come back. Chad shut the water off and ran to the door. "What's wrong?" he asked as he pulled the door open.

Brian stepped inside and closed the door behind him. "I think we need to talk."

The delicious supper he'd made turned to a lump of lead in his stomach. He moved to the side, but his feet wouldn't obey him to walk into the living room.

Brian waved one arm in the air in the direction of Anna's house. "Why did you not tell me she was planning to leave our town? She tells me you have been helping her take courses over the Internet to become more skilled to get a good job in the cities. *Daut es soo domm.* That is so stupid. Are you a person who is going crazy?"

"But . . . I . . ."

Brian crossed his arms over his chest and glared at Chad through narrowed eyes. "Waut denkje dü? She cannot go alone to the cities to work and live. She will be eaten like a young rabbit being chased by a cougar in the spring."

Chad shuddered, the mental picture worse because he'd also compared Anna to a rabbit earlier that day, only Brian's ending was much more graphic. "I know. I'm trying to get her to stay."

"I have seen no evidence of this from what she has said."

Chad dragged one hand over his face. "I haven't specifically asked her to stay because I can't risk that she'll think I'm not on her side. If . . ." He shuddered and shook his head. "When she decides to stay, the decision must be her own, not because I've asked." He also feared he wouldn't merely ask—he'd probably beg. "I promised that I'd help her upgrade her skills, so that's what I have to do."

"Why did you make such a promise, to help her learn more so she could leave us?"

"When she asked, I didn't know her. I also didn't know how isolated this community is. Most people here really have no idea what it's like beyond the surrounding farms. Except for a few, the farthest big city everyone's been to is Bemidji."

"Actually, most of my people have not been that far." Brian studied Chad's face. "You care for her very much, is this true?"

Chad felt himself sag. He wanted to tell Brian he loved her, but he wanted Anna to be the first person to hear it from his lips, not Brian, so he nodded.

"Then you must tell her what she will be facing there. I have already told her of my experiences at college—I did not go to a Christian college—but I came back, and I would not live any place else. But many of our people have left and not returned. The thing is that those who do not come back have not left alone. Either they go as a couple, as have Theresa and Evan, or they go to college and meet someone there and have the strength of a Christian brother or sister. This is like Leonard and Lois's daughters. They planned to come back but met the men whom they married while at a Christian college. They did not move back to Piney Meadows."

"I know. But I don't know what to say to Anna. Some of the stuff most people consider to be normal, she'd never believe. But it's not all bad. If you hang with the right crowd and stay away from the wrong places, you'll be fine. It's not all bad there. Just different. Really different than here."

Brian gave Chad such an intense stare, Chad almost felt himself melt. "You say that she still may be fine. But you do not look like you think she will be fine."

Chad sighed and looked blankly at the wall, in the direction of her house. "No." The day Anna left, she would take a piece of him with her—and he *was* afraid for her. She had such a trusting heart, it would be like sending a sheep out to a pack of hungry wolves—an image not much different than the one Brian had used earlier. "I need to do something to convince her to stay, and for her to think it was her decision."

"Then let me warn you what I have seen. Anna's parents acted different when I left her at home. Something has changed there, and it did not feel good."

All his strength and ideas drained from him. Instead of getting better, he'd felt everything getting worse. He'd never felt so helpless in his life. "What can I do?"

"*Ekj weete nijch,* I do not know. The first thing I would say for you to do would be to pray."

Chad sagged even more. "I don't think it will make much difference. I've already asked God a million times to do something to convince Anna to stay. But as every day passes, she gets more determined to leave. I'm not a prayer warrior, I'm not even sure I know how to pray for this." He gulped, barely able to say the words he feared, but he had to say them. "What if God really wants her to go?"

Brian shook his head. "I do not believe that, and I do not think you believe it either."

"But what can I do? I'd really like for God to use me, to show Anna she's meant to stay and that it's the right thing for her to do. But I don't know what to do."

"Then you must let God use you as He wants. You must open yourself to that."

"How? I'm not hearing God telling me anything. Nothing I'm doing seems to make her go the way I want, as though I'm doing everything wrong. I know even the greatest men of God had their flaws. David. Moses. Peter. But they had qualities he could use. I don't."

One corner of Brian's mouth tipped up. "If God wants to use you, He will. You do not need to have great strengths. God used Lazarus, and Lazarus was dead at the time. Although I pray it is not how God wants to use you, my friend."

Chad shuddered at the thought, but at the same time, he felt strangely strengthened.

Brian said, "I must go. I will see you and Anna in church tomorrow."

After the door closed, Chad raised his palms to lean against the door and pressed his forehead against the cool wood. Certainly he was better equipped than a dead man, and now it was time to show how much.

Besides, he still had her bicycle in his garage.

28

$\mathcal{A}$nna didn't know what Brian and Chad had talked about after Brian saw her home, but she intended to find out. She hadn't wanted to go sit in the kitchen with her mama and answer countless questions about what she did at Chad's home, so she'd walked to the window, intending to watch Brian walking until he turned the corner. However, Brian had instead gone back to Chad's house, where he'd stayed for a long time before leaving.

She had a bad feeling the conversation had been about her.

Fortunately, the time she'd spent at the window waiting for Brian to leave had been the right amount of time for her mama and papa to become involved in a conversation that didn't include her, so she managed to escape to her room.

This time.

Her parents hadn't spoken to her about her plans to leave Piney Meadows after she completed her online courses, so she was less worried they now knew. Still, their relationship had changed, and it made her increasingly uncomfortable. Her papa had always been a strict man, but he had become almost obsessive about needing to know where she had gone, how long she had been there, and who else had been there besides

Chad. When she'd asked why he did not ask such questions of her sesta, he replied that Sarah always did what was expected and Anna did not.

Sunday morning she stood at the door, waiting for Chad to knock so they could walk to church together. Secretly, she prayed that Chad would hurry so she could leave before her papa was also ready to leave. Then she could avoid his criticism of her clothing. Instead of plain dresses like those her mama and sesta wore, she'd selected her new pink blouse, because it had been a gift from Chad, and a matching skirt. He'd told her he liked the color on her, making her want to wear it when she was with him.

Again, she looked at her wristwatch. It was unusual for Chad to be late, although just as she'd finished getting dressed she'd heard triumphant squawking coming from the chicken hotel, telling her that Blinkie had laid another egg. Knowing Chad, instead of getting ready, he was at the entrance of the coop waiting for Blinkie to settle down so he could pet her for her accomplishment.

Almost as if she could have timed it with a clock, the clucking stopped, and Chad was at the door.

She opened the door before he knocked to find him with his fist raised and grinning ear to ear.

Anna gulped. She liked to see him smile. He didn't smile enough.

She couldn't help smiling back. "I am thinking that you have another egg this morning."

His smile widened. "Yeah. And this time, it was Waddles. They're both hens. Isn't that great?"

"I suspected Waddles was a hen, but I did not want to say, just in case that was not correct." She looked up into his face, remembering what had happened when Blinkie laid her first egg. He'd kissed her. It had been sweet and exciting and wonderful.

And she wanted it to happen again.

Except this being Sunday, they now stood on the porch of her parents' house. This was not the time, nor the place. She shouldn't have felt disappointed, yet she did.

He held out one hand, as if she needed help walking down the steps. "Come on, we should go. I'm a little later than usual. I had to give Waddles a hug."

"I knew you would do that." Not wanting to think about it too much, she slid her hand into his. His fingers wrapped around her hand firmly, but instead of guiding her down the steps, he gave her hand a gentle squeeze.

"You look very nice today." He smiled again and rubbed the back of her hand with his thumb.

She didn't know why, but her heart quickened at the simple touch. "Danke shoen," she mumbled as he guided her down the three steps to the sidewalk. "You are looking very handsome, as well." Today, he'd dressed in his new pants and a nicely ironed blue shirt complemented by a shiny black tie with a picture of a guitar on it, complete with his new suspenders and his black shoes shined to perfection.

If she weren't mistaken, Chad blushed at her compliment.

When both her feet were on the sidewalk, he released her hand. A pang of disappointment struck her at the loss of his touch.

As they walked, she found herself looking up at him, thinking how much he'd changed since he first moved to Piney Meadows, yet in other ways, he hadn't changed at all. He was still fairly useless with tools, and sometimes a bit dangerous, but he still did his best when asked to help and behaved graciously when the other men obviously gave him only the easy tasks. On the other hand, everyone respected him enormously for his work with all the improvements at the furniture factory. Unfortunately, as he'd told her would happen, since he'd now been there for eight months, his excellence in management had become normal and even expected. He accepted it without complaint, simply happy doing the job he had been hired to do.

She knew he was a talented musician, skilled on the guitar and an excellent singer, yet he was too shy to sing in front of people, so no one knew of his gift. She had also felt the same way when Miranda had asked her to perform in the Christmas play. When the play was over, Anna still didn't like to sing when anyone could hear her, so she and Chad spent much time singing to Chad's guitar accompaniment on evenings when he invited both her and Brian over for supper. Brian was not a very good singer, but he was willing and they enjoyed themselves, and that was all that mattered.

Besides his beautiful singing, Chad's greatest talent was also something no one knew about—his skill at cooking. She could never tell anyone, but Chad was a better cook than her mama—almost the best cook she knew, second only to Lois. Yet because of their culture, so different from his, he couldn't share his joy by inviting guests to his home to share a wonderful meal he had prepared. It saddened her not to be able to tell anyone, but Chad already accepted much teasing about his different ways. When anyone called out "City Boy," Chad answered as readily as he answered to his name. He took it all in stride, always with good humor.

Chad Jones was a kind and considerate man and so different from anyone she'd ever met. Perhaps it was part of his charm. He made her smile, and being with him she felt happy, even at work.

When she left Piney Meadows, she would miss Chad very much. In fact, the thought struck her—she maybe would miss him so much she might want to stay a little longer. He had suggested perhaps she might want to take a few more courses before she left, and she liked the idea because even though she had to face increasing criticism from her parents, it would give her more time to be with Chad.

Pastor's sermon today centered on the balance between judgment and forgiveness, and many times her breath caught. Pastor usually didn't give such a harsh message, but today he held nothing back. Many times she felt like standing and pointing to her papa, to remind him of many of the comments she'd heard him say about Chad when he didn't know she was nearby. However, standing in judgment of her papa wasn't God's will, either. Instead, to show her support for Chad, she brushed her fingertips along his hands, which he clasped tightly on top of his Bible in his lap. Feeling his tension, she splayed her fingers over his hand and gave his fingers a gentle squeeze.

He turned his head toward her, gave her a short nod, and then turned back to listen to Pastor Jake's sermon. At the closing hymn after the sermon, she noted Chad didn't sing with his usual enthusiasm and instead seemed rather quiet, even hesitant.

Usually they lingered in the lobby to chat, but today, he seemed reluctant to talk to people.

His anguish tore at her heart. Even though Pastor had not mentioned Chad's name, it was quite obvious that his situation had been used as fodder for the sermon.

If anyone wanted to talk to him about it, it should best be done in private.

Anna grabbed onto his hand and tugged. "Come. Let us go. I wish to have a picnic lunch today. Let us hurry to your house to get in your car, and we can go to Cass Lake, like we did before." At his hesitant expression, she smiled. "*Donn nijch sorje*. Do not worry. There will not be bears now. It is too early in the day for them to be out in this heat."

He glanced from side to side, as if waiting for people from the hovering circles to descend upon him. "Are you sure?" He let his question hang, and she could almost hear him thinking . . . *what about your papa?*

About to pull his hand again, she froze and looked down at their joined hands. If people were looking—and they were looking—they would think that she and Chad were holding hands like a couple who were courting.

Instead of dropping his hand, she squeezed it tighter and pulled again. "I am sure. Now let us go."

He followed her quickly out of the church, and they continued at a fast pace until they arrived at his house. "Let me throw together some leftovers from the fridge. How about if you wait in the car?"

She smiled at his solution to her not wanting to be inside his house with him without an escort.

He hurried into the house, and within seconds, the garage door began to rise. So amazing.

As she walked into the garage, she saw her bicycle tucked against his, leaning against the garage wall.

Again, she smiled. She should have taken the bicycle home, but leaving it here in Chad's garage would give her an excuse to come back when she otherwise didn't have a good reason.

She barely got herself settled in his car when Chad came out with a shopping bag. "I ended up just making sandwiches," he said as he tucked the bag carefully behind the seats. He started the car and backed out of the garage. When the car had cleared the garage, he hit another button, and the garage door came down. All she could do was watch it close as he continued to drive away.

"You find that fascinating, don't you?"

"Ja." She nodded, then turned to continue watching out the back window of the car until the garage door had completely closed. "I have never seen such a thing before."

"In the city, it's normal. Most people have electric garage door openers. I didn't buy it. I won it as a door prize. Since I had an apartment, I had it in my storage locker, which is probably why Brittany didn't take it." He made an odd laugh. "I'm sure all the neighbors laugh every time I use it. It's got to seem pretty lame, because usually I only use the car once a week when I take your mother grocery shopping. It seems silly in the summertime, but I have to tell you that in the winter, when you take the car to work every day, it's a great thing to have when it's cold outside. Except here, I never take the car to work. But I had it, so I didn't want to waste it."

"I'm sure all the neighbors find it as fascinating as I do."

They lapsed into a silence on the way to Cass Lake, and Anna didn't mind at all. To the contrary, she enjoyed the quiet and found it relaxing. The silence being comforting instead of awkward spoke of a good relationship between them. Here, in the car, they could simply enjoy each other's company without words. She'd never done that with a man before, not even with William, who tended to ramble when there was a silence and he had nothing to do with his hands. Although she didn't know why William should be nervous around her, when they'd been friends since childhood.

When Chad parked the car and turned the motor off, Anna reached behind the seat for the bag containing their lunch, then froze when her fingers touched the bag. "When I first got this idea all I thought of was eating lunch and then going for a walk around the lake, since we did not do that the first time we came. But now, I have realized that neither of us is dressed for such a thing. We are in our good church clothes."

Chad looked down at his new clothes and ran one hand down the smooth fabric of his tie. "You're right. I never thought of that, either. I just wanted to get out of there." He craned his neck and looked down at her feet. "Although, you're still wearing sensible shoes. Back in Minneapolis, on Sunday morning when the women dress up, they wear shoes with insanely high heels. They sure look good, but I don't know how they walk. From the angle of their feet, it's like they're walking on their toes."

She turned to him. "I do not understand. Why would someone wear shoes that are not comfortable?"

He grinned, and his eyes lost focus. "When women wear high heels, the shoes alter the natural posture of the body. By changing the angle at which a woman stands, the shoes make the calf muscles tighter and more firm. But most of all, standing that way makes a woman's . . . uh . . . never mind. I think you have the right idea wearing good sensible shoes like you do. You can walk as much as you want and not complain about sore feet for a day and a half afterward. I've got a blanket in the trunk, so let's find a good spot and have our lunch."

Chad gave the blessing for their food and thanked God for their impromptu time together, and they began to eat. Not only had he made some very delicious sandwiches, he'd also brought some fruit and a couple of cans of soda.

"When we are done, dressed as we are, we cannot really go for a walk around the lake, but we can certainly go to the shore and sit for a while to relax."

"Sure. I'll throw the blanket over that big log we sat on last time, and it'll be nice. As long as there are no bears down there."

Anna nibbled her bottom lip and pretended to concentrate intently on the top of her soda can. "Nein, there should not be bears by the lake, unless they are hot and decide to go swimming to cool down. That is the only way they can cool down in the summer, with all that thick fur." As discreetly as she could, without moving her head, she kept her head lowered but looked up at him.

Chad had been taking a long swallow from his soda can, but halfway through her last sentence, he began to choke.

Anna didn't know whether to laugh or pat him on the back. She ended up doing both. While she did feel a little guilty at making him choke, his life wasn't in danger, and it was pretty funny.

When he finally caught his breath, he turned to her. "Okay, that was good. I know the bears aren't going to go swimming in front of us like they do at the zoo. But you sure caught me off-guard. You made me think. Good one."

When her laughter faded, she looked again into his face. Without commenting again on the bears, Chad reached forward and grasped one of her hands. Her breath caught as he brushed the back of her hand with his lips, then opened her palm and pressed it to his cheek.

His face was smooth, but she could feel the start of the prickles of his beard. It was a sensation she'd never experienced before.

Slowly she ran her fingers across his cheek, and his eyes drifted shut.

She wanted to kiss him again. A lot. Her heart burned with it.

Before she could think too much of the possibilities, his eyes opened, and he reached up and took hold of her hands, enclosing both her hands in his much larger ones. Not releasing her, he slowly rubbed his thumbs up and down her wrists.

"You know, when everything settles down, I've been thinking. I'd really like to get married. The whole thing. The 2.5 kids, a dog, and the white picket fence. And of course, here in

Piney Meadows, chickens in the backyard, complete with their very own chicken hotel. What do you think of that? Not right now, but not too long, either."

Anna had to force herself to breathe. For a second, she could picture herself in that very scenario he'd described, happily married, and very much in love with Chad. Part of her wanted to think he had just proposed to her, but the more sensible part told her that he was speaking in general terms. After all, he was at that age when a man began to think of settling down.

Actually, he'd already thought of settling down and getting married, only not with her.

She didn't know what to say, because she really didn't understand his question, or if it was specifically directed at her.

He released her hands, then reached up with one hand and brushed her cheek with the backs of his fingers. "It's okay. I don't really expect an answer now. When the time comes when I do, though, I plan to ask you with much more flare than this." One corner of his mouth tipped up in half a smile. "That day will come, Anna. I just want you to know." He pushed himself to his feet and then reached down to help pull her up as well. "We've been sitting long enough. Let's put the stuff in the car and go for that walk to the lake. We'll just make a lot of noise on the way there so we don't catch Winnie-the-Pooh skinny-dipping."

"Who?"

He grinned, putting a little flutter in her heart. "Never mind. I just charged the battery in my camera, so just take me to the best place to take some good photos. I'm right behind you."

29

Sitting at his desk, Chad nodded, even though the caller couldn't see him, and entered a few more numbers in his calculations. This would be an important order for the factory if he could get a little more flexibility with the dates. He knew everyone on the crew would be more than willing to work the overtime, but Chad didn't want his staff to become slaves to their jobs, as he'd once been.

Just as he began a new barter for some extras in exchange for more time, his cell phone rang. Again. For the third time in ten minutes.

So he wouldn't be distracted from his negotiations, he reached into his pocket and pressed the mute button without allowing himself to see the caller's name. If it was so important, whoever it was could text him or leave a voicemail.

With a bit more bartering, Chad managed to meet in the middle with the customer. He promised to have a contract e-mailed shortly, then hung up.

He'd barely raised his hand from the handset when Anna ran into his office.

"Chad, this is very important. You must call that detective person back immediately. He has said he has some very important information for you."

Chad's heart stopped and then began to pound.

This was it. According to his calculations, the baby would have been born by now, and this was the phone call he'd been waiting for.

The PI had found Brittany and the baby.

This call would change his life forever. He was a father, and he would use almost everything he had within him to get equal and shared custody.

The only thing he wouldn't do was marry Brittany. For months, he'd realized that he'd never really loved her. It had been a wild infatuation fed by her feminine wiles, which he now saw was just a way to get what she wanted from him, without having to give anything in return. When he'd wanted something in return, which was to be a father to their baby, she proved she'd never intended to marry him.

Now, she could no longer take that from him. Rod had found her. Shared custody would be difficult, but he would do anything to make it happen, including taking her to court.

He turned to watch Anna, still standing in the doorway, shuffling her feet and looking like she didn't know whether to leave or stay with him.

His throat tightened. He needed her now more than he'd ever needed anyone. He needed her not just as a friend but as his soul mate, forever, through good and bad, through joy and tribulations, if she would have him.

Even though she appeared unsure of what to do, she seemed to want to share the news with him and was waiting for him to ask.

He stood and extended one hand to her. "Please, come here. I would like you to be with me when I call him back. Now that the moment has come, I'm feeling a little unsure of myself."

She gave him a shaky smile that was a perfect match to his shaky stomach, and came to him.

Before he reached for his phone, he wrapped his arms around her and drew her in for a hug. When she wrapped her arms around his back and gave him a squeeze, it made him feel both weak and strong at the same time.

Before he could start to enjoy her touch, she dropped her arms and backed up, causing him to release her.

"You had best make that call. The man sounded almost frantic."

Chad's stomach flipped. He hoped nothing was wrong with the baby, but even if there was, he still intended to be the best father he could be. And hopefully, Anna would be there to join him—not as a helper or his administrative assistant, but as his wife and the baby's stepmother.

He sank into his chair, unmuted the phone, and dialed.

As soon as he identified himself, the receptionist put him through to Rod.

"You don't have a lot of time," Rod blurted out without preamble. "I've arranged a meeting for you and Brittany this afternoon—this was the only time she would agree to. I can't divulge any details, but she says she will meet with you today, at one o'clock, in my office. Can you be here by then?"

He looked at his wristwatch. It was just past 9:00 a.m. and he knew it would take about four hours if he stuck to the speed limit—doable, since he wouldn't be traveling in rush hour. "I can if I leave right now. Can I bring a friend?"

"Yes. I was about to suggest that if you could have someone with you, it would probably be a good idea. I believe there will be someone else besides Brittany at our meeting."

"I'll see you then. I have to leave now."

He barely had his cell phone back in his pocket when he turned to Anna. "Will you come with me? I know it's asking a lot, but I'd really like to have you there, as a . . ." his words trailed off as he thought of what he could say to describe her. He wanted to say "fiancée" but he really hadn't formally proposed. He had been working up to it, but right now was neither the time nor the place nor the atmosphere for something that should be one of the most important moments in a person's life. "Friend" was the best he could come up with. He lowered his voice and reached for her hand. Gently rubbing his thumbs against the backs of her hands, he gazed into her eyes. "A very special friend. I'd really like you to be with me for this."

She gulped so loud he heard it. "Ja. I will go with you. I think we must hurry, mustn't we?"

"Yeah. We have to run. Literally."

Anna made a quick phone call to Frank to say they were leaving for the day—an emergency had come up and there was no one to answer the phones. The second she hung up, she turned to him. "As you have said, I am wearing very sensible shoes. We can run all the way to your house."

Just as she'd said, she did run all the way, and at the same time, proved without words that she was in better physical condition than he was, because she wasn't panting nearly as deeply as he was when they reached his house.

For the first time, he called himself a fool for installing the electric garage door opener, because he had to unlock the house, run inside, and go through the door leading to the garage in order to hit the switch to raise the garage door, when it would have been faster to just open it from the outside.

As quickly as possible, they were on their way. They'd left town and were on the highway at full speed before he remembered he hadn't locked the house door when he left. Although in Piney Meadows, it didn't matter. If anyone came to his door and found it unlocked, a person was likely to simply lock it for him and leave a note saying they would be back later.

This time, the drive was not comfortable. He didn't have it in him to chat about nonsense, so he let the silence hang. However, Anna obviously didn't feel the same way. He saw her reach into her purse and pull out a CD.

His brows knotted. "What are you doing with a CD in your purse?"

She smiled at him, then pushed the CD into the player. "Brian has made this for us. It is a collection of some of the choruses we have been singing at your house. He has made a copy so he may sing when he is working alone in his shop, and he said he made a copy for me, so I may do the same. I have no place I can play this except in your car, so I have been carrying it in my purse for the next time I am in your car, and this is today. I think these good songs will give you some peace today."

Of course, she was right. It took a few songs to play, but by the time the fourth song started, the words calmed and soothed him by reminding him that God was watching, and whatever happened, God was in charge.

He didn't know how many times the disc replayed, but Anna, bless her heart, didn't complain. She sat with him, a comforting presence like he'd never had in his life. He felt like asking her right there if she would marry him, but now he had to make the proposal extra special, because she was so extra special.

He pulled into the parking lot of the private investigator's office with exactly six minutes to spare, allowing them to walk in with a grace and dignity he didn't feel.

Chad didn't even try to smile when they approached the receptionist. He reached for Anna's hand and held tight as he looked at the woman behind the desk. "I'm Chad Jones, and we have an appointment with Rod."

"Yes, he is expecting you. You can go right in, third door on the right."

❧

Anna had never been in such a place, and being the first time, she needed to observe how office procedures were handled in the cities. The secretary's manner was brief and blunt, and not at all cheery when she told them to go to the detective's office rather than escorting them. The woman was not at all friendly.

When they reached the correct door, Chad stiffened, gave her hand a squeeze, and knocked, and when a man's voice called to go in, they entered the small office.

Anna nearly gasped when she saw the detective was not alone. In a way, she'd expected to see Brittany already there, but she had not expected to see another man with her.

Since they were holding hands, the man had to be Brittany's boyfriend. Likewise, since Chad was holding her hand in a death grip, they probably assumed she and Chad were in a similar relationship.

She watched him as he glared at Brittany, then looked around the room. There was no baby lying in a basket. However, from the looks of Brittany, she did look like a woman who had just had a baby.

Rod motioned everyone toward chairs he'd set out—two sets of two armchairs facing each other on either side of his desk in the center of the room, with plenty of room between.

Brittany and her gentleman friend sat in one set of chairs, and Anna followed Chad's leading into the other set. The detective remained in the middle, half sitting on the front of his desk.

Rod cleared his throat. "I don't believe we need introductions. This is not going to be a pleasant transaction, so I'm simply going to state the facts and requirements." He pulled some documents out of a folder and laid them on the desk. "I'm going to ask that all parties remain silent until I've finished speaking."

He waited until all four of them nodded.

Rod turned to Chad. "As you can see, the baby is not here. That's because you're not the father."

Chad opened his mouth, but Rod quickly raised one hand to silence him. "Brittany declared on the birth certificate that Mark"—he gestured toward the man sitting with Brittany, still holding her hand—"is the father. Mark insisted on a DNA test, and the results confirmed it. Brittany and Mark were married last weekend."

Chad's entire body stiffened. His grip on Anna's hand tightened even more as he stared at Brittany. "But you were pregnant when we were still living together."

Brittany turned away from him, then looked down at the floor. "Yes," was all she said.

Anna's mind reeled. This was not what she'd expected at this meeting, and she knew Chad was absolutely stricken.

His grip on her hand tightened even more, and he continued to glare at Brittany, despite the fact that she refused to look at him. "How could you? How long was this going on behind my back while we were living together? We were engaged to be married!"

Brittany shook her head. "I'm not going to answer that. If you want to see the lab results, they're on the desk."

Chad stood abruptly, so Anna stood as well. She actually didn't have a choice, because his hand gripped hers like a vice. "I don't need to see them. I'm out of here."

Brittany stood as well. "No. Also in the pile is a document I had my lawyer write up. It's an agreement like a prenup, but retroactive, stating that neither of us will proceed with any claim against the other. You have no claim on anything I owned before we started living common law, and I have no claim on anything you owned before."

Anna watched Chad as he glared at Brittany. She didn't know much about prenuptial agreements, but she'd heard of them.

Chad narrowed his eyes. "In other words, you've got far more money than you told me about, and even though you took almost everything I owned, you're not going to let me have anything of yours in what should have been a fifty-fifty split."

Brittany glared right back at him. "Or you may want to protect any assets you didn't tell me about, and I have every right to take my rightful fifty percent."

Anna held her breath. She had a feeling it was Brittany who had not been truthful about assets. Since Chad wanted to do the right thing if he was the baby's father, she had no doubt he would have done the right thing in a breakup settlement. In her heart, she had no doubt it was Brittany who was again being untruthful.

From Chad's tight expression, Anna could tell he was gritting his teeth as he read the document and then applied his signature. He then extended his arm toward Brittany, offering her the pen. When he stepped back, Brittany stepped forward and signed it, and then the detective signed as a witness, like it had been previously arranged.

Chad turned to Brittany's husband. "Congratulations. I'm sure you two will be very happy together," he said, his voice dripping with sarcasm.

Mark's face paled, and he didn't reply.

Chad tugged Anna's hand. "We're done," he said with his teeth still clenched. He guided her quickly to turn around and began walking.

Behind them, Rod cleared his throat. "Brittany will be paying for this meeting. I could have told you what I'd found over the phone, and this should have been done at a lawyer's office, not here. I'll have my final bill for my services to you in the mail."

Chad said nothing. He simply strode out, straight to the car, almost pulling her behind him. After he unlocked the car door, he didn't open it or seat her but continued on with his fast pace to the driver's side. Anna scrambled in and barely had the door closed before Chad, who was already behind the wheel, started the engine.

He drove in silence, with sudden movements, driving much too fast, until they reached the first rest area outside the city. He pulled abruptly into a parking stall far away from any other cars, turned off the motor, rested both arms on top of the steering wheel, and dropped his forehead onto his forearms.

Anna had never seen such anguish in a person's heart—with the blows he'd just been dealt.

Chad didn't raise his head. His voice shook as he spoke. "I didn't find out if the baby was a boy or a girl. I don't know why I even care."

Watching him, her heart and soul ached for his pain. She'd never felt such a thing before, but part of her wanted to slap Brittany for hurting him so. Retribution aside, more than anything she'd ever wanted in her life, she wanted to take his pain away—to support him and make it all better by giving him all her love, unconditionally, with the promise she would never cheat on him or deceive him.

Anna's breath caught as she backtracked on her thoughts. She did love him. She'd loved him for months, but she'd been too caught up in her goal of moving to the cities to allow herself to admit it.

She also knew that he loved her. In a roundabout and cautious way, he had already proposed to her. She'd been too shocked at the time to think about what he'd really been telling her. Whether he realized it or not, he had opened his heart to her in a way that protected him, in case she turned him down.

For everything she needed or wanted, she didn't have to go two hundred miles—she only had to go next door. She suddenly had no desire to move away for a new start, despite all the courses and work she'd done in preparation to leave Piney Meadows. In an instant, she knew what she really wanted. Not a job—she'd wanted to go to a place where she could find a man who would love her as much as she would love him. She'd read books about couples falling in love and becoming soul mates. She'd never understood what that meant, but like an epiphany, right now, she did.

Her heart burned for Chad, for all the hurt, anguish, pain, and anger rolling through him. She wanted to make it all better, to tell him how much she loved him, but this was not the time. At this time, she doubted he would believe her, perhaps thinking that she would only say such a thing to ease his pain. What he needed right now was for her to hold him up, even though it took all her emotional strength not to cry for his despair.

"I am so sorry," she gulped. "I do not know what to say."

He shook his head without raising it. "There's nothing you can say. I feel so mixed up. Burned. Violated. Manipulated. I feel like part of me has been ripped away, but the baby was never part of me in the first place. Neither was Brittany, either, I guess. All she did was use me for what she wanted. But knowing she was pregnant with another man's baby is really the worst. I feel . . . I don't know. Tainted. I can't describe it. I want to hold you, but I feel like I need to get tested for STDs or something first. Is this how a leper felt when they feared they were unclean?"

Anna bit into her lower lip. Chad's voice was starting to become uneven. If he broke down completely, she didn't know what to do.

While she understood and respected his feelings, he needed to know he wasn't alone.

Anna inhaled deeply, reached to him, rested one hand on the center of his back, and rubbed gentle, soothing circles. "I am sure you are fine, but I certainly understand that you would want to get tested."

He nodded, still without lifting his head. "I should feel relieved the baby isn't mine and I'm in the clear, free to go on with my life. Happy. But I don't. What's the matter with me?"

It made sense most men would feel relief at no longer being trapped by an unplanned baby. However, Chad had accepted it and had made plans to change his life, to make sacrifices, and to be a good father. His willingness to take responsibility in a difficult and unplanned situation was one of the things she found so very appealing about him.

She slid her hand from rubbing the center of his back to his shoulder, leaned over the stick shift and parking brake, reached to grasp his forearm with her other hand, and rested her cheek on his shoulder. "Nothing is the matter with you. You are a good man, Chad. God has blessed you with a good and faithful heart."

He raised his head to look at her, causing her to lift her head from his shoulder and meet his reddened eyes.

Anna's heart melted. Leaning forward a little more, she wrapped her arms around him and gave him a small tug, hoping to encourage him to come the rest of the way.

Chad squeezed his eyes shut, his breathing 'hitched, and before she could catch her next breath, he twisted, his arms surrounded her, his cheek pressed into the top of her head, and he embraced her so tightly she couldn't move. She felt him struggling to breathe evenly, which made her heart break for him even more. Gradually, his body relaxed, he sighed, and he released her.

He slumped in his seat, turned his head as if looking out the window, ran his sleeve across his eyes, and then grasped the steering wheel and turned to her. "We should head home. We've got a long drive back, and I'd like to stop at Dr. Friesen's office before he closes the clinic for the day."

30

Chad stared blankly at his computer screen, unable to type. Except for the low hum of the two computers' fans, the clicking of Anna typing at full speed was the only other background noise in the office.

He couldn't believe how hollow he felt. Of course, Dr. Friesen wasn't sure of what he needed for an STD test. It was the first time he'd ever done one. Dr. Friesen had relieved him of a few vials of blood, more than he thought would be necessary, just in case, plus he took a rather invasive body fluid sample, and then told him he'd have to wait until Monday for the results to come back from the lab in Bemidji.

Chad continued to stare as the screen saver kicked in. Instead of getting back to the quote he should have been working on, his mind drifted as he watched, mesmerized, the colored lines merge and blend as they flipped and turned around.

After getting home from the doctor's office yesterday, he'd taken Waddles and Blinkie into the house and just sat there with them in his lap and phoned Brian. It had felt safer telling his friend that way than having to look him in the face and recount his day. He didn't know if he could have done it in person.

Brian had been so silent so long, Chad didn't know if he'd lost his phone connection. Instead of a shout of victory that it was over and Chad was free, he'd quietly asked Chad what he was going to do now.

Of course, Chad knew the question had been about Anna. The answer was that he didn't know.

He'd thought about it all evening, sitting in his silent living room with two snoozing chickens in his lap, and came up with nothing. At nearly one in the morning, he'd carried them to their box at the foot of the bed and put them on their blankets without bothering to put their diapers on and gone to bed. Instead of sleeping, he'd lain there in the pitch black room staring up at the ceiling almost till dawn, the same way he was now staring at the moving, colored lines on the computer screen. He'd woken up at noon, when the phone rang. Anna had seen no lights on in his house and gone to work without him, then phoned him at lunchtime to get him to come in.

And he'd done nothing ever since. But he'd changed the scheme on his screen saver a few times.

Maybe if he changed it back to the system's logo, it would bore him enough to get back to his quote. Or not.

"Chad?" Anna's voice came softly from the doorway, so he turned to look at her. "It is time to go home." She clasped her hands in front of her. "I hope you are still planning to go to the Bible study meeting tonight. I would not like it for you to stay home alone."

"I don't think so. I'm not very good company right now."

"Then it is more reason for you to come. I have been praying very much for you. I would like you to come." Her voice dropped. "These people, they are your friends. They would want to pray for you."

He looked into her eyes. He'd never seen her so sad, and it made him ache since it was because of him.

Chad moved the mouse to kill the screen saver, clicked the button to begin the sequence to shut his computer off, and stood. "Okay, I'll go."

As they walked home, Chad had nothing to say, but he had a lot to think about. He'd already announced his sins to the church membership, and in comparison, this should be easy, especially since it was closing the door on a section of his life he was glad was over. Somehow this felt worse—instead of confessing his sins, he was announcing his failures.

If he had to find something positive, then once he told this small group, in less than a day the whole town would know, and he wouldn't have to say it out loud ever again.

After he dropped Anna off at her home, being home alone seemed daunting. He'd never had time drag on so long. Even cooking a meal didn't make time go any faster, especially when in the end, he couldn't bring himself to eat it.

Five minutes before they usually left, Anna was at his door, coming to him instead of him walking first to her house, as if she were afraid he had changed his mind.

The more he thought about it, telling the small group tonight would be the best way of spreading the news. Still, he was in no rush to get to Leonard and Lois's home.

He didn't know how they knew, but as everyone greeted him, everyone asked him what was wrong. He almost felt swarmed; even the men seemed hesitant to leave him alone.

The kindness of these good people was overwhelming.

As soon as the last person arrived, as he always did, Leonard welcomed everyone as a group, then invited everyone to share their praises and prayer requests.

Chad waited until everyone had said something, and when he was the last one left, Anna picked up his hand, squeezed it, and didn't let go.

In front of everyone. He could have melted from the stares.

Anna cleared her throat. "Chad has something very important, and very personal that he wishes to ask for you all to pray with him about." She gave his hand another squeeze, turned to him, and nodded.

He told everyone the short version of the meeting with Brittany—not including his trip to the doctor's office—then sucked in a deep breath as Anna gave his hand another little squeeze.

The room fell into complete silence, which was amazing considering there were fifteen adults squeezed into the small living room. Instead of saying more, he stared down at Anna's hand, still joined with his, so he didn't have to look at anyone else looking at him.

Leonard's voice, lower in pitch than usual, finally broke the silence. "Let us now pray."

Leonard prayed for everything that had been mentioned before Chad spoke, then paused. During the lull, Chad felt the warmth of a number of hands resting on his shoulders, then one hand on top of his head. After Leonard prayed for him, many others prayed such heartfelt and earnest prayers he nearly broke down. Behind him, Evelyn's voice cracked, and she sniffled as she prayed for him.

These were good and gracious people.

Of course, there were always a few exceptions in every crowd, but even with the shortcomings of those few, he had fallen in love with the people of Piney Meadows.

After his testimony, he'd been accepted as a church member by most of the membership, even if he wasn't ever going to be in the inner circle of their society. He could accept that, but

Pastor Jake hadn't. Just to straighten out the few who stood on the judgmental side of the fence, Pastor Jake had aimed a whole sermon at those people, and everyone in the congregation knew who they were, including the direct recipients.

Again, his sins were affecting these good people. They would never be as innocent as they once were, because of him. By opening their eyes, he was poisoning them.

Even if he wasn't corrupting them directly, he couldn't fit into their lifestyle. He'd tried and failed. Some of his greatest joys, such as cooking, were his biggest secrets. He simply didn't fit into their culture. Even in his small circle of good friends, he was still an outsider, and he would always be an outsider.

Someone squeezed his shoulder, and a different person began praying for him, for stillness and inner strength.

He didn't have the test results back from Dr. Friesen yet. He shouldn't allow these good people to even touch him, just in case they were positive.

Yet, right now, he thought he'd die if he had to release Anna's hand.

When everyone had finished praying for him, for his healing, and for peace, someone also prayed for Brittany and her husband and their baby. He prayed along with them, and as he agreed in prayer, he started to pray for them as a family as well. Even though the wounds ran deep, and probably always would, his prayers for Brittany, Mark, and the baby were sincere, as were the prayers of all around him.

These were good, godly people, and Chad had no doubt they meant every word of their prayers.

At the closing amen, Leonard picked up his Bible. "I have changed my mind on tonight's lesson. Please turn with me to Psalms 103:2-4. 'Bless the LORD, O my soul, and forget not all his benefits: Who forgiveth all thine iniquities; who healeth all thy diseases; Who redeemeth thy life from destruction; who crowneth thee with lovingkindness and tender mercies.'"

Leonard turned to Chad. "These words are for you, my son. Do not ever forget them, and do not ever forget to praise the Lord for His promises."

Chad gulped. All he could do was nod.

Leonard continued with his lesson as if he'd been prepared for it. At the end, all the men stayed in the living room and all the ladies disappeared into the kitchen to bring out the food. For this, he had to release Anna's hand.

As she walked away, he felt he was releasing more than her hand. She deserved better than him. He loved her so much— he had to let her go.

~•~

Putting the call on hold, Anna nearly spilled her coffee. It had been a long week, and she had felt Chad's tension and something else she couldn't name all week long. He'd been different, quieter, even rather introspective, which for Chad was unusual.

But she couldn't wonder about Chad's moods now. This was the call from Dr. Friesen Chad had been waiting for— early. He'd been told he would have the results on Monday, but today was only Thursday.

She didn't know if that meant the results were very good or very bad.

Either way, he needed to take this call.

She hurried to his office and stood in the doorway. When he saw her, he put the person he was talking to on hold and turned to her. "Yes? Do you need something?"

"It is Dr. Friesen, on line two."

All the color drained from Chad's face. His hand shook as he pressed the button to speak to the caller on line one and told the man he would have to call him back.

Anna turned as Chad touched the button for line two.

"No. Anna. Please stay with me. I need you to be here. He's calling early, and it makes me nervous."

She walked behind his desk and rested her hand on his shoulder. He reached up and covered her hand with his, then answered the call.

"This is Chad," he said. He nodded, then shook his head and nodded again. "I understand. Yes, I can come in at 1:15 p.m. on Monday. See you then."

Anna's heart pounded in her chest. "Would he not tell you on the phone?" Surely that was a bad sign. Her stomach churned, and she wondered if she would be sick. She didn't know how Dr. Friesen could make Chad wait so long. Usually Dr. Friesen was a kind and compassionate man.

He turned to her, smiled, stood, and grasped both her hands in his. "I'm fine. All clear. Well, maybe not all fine. He said while he had so much of my blood, he made the testing worthwhile. He reminded me that I haven't made an appointment for a complete checkup since I've been here and took the liberty of using all the samples I provided. He says everything is good, except my cholesterol is a little high and he wants to talk to me about my diet." Chad grinned. "Maybe I'm eating too many good eggs. I don't know. Right now, I don't care."

Anna grinned ear to ear. "That is wonderful!" she squealed, and she pulled her hands out of his grasp, threw her arms around him, and squeezed him so hard she felt him exhale.

Slowly, his hands rested on her back, and he returned her embrace.

She squeezed him again, her heart racing with the relief that he was fine. With the good results, this day would be the start of a new life for them together, and it was now time to tell him of her decision.

Anna cleared her throat. "As you know, in two more weeks I will have finished my courses."

He squeezed her a little tighter. "Yes. I know that."

She nodded with her cheek pressed into his chest. "I have made a decision. I have decided that when I am done, I am not going to leave Piney Meadows. I want to stay here."

His body stiffened. In the blink of an eye, he pushed her away. "Excuse me?"

The separation felt like he had tossed a bucket of ice water at her. "I said I have decided to stay in Piney Meadows."

He shook his head. "But you can't. What about all your hard work? All your classes?"

"They are good for me here, for working at the factory. Now I can do so much more. I am a better secretary, I mean, a better administrative assistant. This is good for the factory, good for the people of Piney Meadows, and good for me. I have decided to stay."

He backed up a step. "I thought your dream was to find a nice church in Minneapolis, get settled in a new community, and find a good job."

"I have a satisfying job here, and I could never find a better group of people with whom to share my life. I need nothing more." Nothing, with the exception of Chad. Except, she could see him slipping away from her before her very eyes, and she didn't know what she'd done.

She stepped forward; he took another step back. "Why are you doing this?" he stammered. "What's going on? Why have you changed your mind?"

All she could do was stare at him. "Why is this bad? I thought you loved it here . . ." She felt her heart slowly ripping in two as he continued to back away. "And me . . ."

His face paled. "It would never work. I was wrong about this place. I need some time to think. I need to be alone."

Before she could open her mouth to ask what had changed and what had happened, he was gone.

31

Instead of waiting in the living room, where her papa would see her reddened eyes, Anna sat on the edge of her bed, waiting, even though she knew her hopes were in vain.

Since it was Thursday night, they should have been going to the young adults' group. However, it was now half an hour past the time the meeting started, and Chad hadn't come for her. Instead, her mama said he'd arrived home from work in the middle of the day, gotten in his car, and driven away.

He still hadn't returned.

She didn't know where he'd gone. Neither did her mama.

A light rap sounded on her bedroom door. "Anna? Brian is here for you."

She opened her mouth to ask Brian if he'd seen Chad, but his narrowed eyes and tight lips silenced her.

"What is it you have done?" he ground out between clenched teeth.

She cowered at Brian's harsh tone. "I do not understand what you mean."

Brian glanced to the kitchen doorway, where she knew her mama and papa were, probably standing next to the doorway listening to every word they said. "Let us go outside, where we may speak in private."

She had no choice. Brian strode out of the door, forcing her to follow him.

He stopped at the edge of the sidewalk, so far from the house she knew something had to be very wrong.

"I have just received a telephone call from Bart. Chad has just left his home."

"I do not understand. Why does this concern you?" Although she had no idea why Chad would have been at Bart's home. Usually, as the owner, Bart came to the office once a month to go over the financial report she helped Chad prepare, and it had only been two weeks ago. Instead of being a reason for concern, their last month's fiscal report was the best it had ever been.

"Bart has told me Chad has given his resignation. He has not found another job, but has agreed to stay at the factory until Bart can find a replacement for him or if he finds another job that will not allow him to give a longer notice. Why has this happened? Bart does not know and called me to see if I know why Chad is so unhappy. I thought he should not be unhappy. The things that have gone wrong in his life have reached a good conclusion."

All the strength left Anna's legs. She sank to the ground, to sit on the grass. "I do not know. He was very strange today. I told him that I have changed my mind about leaving, that I have decided to stay here. I was expecting him to ask me to marry him, but instead he left so fast I did not even get a chance to ask where he was going." Suddenly she pushed herself to her feet. "We must check something." She ran to Chad's gate, pulled the chain to open it, and ran to the chicken hotel.

As she feared, there was a double portion of seed in the bowls.

Anna's heart sank, and she looked up at Brian. "This is not good. This means he does not intend to be back tonight." However, knowing he had thought ahead and left enough food for his chickens, she didn't have to worry when she didn't see him come home.

If only she knew why he'd gone.

༻

Chad shook Anton's hand. "Thanks for seeing me. I look forward to hearing back from you."

As he turned and walked away, the smile he'd plastered on his face dropped.

Honestly, the response he hoped to hear back was that they had chosen someone else for the position, except the response he needed was an offer for the job.

Today, he'd seen five people from his contact list, and one of them was actually hiring. After crossing this one off his list, he got in his car and started driving to the next, but he only got a few blocks and pulled into the nearest parking lot.

He hadn't realized how much he hated downtown traffic. He hated the crowds. He hated the smoggy air. He hated the concrete jungle. Inside the building, he didn't even like the re-circulated air conditioning. He wanted to work in a building where you could actually open the windows.

He wanted to go back to the peace and tranquility of Piney Meadows.

He missed walking to work in the morning sunshine. He wanted to inhale the clean scent of fresh grass. He almost wanted to smell the manure the farms spread last weekend, but not really.

More than he expected, he missed Blinkie and Waddles.

Most of all, he missed Anna.

Instead of driving anywhere, Chad pulled at the tie threatening to choke him, and looked up at the tall buildings lining the congested street.

More than anything, he wanted to go back to Piney Meadows and pretend everything would be okay, but it couldn't be.

He couldn't work with Anna every day and then go out somewhere with her almost every evening, and not go home with her.

He loved her so much that he couldn't taint her any more than he already had.

Because he'd already made the appointment, he refastened his tie and made his last stop on his list, again with the same no-win feeling—whether he got the job or not, it wasn't what he wanted.

By the time he was back in his car, it was right on the starting edge of the evening rush-hour traffic. He hadn't missed the grueling commute at all, and he didn't need a reminder of what it was like to be stuck in it.

He really wanted to be back home, in Piney Meadows.

Leaving now, by the time he got back everyone would have finished their job at the factory, including Anna, and gone home. With everyone he knew gone to some Friday evening activity, including Anna, he could go back to work and catch up on everything he'd missed. One day wouldn't make that much difference, but it would be better to be busy.

He cranked the music up loud and made his way home, stopping only once at the edge of the city to fill up his gas tank.

The closer he got to Piney Meadows, the more he could feel the tension draining out of him.

Rather than going straight to the office, he first went home to change into something more comfortable. Before heading to the office, he detoured to the yard to give Blinkie and Waddles a short pet.

Just as he closed the door to the coop, Peter's voice came from over the fence.

"I see you are now home. Would you mind if I spoke with you?"

Chad cringed, knowing the accuracy of Peter's words. He had no doubt of who would be doing all the speaking and who would be doing all the listening. He really didn't feel like another lecture about his evil city ways, but the man was Anna's father, and he could respect the man for raising a wonderful daughter.

He forced himself to smile. "I was just about to go to the factory, but sure, Peter, I've got a few minutes. What can I do for you?"

The gate between their yards opened, and Peter walked into Chad's yard, motioning for the two of them to sit at the table on Chad's patio.

Mentally, Chad cringed. The request to sit indicated this would be a longer lecture than he anticipated.

Peter cleared his throat and made eye contact. If it wasn't Chad's imagination, for the first time, Peter appeared nervous.

The hairs rose on the back of Chad's neck. He had a feeling this wasn't going to be good.

"What I need to do is to apologize to you. I have never done this before, but today, I have heard the two of them talking in Anna's bedroom. I had not meant to listen, but when I heard them mention your name, I found myself staying. I heard them talking about Anna's plan to leave us and then to leave Piney Meadows. At first I was angry, hearing that you were helping her, but then I realized you were instead equipping her so people in the cities would not take advantage of her. Even though it is not what I would like for my daughter, I have realized by holding her as we have, we have only been pushing her away."

Chad agreed. Anna had told him of her plan to leave Piney Meadows before he came to know her. Instead of saying so out loud, he nodded once, to encourage Peter to finish what he had to say.

"Listening to them talk, I realized I have been trying to make Anna into something she will never be. Yet she can still be a good wife for the right man who can accept that Anna will never be like her mama or her sesta. Even though I do not agree with your city ways, you are a good and fair man, and if you wish it so, I give you my blessing with my daughter."

Chad's head spun. While part of him was overjoyed that Anna's father had just given him permission to court Anna, his reasons stung.

Chad stood, so he could purposely look down as he spoke to Peter. "Anna is a sweet young woman and has many, very good qualities. It doesn't matter if her biggest strengths and talents are outside of your traditional boundaries. Being a cook and a good housekeeper isn't what makes Anna happy. What makes her happy is to think and figure stuff out. To plan and organize. She's smart, she's strong, she has good judgment and a kind heart." He wanted to point out to her father that Anna was pretty, too. In fact, if she ever wore makeup, even just a little, she'd be knockout gorgeous. But in light of all her other great qualities, it seemed rather shallow. Instead, he thought of the last time they'd spent time together outside of work, at Cass Lake, when she teased him about the bears. "She's also brave and wears sensible shoes."

Peter smiled. "Ah. I am right. I see that you have a place in your heart for Anna. She also has a place in her heart for you." Peter stood, and extended one hand, so Chad automatically returned the handshake. "Make my daughter happy. May I call you 'City Boy'?"

Chad's mind spun. "Sure, you can. But I think I should tell you that I don't plan to stay in Piney Meadows much longer.

I might be getting another job offer, and if that happens, I'm going to take it."

Peter's smile faltered. "Then you must follow where God is leading you. I must go. I did not mean to interrupt your plans for so long. Goode nacht."

Chad watched him go until the gate clicked shut. Where was God leading him? Until recently, he'd thought it was here. Now, he wasn't so sure.

Before he could think too much more about it, he locked up the house, got back in the car, and drove to the furniture factory.

⌘

Anna couldn't believe her eyes. Her papa had just gone into Chad's backyard, they'd had what appeared to be a very serious conversation, and then they had shaken hands and gone their separate ways.

As her papa returned inside, she blocked him from going into the living room. "Where is he going? I must know."

Her papa smiled a very strange smile. "He is going to the factory to work." To her shock, her papa reached forward and rested one hand on her shoulder. "He is a good man, Anna. Go to him."

Anna's head spun. Until today, she'd only met with strong disapproval for spending time alone with Chad, even at work. If her father had changed his mind, she shouldn't do anything to change it back. It would be dark soon, and she could be at the factory in only minutes if she rode her bicycle.

Unfortunately, her new fast bicycle was still in Chad's garage. It took much more effort to pedal her old bicycle without the racing gears, but she still made it in record time.

Seeing Chad's car filled her with relief. She leaned her bicycle against the wall, tossed her helmet on the seat, and ran inside.

Obviously, he hadn't expected her to be there. As she entered his office, he flinched when he raised his head at the movement and saw her.

"What are you doing here?"

"I have come so I may speak with you. Brian has told me today you went to the cities to look for another job. I must know why. You have come to like Piney Meadows very much, and if you move to the cities, you will not be able to take Blinkie and Waddles."

She noticed he cringed at her comment about losing his chickens. All was not lost.

Taking advantage of the moment, she walked behind his desk and rested one hand on his shoulder. "You cannot leave because everyone will miss you too much. Everyone has come to like your city ways."

He shook his head. "Not everyone."

"Everyone who matters. I had a very strange conversation with Papa today, and I have a feeling you did as well."

He nodded, and his brows furrowed. "I did. I still don't understand it."

Anna hesitated. For now, Chad was relaxed and listening to her. She couldn't live if he made a sudden retreat as he had yesterday. It was now, or never, and never was not an option she wanted to contemplate. "Papa has finally accepted you. But it would not matter if he did not. Do you remember what you asked me the last time we went to Cass Lake? I am now going to give you my answer."

She felt his body stiffen under her hand. Anna cleared her throat, raised her hand from his shoulder, and then cupped his cheeks with both hands. "Ja, I would like to get married to you, only I do not know what you mean by 2.5 children. I would like to have at least three *kjinza*, children. I would also like to have a dog, because a dog would be good to help protect the chicken hotel. Also, I do not think I would mind the chickens in their box on the floor by the bed."

He flinched at her words, and when he started to open his mouth to speak, she pressed her index finger over his lips to silence him. "*Dü dast mie nijch aunschmääre*, you are not fooling me. Do not think I do not know you allow your chickens to sleep in the box in your bedroom. I have seen it, because one evening when you were cooking, I followed Blinkie to see where she was going, and she went to have a nap. I have seen you taking them into the house at night after I go to bed."

"I bought chicken diapers on eBay for them. Then they go outside first thing in the morning. My house is clean."

She couldn't help smiling. "I know that, too. Many people know that you have put diapers on your chickens. Some have laughed, but I have also seen at sewing club, two of the ladies are trying to figure out the pattern so that they may try it."

He grinned. "Really?"

"Ja. Piney Meadows is your home. Even though your ways are different, everyone has come to love you." She lowered her voice and looked into his mesmerizing blue eyes. "And I have come to love you more than all of them. If you wish to marry me, then I wish to marry you. *Ich leewe die*, I love you, Chad Jones, and all your city ways."

Anna held her breath, waiting for his response.

He squeezed his eyes shut. "I can't do that to you. You're so pure and innocent. You deserve better than me. You should be marrying one of the good men who live here."

"You are a good man, and we are both God's children in the same way. Do not think of yourself as different. I love you, and if you love me, then that is all that matters."

His eyes opened wide as he studied her face. "You have no idea how much I've thought about this."

"What do you want to do? From deep in your heart."

"I want to marry you and love you until my dying day. Which I hope won't be for at least fifty or sixty years. Or longer."

Anna couldn't hold back her smile. "That is what I want as well. I would like to do that in Piney Meadows. If you really wish to go back to the cities, then I would go with you. But I do think you want to stay here, and I will, too."

He stood and gently cupped her cheeks in his palms. "Are you really sure of this?"

"Ja. I am sure."

He sighed. "I had such big plans to propose properly. I guess we can't pretend this never happened and do it all again, can we?"

"Nein. We cannot. This is done."

He smiled. "I love you. You know, I'd practiced saying that in German, but now that the moment is here, I don't want to embarrass myself because I know I've got the accent all wrong."

"You will have plenty of time to practice your accent, but for now, wait here for a minute."

Before he could protest, she hustled to her desk and pulled a large bag out of the bottom drawer. "Brian has given me this, and he said to give it to you at the right moment." She reached forward and handed him the bag. "This is that moment."

Cautiously, he looked inside, broke out into an ear-to-ear grin, and pulled a new wide-brimmed hat out of the bag. He placed it on his head, wiggled the brim to get it into exactly the right position, and grinned. "I love it. When do I get to wear it for real?"

She leaned forward for a kiss. "After our wedding."

He slipped his arms around her and drew her in for a tight embrace. "Would you like a short engagement?"

She smiled. "Ja."

Discussion Questions

1. The book opens with Chad very unsatisfied with his job and his life. Leaving his job with no notice and nothing in place was extreme and impulsive. Have you ever had such a reaction? Was the fallout better or worse than the situation?

2. Finding himself stranded at Ted's house on Christmas Eve, Chad makes the best of the situation and ends up having a very pleasant evening, even without a television. Have you ever been in an unplanned circumstance? What did you do to make the best of it?

3. Chad quickly finds himself surrounded by a culture that is completely foreign to him, and he feels very much like an outsider. Have you ever found yourself in a situation where you were the one who was different? What did you do so you could fit in better?

4. Anna is determined to leave her roots where she can be herself. When she first asks Chad about living in the cities she has no idea he is going to be her boss. Have you ever said something to someone you wish you could take back? How were you careful not to do it again?

5. In trying to fit in better, Chad's first mistake is to wash some dishes in the kitchen at the furniture factory. Have you ever made a mistake like this when you were trying to fit in? What did you do to make it right?

6. At the office, every time Chad sees Anna coming closer he moves his coffee mug farther away from his keyboard because he knows she thinks he is going to have an accident and spill it when it's so close. Is there anything you do on a regular basis that you try to hide from someone? Do you think you are succeeding?

7. Unlike the rest of the men in the Mennonite community of Piney Meadows, Chad is not handy with tools. However, he swallows his pride and does his best

when everyone else is doing better. Is there something you aren't very good at doing? How do you react when others around you do something better than you?

8. Even though it is contrary to the Old Order Mennonite culture, Chad enjoys cooking, and he swears Anna to secrecy so he can cook for her in an effort to impress her. Have you ever done anything to impress someone? What were you trying to accomplish? Did you succeed?

9. When Chad sees Henry Rempel's chicken plucker in action he nearly faints, which is very embarrassing. Have you ever done something very embarrassing in a crowd? How did you handle it?

10. Telling Anna, then the congregation, about his past relationship with Brittany and that he is going to be a father is the hardest thing Chad has ever done. He knows that some people will never accept him, but he needs to make it known. What is the hardest thing you've ever done? How did you feel when it was over?

11. Even though Anna's father knows Anna is trying to improve her skills, he continues to disapprove of her doing a job outside the realm of what their community terms as "woman's work." Have you ever done something that someone close to you disapproved of? How did you handle it?

12. When Chad finds out that Brittany's baby isn't his, he feels his world has turned upside down. Instead of feeling free to go on with his life, he feels tainted, like he's poisoning the community of Piney Meadows with his past sins, even though he's been leading a godly life since he arrived. Have you ever met anyone who had a tainted past and turned their life over to God? How do you treat people like that; do you keep them at a distance or welcome them into your heart and home with true friendship?

13. When Anna learns that Chad plans to leave Piney Meadows she thinks hard and fast about what she really wants out of life and their relationship. She risks rejection and tells Chad that if he wants to leave, she will go with him. Have you ever left yourself open to rejection? What did it take to be able to take the risk?